"Would you kill for me?"
"Yes."
"Would you die for me?"
"*Yes.*" The word echoed in the empty station.
"Live now. And serve me."
"Yes." And she wept. When she could see once more, she was alone, filled with a love more thrilling and more violent than hate.

"*Enoth!*" she cried. For him, she would savage the city.

Praise for Chet Williamson:
"Disturbing, challenging, and anything but reassuring."
—Ramsey Campbell on *Ash Wednesday*
"Williamson masterfully creates the sense of doom without hope which electrifies the story."
—*Fantasy Review* on *Soulstorm*
"A fine psychological thriller." A richly textured and satisfying novel."
—*Library Journal* on *Ash Wednesday*
"Chillingly good."
—*West Coast Review of Books* on *Soulstorm*
"Both thought provoking and entertaining. I couldn't put the book down."
—*Rave Reviews* on *Ash Wednesday*
"Chet Williamson has done something powerful and new. You will be haunted by this book."
—*Fantasy & Science Fiction* on *Ash Wednesday*

TOR BOOKS BY CHET WILLIAMSON

Ash Wednesday
Lowland Rider
McKain's Dilemma
Soulstorm

CHET WILLIAMSON
LOWLAND RIDER

A TOM DOHERTY ASSOCIATES BOOK

*Certain liberties have been
taken with the New York
Subway system for the purposes
of this story.*

This is a work of fiction.
All the characters and events portrayed
in this book are fictional, and any resemblance to real people
or incidents is purely coincidental.

LOWLAND RIDER

Copyright © 1988 by Chet Williamson

All rights reserved, including the right
to reproduce this book or portions thereof in any form.

Excerpt from "Sorrow-Acre"
from *Winter's Tales* by Isak Dinesen.
Copyright © by Random House, Inc.,
reprinted by permission
of Random House, Inc.

First Edition: August 1988

A TOR BOOK

Published by Tom Doherty Associates, Inc.
49 West 24th Street
New York, NY 10010

ISBN: 0-812-52722-4
Can ISBN: 0-812-52723-2

PRINTED IN THE UNITED STATES OF AMERICA

0 9 8 7 6 5 4 3 2 1

*To Richard Picchiarini,
Child of the City*

" . . . The gods of whom you speak were never all-powerful. They had, at all times, by their side those darker powers which they named the Jotuns, and who worked the suffering, the disasters, the ruin of our world . . . The omnipotent gods have no such facilitation. With their omnipotence they take over the woe of the universe."

—"*Sorrow-Acre*", Isak Dinesen

PROLOGUE

CHAPTER 1

BODY FOUND IN SUBWAY

The body of an unidentified man was found on the Eighth Avenue express track at the 34th Street station at noon yesterday. Though platforms were filled with waiting passengers, none saw anyone leap from the platform.

A transit police spokesman stated that identification would be difficult, as the victim's head was crushed, and the hands mangled.

—*New York Post*, April 7, 1984

MARCH 15, 1986

The air screamed. It shrieked as if something torn, split apart, buffeted by irresistible forces. The wind blew dust and soot and debris left by thousands up into Rags's eyes, making them sting, so that he had to close them. "Muthah," he swore softly. "Ol' muthah train."

The Eighth Avenue local came to a stop with a harsh hissing of brakes, and the small hurricane subsided, leaving the air chill, foul, and oppressive. The doors opened with a grating rattle, freeing several dozen passengers who scurried onto the platform and toward the stairs, eager to be above again, out of the tunnels. Rags waited until the human flood had ceased, then boarded the car and sat in the corner.

A young girl reading a paperback book sat across from him. Beneath her light jacket she was wearing a white uniform. Rags eyed her white stockings, white heavy shoes. "You a nurse?" he asked, as the doors slammed shut.

She looked up for a second, then back down at her book. Rags read the author's name, but didn't recognize it. He patted his right rib cage to make sure his own books were still there.

"Nurses' good people," he observed. The girl licked her lips and kept her eyes on her book. "My sister was a nurse." The girl closed her book gently, got up, and started to walk down the length of the car. At that moment the train lurched forward, making her stumble. Her book fell onto the green tile floor. Rags lumbered to his feet, and with a grace borne of many years in a wheeled and moving home, snatched up the volume and held it out to the girl, who blanched, took it, and moved as quickly as she dared to the door at the end of the car, through which she disappeared.

Rags sighed and maneuvered himself back to his seat. The girl was gone, and he could now see his reflection in the window across from him. He didn't like to see his reflection. That, and the fact that he liked people, was why he tried to sit across from them whenever he could. Most times, though, he couldn't. At night, for example. Of course it was always night in

Lowland Rider

the tunnels, always night if you were a rider. Always blackness outside so you could see yourself against it, part of it, part of the blackness.

"Black man," said Rags, eyeing himself scornfully. "Poor old black fool." An Orthodox Jew in the middle of the car looked up at Rags's words. Rags felt the eyes on him and turned. The Jew wrinkled his nose as though he smelled something bad, and Rags wondered if he had gone to the bathroom in his pants. He wiggled his backside against the hard seat, but felt nothing objectionable. He was glad. He had done that only twice before, and they had thrown him off the train both times.

Now he breathed deeply, trying to smell himself. It was sour, of course it was—what could you expect when you wore so many clothes? But he couldn't part with them, all those reds and golds and greens and bright sunflower yellows wrapped around him like mummy-cloth, on his arms and legs and around his waist, his wrinkled black waist that he hadn't seen for oh sweet Jesus it seemed like months. He sniffed again and reminded himself to wash soon.

The motion of the train rocked him to sleep, and when he opened his eyes again, the old Jew was gone, and Rags was alone on the car. He tried to remember how many stops the train had made while he dozed, and thought it was seven, which meant that 135th Street should be next. But then he felt a jolt and knew he must have counted wrong. That was the bad piece of track between 116th and 125th. He must have dreamed an extra stop.

Now the train slowed, and Rags reminded himself

to stay awake. He couldn't afford to sleep past the 168th Street station. There was an alcove he'd discovered there that the transit cops hardly ever checked. If he got off there he'd be fine, but if he didn't, he'd be stuck in Washington Heights without a token to get back downtown, and little chance of finding one. He hardly ever found them at the Washington Heights station—bastards must all have cast-iron pockets.

The train stopped at 125th, and in the sudden quiet Rags thought he heard voices in the car ahead, then footfalls. He stepped to the other side of the car and looked out onto the platform where he saw six young men—boys really, with the wispy beards and moustaches of pubescence—leap out onto the platform and look around like rabbits. They moved quickly out of Rags's sight then, though he could hear their sneakered footsteps and loudly whispering voices until the doors closed.

It made Rags wonder. The boys sounded almost scared, like they'd done something bad and were trying to get away fast. They weren't the usual jiving and laughing voices that kids had, the cocky, confident, outa-my-way-I-kick-your-ass tone. Instead they'd been hushed, cautious, as if something had gone too far. Rags started walking forward, toward the car from which the boys had emerged. He was just about to open the door when he looked through the window and saw the nurse.

She was lying on her back, her dress pushed up, her white stockings torn and stained with blood. She was not moving. Through the two layers of filthy glass Rags could see that her eyes were open and staring, still clear, not yet glazed by death as old Andy's had been last week when Rags had found him underneath his bedclothes of moldy cardboard. The front of the white uniform was splashed with a deep red that spread outward even as he watched.

"Aw Jesus," Rags wailed. "Aw sweet Jesus, have mercy." Where the hell were the transit cops? Where *were* they? They were always around to kick a poor old nigger in the ankle and tell him to get off the train or get the fuck up onto the street to do your sleeping. But where were they when something like this happens to a nice young white girl? To a nurse yet. *Where were they?*

Rags knew where *he* was. He was in hell, sure enough.

He wanted to go through to the next car, wanted to try and help. But he knew she was beyond help. Dead as hell. And if he didn't want to be blamed for it he'd better get his ass off at 135th, or he'd be napping in the Tombs tomorrow night, and he couldn't handle that. He'd been in jail. Better to sleep in crap and sleep free, he thought. Or even sleep in hell.

Rags was still looking at the dead girl when they approached 135th Street and the rhythm of the wheels grew less frenzied. He was about to move to the outside doors, when he became aware of another *living* face inside the next car. But wait—it wasn't in the *next* car, was it? It was in the one beyond that, two cars up from Rags. That face was looking through a window too, looking at the raped and murdered nurse, and that face was smiling.

It was not a smile of blood-lust, but of contentment,

a soft smile that made the face that bore it angelic. There was also, in the eyes, a hint of sadness. Those eyes came up then, and gazed into Rags's eyes. The face held Rags, and he studied it.

The man was a mixture of racial types—long nose, flat lips like a black man, but straight, light brown hair, rather long, covering the ears. The skin was swarthy, but the eyes were blue. Rags knew his name. Enoch.

Enoch smiled at Rags, and opened the first of the doors that separated them. Rags stiffened, and felt a hot trickle of urine that soaked into the layers of clothes he wore. But Enoch wasn't coming for him. It was the girl he was interested in, the dead and ruined girl on the dirty floor. Enoch stopped when he reached her, knelt beside her, and lowered his face to hers.

Rags saw no more. Choking back a sob, he turned and ran onto the platform through the open doors, which slammed shut behind him like the closing of a tomb.

The train rocketed away into the darkness, and Rags stood alone on the bare platform, shivering in spite of his many pounds of cloth. This town needs a deliverer, he thought. This town needs a Moses.

Then he wondered if a Moses would really help. He wondered what even a Jesus could do.

JESSE GORDON'S JOURNAL:
FEBRUARY 18TH, 1987

I have seen him again, twice in one day now. And both times involved with death, horror.

I have been riding the Lexington Avenue line for the past few days, with the usual side trip to Penn Station. The weather is bitter cold, and this line seems warmer somehow. Rags is faithful to the Eighth Avenue, and I can understand. At his age it's almost like a home. But back to Enoch.

It must have been around 5:30—early morning at any rate. I was dozing when a high scream woke me. We were stopped at a station, but the doors had either closed or not yet opened, I wasn't sure which. I looked out onto the platform and saw two black men in their early thirties assaulting an old woman. One of them was holding her purse, going through its contents, dumping things on the platform until he came to her change purse, which he pocketed. The other was kicking the woman, who lay on her side, her back to him. He kicked her in the buttocks, spine, and the back of her head and neck. I didn't see her moving at all.

Then Enoch walked up to them, with that damned smile of his. The two of them *bowed* to him, as if paying him obeisance, and walked down the platform. The train started off then, but I saw him kneel by the old woman. At the last, it looked as if he were kissing her.

I felt filthy. It was as if the whole subway, the entire system of tunnels, was soiled by his presence. I got off the Lexington at 51st and made my way over to the Seventh Avenue platform. I felt better immediately. Less happens there, I thought.

But I was wrong. Between Cortlandt and Rector the gang piled on. I recognized their colors—the Noisy Boys—and wondered why they were off their own turf. But it didn't matter to the boy with the trumpet.

He was sitting at the other end of the car, a thin kid, maybe fourteen or fifteen, dressed in a winter coat that looked like a hand-me-down. He had on one of those old-fashioned caps with earflaps, though to his credit they were up. Thick-lensed glasses finished the picture. If ever I'd seen a perfect victim, patsy, *schlemiel*, it was this kid. I prayed to God when I saw him that he wouldn't get hassled, but it did all the good my other prayers have done. I knew, when the Noisy Boys came barreling into the car, that the best the kid could hope for was a stepped-on foot.

There were seven of them, big, dumb, white, and Irish, the kind of city Irish that wouldn't know a County Cork man if he bit them in the ass, but who cheer each time the IRA blows up a children's hospi-

Lowland Rider

tal. They sang and called and bellowed, spraying "fuck" like blessings in between their other words. The other passengers in the car—a well-dressed, middle-aged couple who should have been in a cab anyway—got up and left as soon as the Boys entered. But the boy with the trumpet and I stayed.

I stayed for the reasons I always stay. They can't frighten me, not even if they kill me, so they don't try. I don't know why the young boy stayed. Perhaps he felt that moving would only attract their attention to him. He did seem to shrink within himself, as though wanting to merge unnoticed into the hard plastic of the seat. It didn't do him any good. The Noisy Boys had him pegged as a wimp from the womb.

"Whoa, look at this!" one of them said, and I knew the kid was mincemeat. "A moo-*sish*-un!" I've come to the conclusion that with all the media glop kids stuff themselves with today, faulty pronunciation must be studied. "What do you play, kid?"

"Trumpet," the boy said, so softly I could barely hear him.

But the Noisy Boys heard, and went into a rap on sucking and blowing. All the while the kid kept his eyes down, not looking up for fear of what he might see. "Lemme see it," one of the gang said. "I wanta see your horny horn."

"Yeah, come on, asshole," another put in. "Show us your horny horn. Flash your little tooter!"

The boy didn't respond at all. If he had, if he'd started to cry, that might have been enough for them and they'd have left him alone. But he didn't. He ignored them. It was a big mistake.

"You hear me, pussy? I wanta see your *horn*." One of the gang, with a shock of uncombed red hair and several missing teeth, grabbed the case and yanked it away from the boy. He tried to stand up and go after it, but two others pushed him down. The back of his head made a crack against the window, but he didn't rub it. He was a spunky kid, for what that was worth.

Red Hair snapped open the latches and the lid fell open. The trumpet fell on the floor with a hell of a clunk. The boy cried out then, like he should have when he hit his head. He started after it again, and was again shoved back. Red Hair picked up the trumpet, dug the mouthpiece out of the case, and jammed it home. "Listen, guys," he said, "I'm gonna play a tune on the faggot's trumpet." He put the horn to his lips and a cowlike braying came out. "What *is* this shit?" he yelled, while his buddies laughed and hooted. "This horn's a piece of shit, it don't work!"

The rest of them took up the cry then. "If it don't work, bust it!"

"If it don't work, bust it!"

"What fuckin' good is it? Smash it!"

Finally the boy yelled in a thin voice far higher than the Noisy Boys—"You don't know how to *play* it, you stupid . . ."

He didn't finish. The ferocity with which Red Hair glared at him wouldn't let him, and the car got very quiet.

I suppose I could have said something, have told them to leave the boy alone, have pulled the emergency brake cord and toppled them on their fat asses, but if I'd done either of those things, anything, really, but

12

Lowland Rider

what I did, which was to sit there quietly and watch, I'd have been so much dead meat. Besides, I was an observer of the passing scene. I wasn't there to intervene. I was only there to watch.

So I watched, as Red Hair went up to the boy and stuck his face only an inch away from the boy's own. "You know how to play it, smartass," he leered at the boy, and something in Red Hair's face or voice or breath or all three made the boy's face sour, and he tried to look away. But Red Hair grabbed the boy's ear and twisted, so that the boy was looking at him once more. "You know how?" Red Hair snarled.

"*Yes*," the boy said, with more spirit than I would have shown under the circumstances.

"Then you play somethin' for us. We wanta hear a tune. Right, boys?" The rest of the gang jeered and whistled. Red Hair looked at me for the first time. "Right, Mr. Easy Rider?"

I nodded. Actually I thought it would be nice to hear the sound of a live instrument again. My only source of music for a long time has been ghetto blasters.

"You got a command performance, my man," Red Hair said, handing the boy the trumpet. "You play requests?"

"I can play anything," answered the boy, the brave, gutsy, abysmally stupid and suicidal boy. He might have been from Mars for all the sense he showed handling these cretins.

"Wowie zowie," said Red Hair. "Anything, huh? Okay then, how about Taps?"

"That's just a bugle call," the boy answered.

"I *like* Taps," Red Hair said. "Play it."

The boy looked at Red Hair like he wanted to jam the trumpet up his ass, but he raised the horn to his lips and started to play.

It was beautiful. The notes, long and full, made the car sound like an echo chamber. It took me out of the tunnels, above ground again, over to Union Field Cemetery in Queens, where we'd go with Grandpa Gordon every Memorial Day when I was a kid, and we'd stand under the late spring sun and look out over the graves and hear the soldiers fire their salute and then listen to the bugler play Taps so sadly you thought your heart would break. Even the Noisy Boys seemed entranced.

All of them except Red Hair. Just as the boy was letting the last note of "God is nigh" fade away, Red Hair brought up his foot fast as light and kicked the bell of the horn as hard as he could.

The mouthpiece disappeared between the boy's lips and I saw teeth splinter and fly. Red Hair kicked again, straight in as before, and the rear curve of the horn snapped the boy's jaw down and the brass tubing went in until the valves hit the kid's upper lip. There was a gagging, choking sound, and the boy went down, his earflapped cap still tight against his head. Even the Noisy Boys gasped.

But Red Hair barked, "Come on," and led the gang through the car toward me. At first I thought I was next, and I tensed, ready at last to fight for self-preservation if nothing else. But I didn't have to. As Red Hair passed me, he leaned in my direction and said, "You got a lousy memory, don'tcha?" to which I

Lowland Rider

tacitly nodded agreement. He was just about to open the door to the next car when he froze, and I thought with joy that maybe a transit cop with a big fat gun had his paw on the handle of the other side.

It wasn't a cop, though. It was Enoch. He opened the door and walked in, no coat on, looking warm as could be in just that thin white outfit he always wears. The Noisy Boys all looked as though God had just entered. They got deathly quiet and nearly all bowed their heads and looked down at their feet. Only Red Hair kept his eyes on Enoch, nodding to him and then gesturing back into the car, as if to indicate the boy lying there bleeding, his feet still weakly beating on the dirty linoleum.

Enoch looked at Red Hair and nodded a short, sharp nod. That seemed to be all Red Hair had been waiting for. He edged past Enoch as though he were afraid to touch him, as did the others, and in a moment only Enoch, the dying boy, and I were in the car.

Enoch stood next to where I sat, watching the boy's life pass away, and then he turned toward me and smiled, not saying a word, only looking at me as if he expected approval, even worship. I looked away. For all that I've seen since I've come down, the look on his face was the worst of all. The irony of it is that I saw there what I myself have been trying to achieve—a complete and total separation from my surroundings, the ability to look on all horrors unscathed. But what terrified me, gave me such nausea, was the implication that he not only rejoiced in the act, but had caused it as well.

And I foolishly thought of Moriarty then. Sherlock Holmes's old enemy, that "Napoleon of Crime" who ruled the underworld of London like a spider rules its web. What better image for Enoch, whom I have come to think of more and more as a ruler of this *true* underworld, this human cesspool to which I've confined myself?

He looked away from me then, and went back and sat next to the boy. He waited until all movement had stopped, then knelt beside him and pulled the trumpet from the split throat. It was bent and dark with blood, which lay in a pool around the boy's head. Enoch put his face to the boy's, and I was glad it was turned away from me so that I could not see it. Yet I felt powerless to look away. It seemed, as it had with the old woman, that he was kissing the dead face. Yet, when his face came up after a few moments, it was free of blood.

He rose, smiled again in my direction, and passed on to the next car. I retreated, not wanting to be found in the presence of the dead by some transit cop.

I'm beginning to think of Enoch as the Devil himself, who rules this particular hell. Maybe I'm starting to flip out all the way. The thought scares me, scares me even more than Enoch does. I can just picture myself like Baggie, with her dead rats and her worn shopping bags, prowling these tunnels and trains like some frizzy-haired Charon. Even the thought of becoming Rags is appalling. There is a sense of the grotesque that I like to think I've avoided in my appearance and bearing, even though I've been down here for half a year, and still feel that nothing will

Lowland Rider

make me ascend. I think I will die here, whether soon or many years from now I have no idea. I only know I'd like to die like a man.

My self-disciplined inaction is starting to rankle as well. I hate Enoch. I would like, in some way, to cause his destruction, to kill him as painfully and mercilessly as he has, not *killed*, perhaps, but *caused* the deaths of others. I'm certain he *is* responsible. Maybe he's why I came down here. Among other things, so many other things. I still look for patterns.

I ate well today. I bought a hot dog, and had the man put everything on it. I asked where Bennie was, and he said that Bennie had retired. I'll miss him. This new man doesn't seem as happy as Bennie was, not happy at all. I'll miss the way Bennie would smile and say, "Run it through the garden, right?" Through the garden. That always made me laugh.

How can you have a garden where no sun shines?

I'll get some sleep now. I'm tired.

PART 1

Oh, there was a rider daring,
Yes, there was a rider bold,
Who hadna need for silver,
Nor had he need for gold.

His name was Jamie Gordon,
And frae glen to glen
'Twas the name most feared
By all the lowland men.

Death rode on his saddle,
And death rode by his side,
For death was a' there was to him,
Nae pomp, nor peace, nor pride.

This man, sae guid in years lang syne,
Sae kind to one and a',
Was pulled sae low by murther foul,
The sin of Cain's great fa'.

He had twa daughters very dear,
Whose eyen shone like the sun,
Also a wife, whose bonie smile
Could make the Isla run.

The love he bore for these fair three
Was like unto the love
That Jesu bore for man below
And his great Lord above.

One day when Gordon traveled out
About his lowland farm,
A band of outlaws sought his kin,
Purposed to do them harm.

They had their way with Gordon's wife,
And then they cruelly slew
His lovely wife, light of his life,
And both the daughters too . . .

—*Jamie Gordon, the Lowland Rider*

JESSE GORDON'S JOURNAL: SEPTEMBER 24, 1986

I have descended. I have come into Hell. I am here for eternity, or until I die, whichever comes first.

I loathe it, and that *is* good. It is damp and dark and the air is filthy. You chew it as much as you breathe it. It stinks too. It smells of sour bodies and shit and urine that's puddled too long, that's dried so it's smelled forever.

I'm here forever. It's been only three days, and already it feels like forever. I wonder if this is how prisoners feel when they know there's no hope of parole. I know there isn't, no hope at all, and I know because it's in no one's hands but my own. I'm my own jailer, and I've sentenced myself, though I'm still not sure why, and I don't know if I will ever be sure.

Why do we do things? Why take this job and not that one? Why marry *her* and not *her*? Why take *this* way home? Why love this man, hate another? Why live? Why die?

I used to believe it all had purpose, that the things I

did I did for a reason, that I was guided, even, if not by the good old Judeo-Christian white-bearded God, then at least by some *thing*. Even when bad things happened—a relative's death, a car engine blowing a gasket, throwing up my guts for no logical reason—I thought it was undoubtedly for the best. Somehow I would worm and weasel around until I had an answer, until I could rationalize it to myself.

But this I cannot rationalize. There is no reason for this. A merciful god, even a stupid, inept god, would not have let this happen. There is no *reason* for it, for any of it. And that means we live in Chaos, we reside in Hell, and we are all ultimately *alone* there.

And it is because of that aloneness that I write in this notebook. I bought two of them less than an hour ago. It was the first human contact I've had for three days, ever since I walked down the steps of Penn Station and said good-bye to daylight for good. I suppose it was the kind of human contact I may as well get used to here—detached, cold, hostile. Not one word was spoken. I merely put the notebooks down on the counter, laid two dollar bills beside them, and received my change. Very simple. A machine could have performed both functions.

So I write, and I wonder if anyone will ever read these words, come across them in the locker and care enough to see what they say. If so, I suppose I should start at the beginning.

My name is Jesse Gordon, and I am thirty-four years old. I have lived all my life in New York City—in the Bronx until I left my parents' home, and then in Manhattan. My father was an antique dealer —at least that's what the sign over his shop said. But beneath it in smaller letters read, FINE ART—FARE BOOKS, and that was where his heart was.

The old man had a good heart. That's why he never got out of the Bronx. It's also why my mother died when she did—of worry, and of fear.

The Bronx is Shit City. It's filled with junkies and thieves and people who would shove a knife into you for a dollar. My father's store was on Castle Hill Avenue in a neighborhood that got uglier and uglier over the years. When I was at NYU in the seventies, it got so bad that if I was involved in a school activity that would keep me in Manhattan after dark, I would crash at a friend's place rather than take the subway and walk the two blocks to my folks' apartment house.

Mom died of a heart attack in 1972, my sophomore year. It happened two days after Pop's most recent burglary—he had at least one a month. She had wanted Pop to sell the shop and find a place in Manhattan, or maybe Brooklyn, but he couldn't. It wasn't because he didn't want to, but because no one would buy, and because he had *no* money saved, none at all. He *could* have, if only he hadn't been so generous. The junkies, probably the same ones who had robbed him the week before, would come in with books mostly, and probably stolen at that, and Pop would give them a fair price, a damn *good* price, when they would've been content with a small fraction. I was in the shop with him one time when a woman came in with a baby. She was Hispanic.

Jesus, after what they did I still write that—Hispanic. Fuck it. She was a grease-ball spic who was probably thirty but looked fifty, her baby wrapped in a blanket that looked like it had lain under an old car for a month. She had three books with her, Reader's Digest Condensed Books from the sixties, utterly worthless, water-stained, smelling of mildew. She held them up to my father and asked in Spanish if he'd buy them. He understood her. He'd actually thought enough of those people to learn their language. This bittersweet, foolish look came into his face, and he just nodded and unlocked his cash register and gave her three dollars. I tried to stop him, to make him come to his senses. "Dad," I said, very reproachfully, and he just looked at me and shook his head. The woman didn't even say *gracias*, but scuttled out of the store as if she were afraid he'd change his mind and ask for the money back. She didn't know my father very well.

I was angry. I told him that that money was probably going to go right into her or her boyfriend's arm. And he just looked at me and shook his head again like he pitied me, and he said, "You've got to believe in people, Jesse. They're the only thing you *can* believe in. I want to think I helped feed her child, not her habit."

That was my father, that was what he thought, and that was what killed him.

After Mom died he insisted on keeping the store open, insisted on living in the apartment they'd always lived in, and over the years the neighborhood

Lowland Rider

deteriorated even further. By the time he was killed it seemed as if all the structures of his life had ended and were being replaced by the structures of my own. I had a wife, a child, a job, a home.

My wife was Donna, and even now, after so short a time, I struggle to remember her face outside of the memory of photographs. She was short and very pretty, with dark hair and a rather pale complexion. I remember that when I was falling in love with her, she struck me as looking like one of Poe's heroines, except that I had always thought of them as taller than Donna. When I graduated from NYU I got a job at a small advertising agency, a "no account" agency, as we referred to it, where I became a copywriter, and met Donna at one of the parties the agency threw for their clients. She worked for a finance company we did print ads for, and she was my liaison when I worked on the account. We started seeing each other and before too long we decided to get married. It was all very old-fashioned, very un–New Yorkish. There was no living together first. In fact, I had pretty well made up my mind that I loved her even before I talked her into bed. Once we were there I was sure of it.

We both kept working after we got married, until we decided we wanted a child. It was a decision that was long in coming, but we wanted to have a baby before Donna was thirty. Almost nine months from the first day we tried, Jennifer was born. She was a beautiful baby, and I know she would have been a beautiful little girl, a beautiful woman, if they hadn't killed her.

It hurts so much that I don't think it will ever stop

hurting. It's been three days now. It was Sunday when it happened. My whole family taken, so quickly and in such a way. Have there always been madmen? Has there always been evil in the world? I suppose so. But it seems as if now is their time, as if they have been hidden all these centuries and at last they are surfacing until each one of us comes face-to-face with them, and must cope or die.

Perhaps there is a third way. To build a wall around yourself. To harden yourself. To sink into the furnace and, instead of burning, to be annealed. To become one with steel, so that you never have to feel pain again, and, though you remember past pains, future ones can never hurt you. That is why I have come down to this, why I am where I am, and if I am to be burned instead of hardened, then even the flame holds no fear for me. I can't be hurt more.

I'm babbling. Putting these half-formed thoughts down on paper only makes me feel more confused than I already am. It isn't simple. There are reasons, but there are also irrationalities about what I've done. I realize that, and because I do I think I'm still sane. Whether or not I can maintain my sanity down here—there I'm not sure. I pray to God I . . .

That's very good. "Pray to God." It dies hard, faith. That I should use that term now is perhaps the most irrational thing of all. Pray to God indeed.

Finish, Jesse. Finish the story.

Yes. Here:

My name is Jesse Gordon and my family is dead.

My father died on the street, stabbed.

Lowland Rider

My wife died, raped and shot, on the floor of my father's back storeroom.

My baby died with a bullet in her head.

That is how simple it all was. That is the truth, that is my story, that is why I am here.

CHAPTER 2

Jesse Gordon was making love to his wife when the phone rang and they told him that his father had been killed. Donna stayed in the apartment with the baby while Jesse took a cab to Harlem Hospital on 136th Street, across the Harlem River from the Bronx where his father had lived. The cabby was reluctant to go so far uptown after midnight, but Jesse handed him a ten dollar bill that stopped his protestations. At the hospital he was met by a Detective Pinehurst, a dour looking man with pockmarked cheeks and a black moustache flecked with gray. "Mr. Gordon, I'm very sorry," he said perfunctorily.

"How did it happen?" Jesse asked. His voice was steady, but inside he felt as if he had fallen from a high precipice and not yet landed. Apprehension filled him, as though he were waiting for himself to cry or scream or both. Memories of his father slipped through his consciousness like thieves across a black rooftop: Coney Island and his father's boxlike, knee-length trunks, the whiteness of his inner arms as he threw himself above a wave; playing baseball on

Lowland Rider

Randall's Island, his father laughing when Jesse hit one over his head; the dry hack as the old man blew the dust from the fore-edges of his precious books, redistributing the colloids instead of effacing them, then taking a drag from his Lucky Strike and coughing again; the feel of the leathery skin, the wiry stubble against his own smoother cheek the last time he embraced his father in a good-bye.

Detective Pinehurst led the way into a small examining room and closed the door behind them before he answered Jesse's question. He indicated that Jesse should sit in the sole chair, a dented plastic and chrome affair. Pinehurst took the examining stool. "It shows every indication of a mugging," the detective said. "Apparently your father was walking home—he was found half a block from the entrance to his apartment house." Pinehurst stopped at Jesse's explosive sigh, then went on. "His wallet was beside his body, but there was no money in it."

"How was he killed?"

Pinehurst shrugged. "By the mugger, we assume."

"I mean *how*," Jesse pressed. "A gun? A knife?"

"A knife. He was stabbed."

"Did he suffer?"

"I'm afraid the doctors will have to answer that."

"But you know, don't you?"

Now it was Pinehurst's turn to sigh. "Preliminary examination seemed to indicate a stab wound in the left lung. That's not necessarily an immediate cause of death."

"Then he might have lived for a while?"

"He might have. Then again, maybe not. Mr. Gordon, the doctors and the medical examiner can answer these questions a whole lot better than me."

"All right then. Let me see the doctor."

The physician who had made the examination had gone home at midnight, but at Jesse's insistence, a phone call was put through. The man did not sound as if he had been sleeping. "The point of entry was between the fourth and fifth rib, just missing the heart," the doctor said gruffly.

"He didn't die immediately?"

"I doubt it. Death from this type of wound . . . are you sure you want to hear all this?"

"Yes."

"Well, death probably came through asphyxiation rather than loss of blood. Your father might have lived, oh, say twenty minutes after the attack."

"Now wait a minute." Jesse's voice was edged with iron. "Does that mean that he could have lived if . . . if someone had called an ambulance, gotten help?"

"That's hard to say."

"But it might have been possible."

"Maybe. Maybe not. It's really beside the point now. I understand Mr. Gordon was dead when they found him."

"I . . . didn't know that."

"If it's any consolation, I doubt that your father suffered very much. He probably went into shock right away. It's . . . a fairly effective defense the body puts up against pain." There was silence on the other end of the line. "Mr. Gordon?"

"Yes. Thank you."

Lowland Rider

"That's all right. I'm very sorry about your father."

Jesse made the necessary arrangements with the hospital, and Detective Pinehurst drove him back to 72nd Street. Donna was sitting at the kitchen table with a cup of coffee when he came in. She had been crying, and when she saw Jesse she cried again, went to him and embraced him. Exhausted, he wept at last. She led him to the sofa and sat with him, holding him, until the tears were gone. "The bastards killed him, Donna," he said. "I guess I always knew they would. He had to know too." When he fell asleep, she covered him with the afghan, then went into the bedroom and lay awake for a long time.

In the morning Jesse Gordon awoke with the feeling that everything had been a dream, that he had sweated through one of those tyrannical nightmares in which a loved one is taken and comes back to say good-bye and so makes the parting all the more painful. But when he found himself on the couch, he knew that it had all been real, and he wrapped the afghan's tired fringe around his fingers and tightened the cords until his fingertips turned red, then cried again.

He made the funeral arrangements mechanically, and buried his father on a bright and sunny Thursday afternoon. He was surprised at the rapidity and ease with which his father's life insurance company paid off the fifty thousand dollar policy of which his father had made him sole beneficiary, and rather dazedly deposited it in a low interest, easy access savings account until he could decide how to invest it.

Two weeks later he received a call from the assessor, who wanted to meet with him at his father's store. "I imagine it'll take more than a few hours," Jesse told the assessor, a soft-voiced man named Rhoads.

"We can make several visits until I'm finished," Rhoads said. "I suppose evenings would suit you best?"

"A weekend would be better," Jesse answered.

Rhoads sighed. "It always is." They arranged to meet Sunday afternoon at the store.

Just as Jesse was slipping on his jacket prior to their meeting, Donna decided she wanted to go with him.

"What about Jenny?"

"I'll bring her along."

"It's such a bad neighborhood . . ."

"It's always been bad, and that's never stopped me from going along to visit your dad before. What's the difference now?"

She had a point. But there *was* a difference. His father, the protective totem, was gone now, and he realized that as long as his father had been alive, he'd felt assured that the Bronx was not a jungle, that if an old man could live there and remain happy, then he and his family could walk there unscathed as well. Now that totem had been toppled, evil had drawn too near, and he was afraid, afraid for his wife and child, afraid for himself, afraid for anyone human who walked the streets where his father had betrayed him by dying.

"We'll be all right, Jesse. We'll be going down in daylight, and be out before dark, won't we?"

"There's no reason for you to go."

"It'll be the last time I see the shop," Donna countered. "There's so much of your father in it. It'll be like saying good-bye for the last time."

If he had not been so weary, so full of grief, he might have argued with her, but his soul-sickness had sapped his will, and he only nodded acquiescence.

The day was cloudy, but no rain darkened the city's concrete floor. They went by subway, taking the Lexington Avenue–Pelham Bay Park line, the fastest way to the Bronx. Jesse had no feeling one way or another about the subway. It was merely a part of New York life the same way as was standing in lines, or not taking your hand off your briefcase, not even for an instant. You watched out for crazies, but you learned that most of them were harmless—the weak, the poor, the dwellers in the jungle who had lost everything but the will to survive. There were bag ladies and winos and junkies, beggars slick and roughhewn. Generally the worse the appearance, the less cautious one had to be. Nevertheless, caution was the watchword. There had been plenty of times when he and Donna had moved to a new car because of a truly threatening presence at the other end of theirs, and even a few episodes in which they had left a train entirely, after which they would laugh away their discomfort, shake their heads, and murmur, "Weird . . ." trying to forget the fear that had palpably driven them from their car, *theirs*.

Still they rode. It was a compromise between them and the evil in the city, not the city itself, for it was not the city that bred the evil, but the people of the city. It was the people who robbed and raped and killed, and if the city acted upon them, it did so only in the same way that the sea acts upon sharks.

They got off at the Castle Hill Avenue station, and walked up into daylight. The odor of decaying garbage hung heavily in the air. Plastic bags the color of deep forests lay on the curbside, split by pressure or by claws, bottles and cans and boxes strung out through the rents like entrails dragged from carrion. Rusted autos, tireless, sat here and there, abandoned forts on some new frontier of civilization. Even in daytime, there were few pedestrians abroad. A sixtyish black couple walked past the boarded-up storefronts. The man, stout but muscular, wore a bright, lime-green leisure suit with a zebra-stripe shirt, and the woman, uncontrollably fat, wore a red pantsuit that circumnavigated her rolls like a second skin. The sartorial air of fiesta was belied by the pocked and pitted mine fields of their faces. Eyes were hollow, mouths drawn in flat, firm, and unyielding lines. The couple glanced at Jesse, Donna, and the baby, then looked quickly away, as though they expected the innocent white trio to transmute into apocalyptic beasts if gazed at for too long.

Jesse's father's shop cupped a corner of a street, its windows facing west and south. The glass, which had before always been polished, now brooded dully under a layer of grime behind the security bars. An illegible scrawl of yellow spray-painted graffiti coated both bars and glass. The legend, "Gordon's Antiques," painted in the fifties on the inside of the glass, was completely hidden from view.

Jesse fit the first of the three keys into the heavily paneled door. It took several minutes of turning the keys in different directions, but finally the door swung

Lowland Rider

open. He fumbled for the light switch, flipped it on, and Donna followed him in with the baby. He closed the door behind them, locking the sturdiest latch.

The interior of the store was cluttered but neat. The stock consisted primarily of furniture and bric-a-brac, each item bearing a card on which was written the price and a letter code beneath, telling what his father had paid for each item. "You should have seen this place twenty years ago," he told Donna. "It was loaded with treasures, not all this junk."

In truth, the shop had ceased being profitable years before. But Jesse's father, in the days in which the neighborhood had had a certain gentility, had saved and invested wisely enough to run the business as little more than a hobby in his later years. Only, at the time of his death, instead of selling marble-topped tables and Louis Quinze settees, his inventory had been reduced to old television cabinets and overstuffed sofas, hulking, upholstered lumps that he bought for five dollars and sold for ten. The books and art still in stock were likewise negligible, mostly book club editions and forgotten bestsellers of the thirties and forties, worthless, though carefully dusted and free of mildew.

The only remaining pieces of value were secured in a half-closet, half-safe, which had always stood fast against occasional burglars. It was on the second floor in a back room which was itself kept locked. As Jesse opened the door and stepped into the room, he remembered when its shelves had been filled with richly bound books, magnificently illustrated. But now those shelves were bare. He tried not to look at them as he picked out the key for the closet and slipped it into the lock.

He was not disappointed by its contents. There were framed Icart etchings, some fine Parrish prints, and several original oils by the more obscure members of the Hudson River School which Jesse thought might be worth five figures each. For a moment he toyed with the idea of hiding them in the basement so the assessor would not see them, but then decided not to, whether out of morality or fear of being caught he was not sure. There were books as well, duplicates, he imagined, of those in the collection in his father's barricaded apartment. He slid a volume from the shelf and examined it, an early edition of *Percy's Reliques* rebound in leather. He remembered reading a popular edition of the work when he lived with his father and mother. As he glanced over the contents he recalled the titles more vividly, and felt a touch of the same chill that the ballads had inspired in him when he was eight—"The Bride's Burial," "The Witches' Song," "Admiral Hosier's Ghost," and "The Lunatic Lover."

There was a bookmark further back, and he opened the volume to "The Lady Isabella's Tragedy," and let his eyes roam over the verses about a stepmother who caused her stepdaughter to be killed and baked into a pie for her unsuspecting husband.

Thou art the doe that I must dresse;
See here, behold my knife;
For it is pointed presently

Lowland Rider

To ridd thee of thy life. . . .
For pitye's sake do not destroye. . . .
My ladye with your knife;
You know shee is her father's joye,
For Christe's sake save her life.

Then came the slaying of the daughter, the making of the pie, the accusation of the kitchen boy, the burning to death and boiling in zinc of the treacherous stepmother and master-cook. Jesse began to think that perhaps New York was not the worst conceivable place in which to live.

An unfamiliar sound jarred him from his reverie, a clattering from down below, and it took a second for him to realize that it was the crash of knuckles on glass, someone knocking at the front door.

"Donna!" he cried, and ran out of the room, the book still in his hand. He pictured her innocently throwing the door open wide with one arm, the baby in the other, revealing the man who had killed his father, come back to claim the rest of his family. "Donna! Wait!" he called, dashing down the steps three at a time, feeling them wince under his weight. "Don't open it!"

When he saw her standing beside a playpen she'd made from sofa cushions, he realized she had had no intention of opening the door without him being there. Jenny, clad in a bright green sleeper, was bouncing from side to side of her temporary confines, gurgling with amusement at the novelty of her surroundings.

"I waited," said Donna, as if puzzled by Jesse's alarm. "It's probably just the assessor."

Jesse went to the door. Through the murky glass he saw a hatless man in a trench coat. He was clean shaven and nearly bald, and a red-striped, regimental tie peeped from beneath his drawn-together lapels. His eyes were small and sharp, and narrowed when he noticed Jesse observing him. "Rhoads?" Jesse said through the door, stretching his mouth around the word. The man nodded, patted a briefcase at his side, and Jesse undid the latch.

"Come on in," Jesse said. "Sorry to be so cautious."

"Can't say I blame you," said Rhoads. "I wouldn't be so quick to open my door in this neighborhood either."

Introductions were made, and Rhoads said that he preferred to start on the first floor. Within a few minutes, the short, balding man was quietly appraising, Jenny was sleeping, and Donna was looking through a pile of old *National Geographic*. Jesse slipped upstairs, locked the closet with its treasure of artwork and books, and put the key back into his pocket. He spent the rest of the afternoon helping Rhoads, pulling furniture out from dark corners so the man could see what lay behind.

When they were halfway through the goods on the second floor, Rhoads stopped. He had been chain-smoking all day, and now looked at Jesse apologetically. "Out of smokes," he said, carefully extinguishing a Winston. "There a store around here?"

"There's a bodega two blocks west. But it's getting

Lowland Rider

dark. Want to knock off?"

Rhoads shook his head. "I can finish in another hour. Took less time than I thought. Frankly, a lot of this stuff only has salvage value. Now the books and artwork in the closet I can only list. They'll have to be appraised separately later." He sighed. "But I'm not gonna get there without my smokes."

"All right, look. You just keep going, and I'll go for the cigarettes."

"Winstons. Two packs, huh?" Rhoads took out his wallet, but Jesse waved a hand.

"On me," he said.

"Thanks, but a man's got to pay for his own vices." Rhoads thrust three dollar bills in Jesse's hand.

Jesse went downstairs, where Donna was napping on a fifteen dollar foam rubber couch. He shook her gently till she awoke. "I've got to go get Rhoads some smokes. I'll lock up." She nodded sleepily and closed her eyes again.

He stepped outside into the dusk. The street was quiet and empty, with only an occasional car passing. If the three of them walked to the subway with Rhoads, they would probably be all right. There was little profit in accosting three adults, or at least he hoped any prospective muggers would see it that way.

Jesse turned the key in the top and strongest lock, and jiggled the door handle. Then he started down the street, squaring his shoulders and drawing himself up to try and look even bigger than his six feet two, 190 pounds.

The bodega was still open, and he entered its

painted-over door thankfully. He had seen no one on the street, but had felt watched for the entire two blocks. The interior of the store was stuffy, cluttered, and hot, and the overpowering scent of spices nearly staggered Jesse. Unsure if the proprietor, a thirtyish, whipcord-thin man with onyx hair, spoke English, Jesse held up two fingers and said, "Winstons. Two."

The man, with an air of insouciance, turned and pulled a pair of the red packs from a plastic dispenser. "Anything else?"

"No." Jesse handed him the three bills. "That's it."

The man unlocked the heavy register and fitted the bills inside, then closed the drawer. He looked at Jesse, who was still standing in front of the counter. "Matches?"

"Uh . . . change?"

"Buck-fifty a pack," the man said, then smiled. Jesse looked at him a minute longer, then turned and walked out, wondering if the man ripped off his own people as well, or just whites.

Through the rapidly growing darkness, the antique shop windows glowed with a dull yellow light as Jesse approached them, as though it were aged oilcloth rather than glass in the windows. He could make out nothing distinct within. He fitted his key into the lock and pushed. Suddenly the door swung inward far faster than his gentle shove could have caused it to, and he felt his right forearm grasped by a powerful hand that tugged him forward so that he lost his balance and fell heavily onto the floor. There was a roaring in his ears through which he heard the crash of

Lowland Rider

the door closing like a scream through deep water. Then there was laughter, slow, cool, and methodical. Jesse Gordon looked up.

There were six of them. They were Chicanos in their late teens or early twenties, and they were big, with none of the bantam size that Jesse had always associated with Latins. They wore no identifying gang colors, but Jesse received a dominating impression of leather and metal. "Welcome back, baby," a voice said, coated with a Spanish accent, and there was more laughter.

"Thought you was never gonna leave," sneered another voice.

Jesse got to his hands and knees and shook his throbbing head. He looked directly at the largest man, whose hair was oiled in a cock-fighting pompadour and who wore a thin wisp of moustache like an ancient scar. "What do you want?"

"Everything," the man leered. "But first, money. You know?"

"Where's my wife? Donna!" Jesse leaped to his feet and was grabbed immediately by three of the men. The leader, to whom Jesse had spoken, smoothly took a pistol from his jacket pocket and trained its black eye on Jesse's own.

"Your wife's fine. Take a look." He gestured over his shoulder, and in the shadows of the strangers he could see Donna lying on an old davenport, her hands bound behind her, a dirty gag jammed in her mouth. Her eyes were wide with terror. "No harm done, man. Not yet."

Jesse looked around frantically and saw Jennifer, still sleeping serenely in her jury-rigged crib. "Don't you hurt them," he snarled.

"No way," the man with the gun said. "Not as long as you help us out."

Then Jesse remembered Rhoads. "The man. The bald man. Where is he?"

The leader jerked his head upward. "Upstairs."

"Is he . . . did you hurt him?"

"Don't know. I guess we hurt him. Chico." He turned to the boy at his right. "Bring that guy down. Let's see if we hurt him." The boy disappeared into the back, in the direction of the stairway. "Whyn't you sit down? Sit down by the lady, huh?" Jesse moved to the davenport and sat, touching Donna's head with his hand, smoothing back the hair from her sweating brow. "Sure is a pretty lady. Your wife, huh?" Jesse nodded. "And your kid." He nodded again. "Be a shame anything happen to them."

"Just leave them alone. You take what you want, but you leave them alone."

"All depends on you."

Somewhere in the building there was a rhythmic thumping, as if something hollow were being struck over and over at regular intervals with a stick. Or a bone. Jesse looked around in confusion, but was unable to determine exactly what the thumping was. Then it stopped, and in its place came a swishing noise. The curtains to the back room parted, Chico appeared with a pair of feet and ankles jutting from beneath his arms like some monstrous growth, and

Lowland Rider

Jesse realized that what he had heard was Rhoads's head striking each step as he was dragged down them.

"There he is." The leader smiled. "You think we hurt him?"

Jesse got up and ran over to the prostrate form. Rhoads's bald head looked like a cracked egg with an aborted bloody yoke seeping out. His eyes were opened so that only the whites showed. His mouth was also bloody, and his front teeth were cracked. Jesse listened for the sound of breathing, but it didn't come. "You *killed* him!" He reached for a pulse, found none.

"A little accident. He wouldn't help us out. But you will, won'tcha?"

Jesse's gut cramped. He knew beyond doubt that he and his family were in the hands of madmen who were capable of anything. His first response, barely contained, was to attack, to take as many down with him as he could before he died. But that, he knew, would do nothing for Donna and Jennifer, and they were the ones he had to think about, the ones who must *not* end up like Rhoads, poor dead Rhoads who had come with his box of sharpened pencils and legal pads to perform a sane act of toting up in a nest of insanity; oh God bless poor, foolish Rhoads, who was dead and could not be helped, and *that* was what he had to remember.

"What do you want? I'll give you whatever you want."

"The money. All the money the old guy had."

"There's . . . there's no money here. No cash."

"Bullshit, man. The money in the room upstairs. The room this guy"—the leader gestured with his gun to Rhoads on the floor—"wouldn't open."

"Oh Jesus . . ." Jesse rubbed at his mouth nervously. "He *couldn't* open it. He didn't have the *key*."

"Who does?"

"*I* do." He fumbled in his pockets, wondering if he had been there, would Rhoads still be alive. All for the want of a key. He found it and held it out to them. "Here! This is it!" The bright key shone, graillike.

"Uh-uh. *You* come upstairs and open it for us."

"But there's no money in it, just pictures and some books."

"Don't piss me off. This guy here, *he* pissed me off. *You* piss me off, *they* pay for it." He gave an airy wave of his arm toward Jesse's wife and daughter.

"Leave them out of this," he warned coldly.

"Upstairs then. Manny, Juan, stay down here and watch them."

Jesse and the other four ascended the stairs then, Jesse leading the way. He was glad the stairs were dark, so that he did not have to see the bloody spots where Rhoads's head had bounced, but once he nearly slipped on a small patch of wetness, which he imagined as being only one thing. Soon they were in front of the door. The leader gestured, and Jesse unlocked it, swung it open, and stepped back.

The leader walked in and looked around like a sergeant inspecting raw recruits. He passed his fingertips over the gilded frames as if searching for dust, picked up a few books and thumbed through them, tucking them under his arm. He looked up and down,

Lowland Rider

weighing the situation judicially. In an instant he changed.

Fury took him, and he flung the books at Jesse, who staggered back, angry and confused. "What is this *shit*!" the leader shouted, spraying spittle with each word. He thrust his pistol under Jesse's chin, pushing it up, making him growl from the pain. "The *money*, motherfucker! Where the money?"

Jesse's arms jerked spastically, wanting to push the gun away, to ease the pain that arced through the veins and glands of his jaw, but knowing that to touch the prodding metal would mean his death. "No money," he gritted out.

The gun came down, giving relief for an instant. Then the barrel cracked along his jaw, and the pain turned his legs watery so that it was an effort to remain standing. As he brought his head back up, he saw in slow procession the leader's studded belt, the gold cross nestled in the hair of his chest like an altar in a jungle, the constellation of too white teeth set in the dark sky of the face.

"One more time. One more. The money."

"You can have all I've got. Or I'll get more. But there's nothing here, I sw—"

Jesse was powerless to stop the second blow. The pain of the first had terrified him and taken away any sense of quickness with which he might have reacted. The backhanded metal caught him beneath the cheekbone, smashed his eye closed, ripped a gash from beneath his brow to his hairline. He fell back, the room dancing, and felt himself kicked, poked, half-lifted, half-dragged until the floor fell away and he knew that he was thundering, rolling down the stairs, the same stairs down which Rhoads had been, in comparison, so much more carefully transported. Wooden swords hacked at him from beneath, while on each side the walls bludgeoned him. He tried to cry out in his terror, to ease his pain in words, but he was capable of only a dry hissing.

The cessation of blows told him he had reached the bottom, and then rough hands were on him again. Blood stung his eyes as he strained to see where he was and what was being done to him. His body ached in a hundred places, but through the agony he felt more delicate, refined torments, and, blinking away the blood, isolating the sensations, he knew that he was being bound to a chair. Cords sawed into his wrists and ankles, and another, like a snake, coiled round his neck so that, to breathe, he thrust his head up and back, and expanded his windpipe in a desperate way of which he had not known he was capable. His throat went raw with the effort, but he could breathe, noisily and harshly.

"Looser," someone said, and the pressure on his throat slackened, the rough sound of his breathing grew quieter.

"I told you, asshole. One warning, and that's all."

Jesse's eyes cleared so that he could see the couch on which his wife lay. Knives flashed, and his body tensed, every muscle surged against their bonds, even though he knew he was helpless to intervene. But the knives descended on rope, not flesh, and in the place of the rope dark hands held Donna's arms and legs, pulling them apart, spread-eagling her. The knives sparked again, dove and rose like silver gulls, pecking away the surface of seawater to reveal fleshy sand beneath. Her bare limbs trembled, and he could see how desperately she tried to draw them together. But the dark hands were steely, holding her open, obscene in her accessibility.

Jesse cried out in protest, in horror, and in love. But they jammed a cloth into his mouth so that only his eyes screamed as they did to her what he had never done, and he heard, like songs of dying men, the breath pass into her and out of her, through nostrils made huge by hidden hurts.

Humiliation and sorrow and rage all warred within him, and he wished for death rather than the contemplation of the mystery of things to be. But death did not come, not yet. Only the repetitive, eternal abuse of the woman he loved, only the death he read in her eyes.

The leader came over to Jesse, grabbed him by the hair, and swung his head up so that Jesse stared directly into his face. "All right, fucker, you just lost something. You want to lose more? Money worth that much to you?"

"I swear . . ." Jesse grated out, "no money . . ."

"We kill the bitch, man. I'm not shittin'."

Jesse began to cry, but as he sobbed the rope dug more tightly into his throat, and he was forced to stop in order to breathe. But the tears still ran down his face.

"That what you want?" The leader pulled his pistol

from his waistband and brandished it. "Get offa her," he told one of the others.

"I ain't *done*, man!"

"Asshole, I said get *off*!" The boy fell back at the leader's push. His pants, tangled around his ankles, tripped him up, and he sprawled on the floor, knocking over part of the makeshift crib. Jennifer began to scream.

The men laughed, all except the leader. "Shut up," he said, and they obeyed. "I hate kids that scream, man. I got screamin' kids around me all the fucking time. It drives me crazy, you know?" He knelt by Jennifer's side and pointed the gun at her face. "Shut up, kid."

"No . . ." Jesse said. "Oh dear God, no . . ."

Jennifer shrieked on, louder now.

"I told you to shut up." The leader's thumb brought the hammer back with a dry *click*.

"Luis, don't."

The leader looked up at the boy who had spoken. He was tall and thin, and looked younger than the others. "Did you say something to me?"

The boy's hand jittered nervously at his side. "Not the kid, Luis, huh? Please?"

"Why not? Tell me why not, Carlos? Tell me why I shouldn't blow *all* these motherfuckers to hell. Go ahead, you tell me."

Carlos's mouth opened, but the sound of the shot drowned out anything he might have said. Everyone but Luis, the leader, jerked as if an electric shock had struck them, and Jesse surged against his ropes, his

Lowland Rider

eyes closing with the effort. When he opened them, his daughter was dead.

"You gotta talk faster than that, Carlos." Luis got to his feet, grabbed an afghan from a chair, and threw it at Carlos. "Cover up that mess."

Jesse was hollow. At that moment he felt as if an icy shovel had dug out his chest, and he wondered weakly if he was in shock, or dreaming, or dying from having the light taken from his life. He only dimly saw Carlos kneel and gently cover his little girl's broken form, heard as if from a far distance Luis's voice saying, "It's war, man. The fortunes of war. Us against them."

Then he remembered Donna. She already looked dead, her eyes opened wide, staring at the ceiling, unable to accept the reality of what had just occurred.

"No money now," Luis said. "I believe you now, man. Shit. What a wasted day. I hate to waste my days." He put the pistol against Donna's head and pulled the trigger. Everyone jumped again.

"*Madre dios*, Luis!" Carlos cried, his hands held out in supplication.

"You want to let them live, you asshole? Identify us? That would be fucking smart, wouldn't it?"

A short, stocky boy stepped forward. "What about the stuff upstairs? Paintings and shit."

"Fuck it." Luis shook his head sharply. "Can't move that shit."

Jesse sat, stunned, no longer aware of the ropes biting into his wrists, his neck. He was shocked beyond tears or screaming. The realization that his family was dead, and that there existed such men in the world who could unhesitatingly perform such an act had poleaxed his mind. He had believed, had known there were such people in the abstract, but to actually come face-to-face with them, to have them destroy *your* wife, *your* child, was unfathomable, unbelievable, unbearable. The world had become, all too suddenly, a mass of corruption, a cancer. Jesse Gordon was drained of love, of compassion, of sanity.

"Let me die," he said clearly, seeing nothing but the great abyss before him.

"What, man?"

"Let me die. Kill me."

He hated them, but it was a weak hate, enervated by despair. He had fallen so far that the desire to strike the darkness at the bottom was far greater than his hatred.

"Kill you? That what you want?"

"Yes."

"Man, what you wanta die for? Man, that's *sick*."

"Spic. Spic asshole. Motherfucker." Jesse said the words dully, to enrage Luis, to make him throw up the gun and fire and send Jesse into that deep, welcoming dark he so craved.

"Nice talk. Listen to this. This guy's, what is it, suicidal. You wanta die, huh? You feel pretty bad, right? Okay, you die. But we make it take a while, huh?"

"Luis," the short boy said, "we gotta get out of here. Somebody hear the shots and—"

"We go. But we burn this shit first. Manny, I seen some kerosene in the back. Get it." Luis narrowed his eyes and looked at Carlos. "You got some problems, chickenshit?"

"I got no problems."

"Then you get that chickenshit look offa your face."

They stood in silence until Manny came back with a two-gallon can of kerosene. "Throw it around, man. Get the place nice and wet . . . good, that's good. Hey, careful! Don't get any on our man here. We don't wanta grill him, we just wanta roast him slow like."

When Manny was done, the smooth surfaces of the room gleamed, the fabrics were darkened, the smell was sharply sweet. "Who got a pack of matches?" One of the boys handed a dog-eared book to Luis, who tossed it back into the boy's face. "A *full* pack, man! Got to be a *full* pack." He accepted another, examined it, and nodded approval. "Good. Okay. Now who got the purse and the wallets?"

"Yo." A hand held up the booty.

"All right. Out." They left obediently. Luis stood in the doorway and looked at Jesse. "You wanta die, you go ahead."

He struck a match, set fire to the pack, and tossed it into the room. It landed on a kerosene saturated couch, whose upholstery sprang into fiery life. Jesse watched it burn, watched as the yellow-blue flames crawled onto and across the carpet, enveloping more and more of the room. A door slammed, and when he looked back, Luis was gone. Jesse got ready to die.

The heat seared him, and he imagined his flesh was already burning, popping out in big bubbles that splashed blood geyserlike into the air. He saw the couch on which Donna lay burst into flame, and watched as her body glowed and darkened and disappeared in flame. He thought of nothing. His mind was empty of all but death, blasted by what he had seen and heard in what he expected to be the last hour of his life.

The fire had just begun to touch his daughter, and his mind was slowly becoming aware of how much the individual flames looked like fingers gently cradling his little girl, when the front door flew open and a breeze rushed in, making the fire leap up and roar dully. Then someone was at his side, and a knife flashed, and there was new pressure at the places where the ropes held him, and a voice:

"Fuck him, man, can't do this, ain't right, get you out of here, man, get you out . . ."

Carlos sawed at the ropes haphazardly, so that several times the knife slashed Jesse's wrists and legs, and each sharp pain sparked him, galvanized him into a clearer recognition of what was happening, what had happened, and why, so that by the time the ropes were off him, and he knew that he would not burn, he had become alive again, alive and full of hate.

His legs, though free, would not function, and he toppled sideways out of the chair. A grunt of pain escaped him, and he reached out toward the fleeing Carlos, who turned, looked back, hesitated, then came once more to Jesse's side. "Come *on*, man," he said, fitting his hands beneath Jesse's armpits, "we gotta get *out*."

Suddenly Jesse twisted in the boy's grasp, grabbed Carlos's left wrist with his right hand, and pulled him

Lowland Rider

across the front of Jesse's body so that the body fell on his left side. As he scrambled for footing, Jesse's arms came up and down, smashing into Carlos's face. The boy moaned and went limp long enough for Jesse to find the knife. He opened the blade and began to stab.

Carlos squealed and tried to stop the knife, but it was useless. Jesse was far stronger, and Jesse was mad. The twists and turns of life and death had sidetracked rationality. He did not care that Carlos had come back at the risk of his own life to save him. The only thing that mattered at that moment was that Carlos was one of them who had done it, who had done everything, and he plunged the blade into the boy's face and chest and neck over and over, until they were both soaked with blood, and Carlos lay still.

By then, the flames were crawling around Jesse's feet. He folded the knife, jammed it into his pocket, and staggered out the door. Halfway down the street, he heard the first siren, and shambled back into an alleyway. It was dark and empty and cool, and he closed his eyes and fell onto the stones, letting their chill dampness soothe his aching body. He slept.

When he awoke, it was still night, although the dim light in the alley had another quality now. It was of a dark redness, like blood, and in its light Jesse's bloodied hands were black with a blackness one could fall into. He looked at his hands and remembered everything. Then he rolled over and vomited. When the sickness passed and he could think again, he thought first of Donna and Jennifer and of the fact that they were dead, gone away from him forever, and he began to weep. Rage took him, and he slammed his fists against the unrelenting stones until the sides of his hands began to bleed. Then he stopped, and remembered that he had killed the boy who had come back to help him.

The world was an open sore, and now he was no better than those who had hurt him. He saw the city as a great wound in which maggots teemed, thirsting for blood, and he was one among many, one of the filthy white grubs that clawed and burrowed. The killing had dehumanized him, and he felt filthy, as if he would never be clean again, regardless of whether or not the blood would come off his hands. He felt soulless. He felt dead.

He would bury himself.

He evaded the crimson eyes of police cars and fire engines by leaving through the other end of the alley. There was still change in his pocket, enough to get a subway token with which to get back to his apartment. He went through the night, all the way from the Bronx to Manhattan, with blood on his hands and clothes. But no one said a word to him about it, so he knew that he was dead and unseen. No one who shared his subway car looked at him, no one noticed him on the street, even the doorman in his building sat with his back to him and did not look up as Jesse stepped into the elevator.

In his apartment he stripped off his clothes and washed until his body was clean. Then he walked naked from room to room. He picked up things that had belonged to Donna, that she had touched every

Lowland Rider

day. He stood over Jennifer's crib, looking into it and seeing her there. He looked into the mirror for a very long time, memorizing himself, knowing that he would never be naked again.

From his chest of drawers, he took three pairs of underwear and three pairs of socks, two short-sleeved cotton T-shirts for summer, and two black wool turtlenecks for winter, two pairs of jeans, a wool stocking cap, and a lightweight, down-filled jacket. He picked up a color photograph of Donna and Jennifer from the nightstand, set it on the bed, then put it back where it had been.

"No," he said quietly, even that small word making his battered jaw ache.

A brown leather shoulder bag was in his closet. He got it out, opened it, and fit the clothes inside. As he zipped the bag shut, the telephone rang. He looked at it, but did not answer, and eventually it stopped ringing. Then he sat down and waited for morning.

Just after dawn, he drank some milk and ate a few slices of bread. At nine o'clock he dressed in a suit, and put the bag over his shoulder. The last thing he ever did in the rooms he had shared with his wife and child was to take the bankbooks from the china closet and put them into his pocket.

His bank opened at ten o'clock, and he closed out the checking account and the savings account he had opened with his father's insurance money. The bank employees were doubtful and suspicious, but Jesse's credentials were in order, and they gave him the money grudgingly, over fifty thousand dollars in twenty dollar bills and ten rolls of quarters. These he added to the contents of his shoulder bag.

The morning was cool as he walked the twenty blocks to Penn Station. He watched the people he passed more closely than he ever had before, and saw greed in the grim faces of the men, hardness in the painted faces of the women. He was glad to be dead, glad to be going under the ground where they all, every one of them, were dead.

The station was crowded with people hauling suitcases on wheels, and Jesse though the noise they made sounded like hundreds of squealing rats. He went down a hall toward a subway entrance until he came to an alcove housing a wall full of metal lockers with a decal of an eagle, wings spread, on each one. There was a rest room nearby, and he went into it. A young black man stood at a urinal. He glanced at Jesse, then back at his own reflection. Jesse entered the booth at the far end of the row and took off the suit, folding it neatly, and put on one of the pairs of jeans and black turtlenecks he had in his bag. Then he put a small wad of twenty dollar bills and a handful of quarters into his pocket and zipped the bag shut. When he came out of the booth the black man was gone.

Jesse left the rest room and walked back to the lockers, where he selected one in the top row. He put the folded suit and shoulder bag into it, dropped two quarters into the coin slot, and closed the door. He drew the key from the lock and looked at the number on both it and the locker itself. 4602.

Lowland Rider

He put the key into his pocket and walked to the subway entrance, where he purchased a dozen tokens. Pushing through the turnstile, he walked to the platform for the IND uptown local. When it arrived, he stepped on and sat down.

The ballad of the Lowland Rider had begun.

PART 2

Home he did ride, and woe betide
When he saw what was done.
He swore to rend the killers' flesh
Before the day was done.

Then did he ride ower countryside
Until the murthering crew
Came into sight, and he did fight,
And every man he slew.

But in the midst of bonie brawl,
A young child by perchance
Did enter in, and bold Gordon
Nae gave him half a glance,

But struck with speed, too late to heed
The father's warning cry.
In coldest grue the child he slew,
And tears came to his eye.

Loud Gordon wailed when he beheld
The boy to whom he'd giv'n
A deadly blow, and made to go
Unto his Lord in Heav'n.

"I have brought death to this sweet bairn,
As death was brought to me.
For Jesu's sake, the law should break
Me on the gallows tree."

Away he rode into the night,
And stopped within a glen,
And there he swore to hide away
From sight of living men . . .

—*Jamie Gordon, the Lowland Rider*

CHAPTER 3

There was no poetry in the subway. It was composed of surfaces with no rhythms. In the stations, tile predominated, the color of old men's teeth, and beneath one's feet cement, never clean, stretched snowlike in all directions, into distant chambers, up toothy steps, down into maws that seemed volcanically lit, with tongues of yellow fire. It was a cavern of flatness, with the omnipresent crevasse of the tracks, a canyon dropping into darkness.

Within the tile walls, and deeper in—inside the glass and metal tubes that burrowed through the lightless tunnels—the people moved, and stood, and sat, each of them lost within themselves as well, twice-buried. The floor drew their sight, or books, or newspapers, the concentration on which steadied them, held their center, while without they were rattled and whirled down black paths, shunted from one dark region to the next. Eventually they rose, left the false light, and ascended into day.

But there were some who never ascended, or, if at all, only infrequently. The pit was their home. They had learned to live with walls all around them, the stench of urine, the grayness at their feet, with the sounds of crashing wheels, of huge blocks of air displaced by the rush of the trains. They survived on the debris of the surface dwellers, of food discarded, money lost, occasional generosity. Often they stole, often they were caught, and just as often were set free again to scurry back to their holes. Most of them were mad, but the city had run out of room for its madmen, so they wandered the streets, and sank like stones into the tunnels for shelter from the rain and snow, and the discouraging presence of the sane. The passengers feared them. The transit police tolerated them and pitied them, and sometimes fed them. They dubbed them "skells," walking skeletons, dwellers with death, denizens of the city's large grave.

Gladys H. Mitchell had been a skell for fifteen years. Prior to that, she had been a prostitute. She had come down into the subway when she was thirty-eight years old and looked fifty. Her skin was etched with wrinkles, and her breasts hung low. Makeup alone could no longer hide the ravages of her past, and there had been fewer clients every month. So she had descended to undertake cheap services of oral sex in shadowed corners or vacant end cars, kneeling with her back to the storm door while the men stood gazing through the grimy window into the car ahead. Few men wanted her any other way. She had become an alcoholic, and carried syphilis.

Early one morning it occurred to her that it would be convenient and economical to sleep on the train instead of returning to the surface and seeking out one

Lowland Rider

of the transient hotels she usually tenanted while the rest of the city awoke. Rush hour, when it came, jarred her, and she had to transfer three times. But she slept, and, if she was not as refreshed as she would have been after sleeping in a bed, she was at least rested, and spared the five dollars her landlords would have assessed her, now that they were no longer willing to accept the levy in services rendered. So the next morning she spent on the trains as well, and the next, and the next. It was the end of her. She never went back to the surface.

She was cheated many times, was raped occasionally—incidents she never reported—and slowly grew to detest men far more than before. The day quickly came when she could no longer command even the smallest remuneration for her favors, and from that time on her descent began in earnest. The only benefit with which her subterranean existence provided her was the abatement of her alcoholism. As her finances decreased, so too did her opportunities to buy liquor. Of necessity, she drank less, and slowly the bottle loosened its hold on her. However, by the time the pressing demand for alcohol was gone, something quite different had muddied her mind, stolen her sanity.

For years, as long as she could remember, she had been a counterfeit of love, a mere repository into which men could, without emotion, void their lust. She had not wanted it that way, but she had borne it all, every indignity, every rough word and act, until all the love had been burned out of her. She hated not only men, but love itself and its consequences, with the concentrated hate one feels toward the object, once deeply sought, that one can no longer hope to possess, as the irredeemably poor grow to hate not only the rich, but gold itself.

Gladys H. Mitchell carried a knife, which she had taken, unbloodied, from the side of a wounded, unconscious boy at the Rockaway Avenue station on the IRT Brooklyn line. She liked the knife. It had a shiny steel blade that leapt out of the white pearl handle when she pushed a little button. The blade was long, as long as from the tip of her thumb to the end of her little finger when she stretched her hand apart. The arthritis which had begun to twist her fingers had, over the years, lessened that distance, but the blade stayed as long as ever. The shine never left it. After she had made a kill, she could wipe it on her skirt and look into it, and see her own face glowing back at her, her eyes looking into her eyes. She hardly ever looked any more, though. She no longer knew the woman who looked back at her.

Her kills were of little concern to the transit police. In their eyes, Gladys H. Mitchell, whose name they did not know, and who came to eventually forget it herself, performed a valuable service which more than made up for her sometimes frightening eccentricities. Vermin, of the animal variety, were a frequent annoyance beneath the city. Rats, despite the best efforts of the exterminators, ran abundantly, and stray cats crept below, much like the skells themselves, to seek a less harrowing cold in winter. Dogs roamed too, less frequently, for their natural skill in concealment was far inferior to that of the cats, and light years away

Lowland Rider

from the rats' highly evolved efficiency. All these creatures were fair game for Gladys H. Mitchell, now known solely as Baggie.

Transit police new to the beat assumed that the nickname was derived from the obvious categorization of the woman as a bag lady, one of those pieces of urban debris who carry all their possessions in shopping bags from one temporary haven to the next. There was more to it than that. Shopping bags served Baggie not only as luggage, but also as a method of execution.

The technique had taken months to conceive and years to perfect. She performed, as she always had, late at night and early in the mornings, when stations were bare, empty of all humanity but the predators to whom Baggie offered no rewards of a financial or sexual nature. She was even too mad to terrorize, so was left alone.

Alone she sat, on a folding chair of gray metal with a tattered seat cushion that had once been green. She sat out of the light, in the deepest shadows she could find, four or five shopping bags beside and behind her, and one empty at her feet, its open mouth grimacing dumbly toward the tracks, a strong odor telling of something small and delicious within. She sat, and she waited.

It was this intense patience that had come hardest to her, but she had mastered it fully, sitting still for hours if need be, watching the platform, the tracks, the open bag. Eventually one would come, disguised, of course, as cat or rat or dog, slinking close, scuttling away, its claws chattering on the dirty pavement, then coming nearer, eyes clicking from woman to bag to woman to bag, from where the smell of food was coming, and finally, finally, if she just held still long enough and breathed quietly enough, the furry head would vanish into the bag, and then the shoulders, and more, until only the tail, that long, sleek devil's tail that all men have, tucked into the cleft of their buttocks, remained visible.

Then, only then, did Baggie, self-forgotten Gladys H. Mitchell, come to life. The knife, its blade already exposed, sparked down, piercing the brown paper with a dry snap, impaling the beast within with a wet, squelching impact. It often squealed, and she laughed when that happened, wrenching the knife free and thrusting down again into the thrashing brown paper, into the trapped body of the longshoreman who had torn her anus, twenty years before, under the Queensboro Bridge, or the writhing forms of the six trade school boys, now magically fused into the shape of one small dog, who had paid her for one fuck only—for the youngest of them—then had all taken their turns, and the ten dollars back as well, leaving her bruised in an alley.

She killed them again and again, until nothing moved for the longest time, until her own heavy breathing and the awesome trembling of a train far down the tunnels were the only sounds to touch the station. Then she would rest for a moment, spent as if after a long ago tussle on some unmade bed. She would wipe the knife and turn it, smiling as it caught the few traces of light that invaded her dark haven, and then lean down, pick up the perforated bag and its contents, warm and dripping, and place them carefully into another bag, this one with handles of white, twisted twine.

"I have you," she would whisper. "Now I have you."

A train would come, she would board it, fold her chair and lay it down, array her bags on the seat beside her, the most precious at her right hand, and go to sleep, her pale, creased face as guiltless and untroubled as a child's.

JESSE GORDON'S JOURNAL: OCTOBER 3, 1986

There is so much misery here. Today—around five in the morning—I was riding in the last car of the Number 6 train on the Lexington Avenue IRT. I was alone in the car except for a transit cop who was sitting, half-dozing, at the other end. At 103rd Street an old woman got on. I say old, but I suppose she could have been anywhere from forty to eighty. When they're in her condition it's hard to tell. She wore a heavy cloth coat that fell below her knees, absolutely shapeless, making her look like a big block with arms and a head. She had a bunch of shopping bags with her, and one of them gave off a stench much worse than urine or feces, a smell like rotting meat. The cop got up right away, wrinkled his nose at the smell, but smiled a little too. "Okay, Baggie," he said. "Which one is it?"

She didn't say a word, just plopped down in a seat, her arms still holding all the bags. I could see that one of them had a dark, wet spot at the bottom of it. She

Lowland Rider

looked at the cop, and her face went sour. There was real hate in the look.

"Come on now," said the cop. "You'll get your bounty." He pulled a wrinkled dollar bill from his pocket and gestured with it to the stained bag. "That one, isn't it?"

She shook her head in short, sharp jerks. "Fuck you," she said. "Oh, fuck you." Her voice sounded like it came from the bottom of a mile-deep gravel pit, like the inside of her throat was caked with scars.

"Come on now, we treat you good. Lemme have it now . . ." He reached out and grabbed the handles of the bag, but she pressed her arm tight against her body and made a sound almost like a growl.

"Get away, fuck you," she spat at him. I could see the drool sliding down her chin.

"You know what'll happen," the cop went on calmly, still holding the handles. "You know. You'll have to go up. Up above. And we won't let you come back. You'll have to stay up there. You can never come back. Not ever, Baggie. You let me have it now."

The old woman muttered and mumbled, but she let the bag slip off her arm. The train was moving now, heading uptown to 110th Street. The cop held out the dollar, but the woman, Baggie, wouldn't look at it, just looked down into her lap. I could hear her teeth grinding together—what she had left of them anyway. The cop tossed the bill onto her lap, and she spat on it, spitting on herself in the process. And the thought crossed my mind, as it has every waking hour since I've been down here, that I really have condemned myself to hell.

The cop looked down into the bag, gave a *tsk tsk*, shook his head, and closed it up again, then glanced over at me and gave a little smile as if to say, Boy, there's all kinds, ain't there? and I gave him back a look of humor and regret, as though I pitied her, and agreed that the cop and I were better than her. I knew that that, in my case, was a lie. Still, the look came easy to me.

The train stopped at 110th Street and the cop got off. Through the window I saw him go over to a trash can and dump the bag inside, then move on down the platform. That station would stink like rotten meat all morning, but I guess the cop didn't care. He figured 110th Street was trash anyway. I found myself hating him for that, but then I remembered, and agreed with him. It *is* trash. They could take everything from 110th Street on up, including all of the Bronx, and shitcan it. I wouldn't shed a tear. Not now. Not after what happened.

Hell with it. Back to the woman, the crazy woman.

The doors closed and we rattled off toward 116th. Right away, as soon as the closed doors are between her and the cop, she begins to scream, very loudly. Doesn't move, just yells as loud as she can, what I assume were curses against the cop for taking her bag. I could make out "cocksucker," and "motherfucker," and a few more, but most of it was unintelligible, though it all sounded obscene because of that rough, scratchy quality of her voice. Then finally she saw me.

She stopped dead, why I can't say. There was nothing about me that could have been considered remarkable. I was wearing jeans and a black turtle-

Lowland Rider

neck, and I suppose the expression on my face was one of pity and curiosity—surely she must be used to that. But she looked at me with terror, as though I were a ghost, or a walking dead man (not so far from the truth), or someone she thought would kill her in the next few minutes. The intensity of her gaze rocked me, and I must have looked as frightened of her as she seemed to be of me. We sat there, the train trembling, our eyes locked on each other. I think we might have sat there until the end of the line, if the black man had not come in . . .

CHAPTER 4

When Rags stepped into the car and saw Baggie, his face tightened so that in both texture and color it resembled a prune. "Ol' bitch," he said quietly, and then, louder, "Yo! Bitch!"

She looked up at him cautiously, like a cat unwilling to draw her eyes away from one enemy to confront a lesser one.

"Get on out," he growled, and now her attention grew more fixed on him, less on the white boy, though her eyes still flashed back and forth between them. "Gwan, get outa here. Gitcher ass out."

The white boy opened his mouth, but Rags shot him a quick look, gestured him to silence.

"Fuckers . . ." the woman whined, gathering up the loops of her shopping bags and slipping a tattered arm through them, while with her other hand she grasped her folding chair. The car lurched as she pushed herself to her feet, and she sprawled on the green and yellow linoleum, her knee striking the floor sharply. The white boy staggered to his feet to help, but Baggie shrieked a short, high, piping scream, and scuttled

Lowland Rider

back, ratlike, from him.

"Get away! Get thee behind me! Evil, evil . . ."

She repeated the word, crooning it over and over as she pulled herself to her feet, picked up her things, and, bouncing off the hard, plastic benches, moved toward the cars in the front. When she drew near Rags, he pressed against the wall. As filthy as he was, he could not bear to have her brush against him.

The door clattered shut behind her, and Rags relaxed, turning to look at the white boy, who, he saw now, was older than he had first thought. "Devil can quote scripture, they say . . . I think we jes' heard it." He walked the length of the car and sat down across the aisle from the man. Rags couldn't categorize him, and that made Rags curious. He wasn't just a passenger, he looked too settled in for that, nor was he an undercover cop—the shoulders weren't set right, the eyes didn't poke and probe—and he looked too clean, smelled too good to be a skell.

"She a crazy woman," Rags said.

The man nodded in agreement.

"She kill things."

The man cocked his head, and Rags saw him frown.

"Not people. Rats and stuff."

The man spoke. "Cats? Dogs?"

Rags nodded and smiled, pleased that a conversation had begun. "Yeah. Sure. Cats, dogs, any of that shit."

"She had a bag. Something dead in it."

"Yeah. Sure. Baggie, they call her. Leave her alone mostly, just gets ridda crap animals, they don't bother her. I hate her, though. She ain't right. She say evil, but there inside, that's where *she* got the evil. Bad through. Lotta hate."

"She must hate animals anyway."

"Yeah. Breeders, she calls 'em. I useta talk to her before she went way off. See a rat or somethin', she say them damn *breeders*—funny word."

"Funny lady."

"*Funny?* Not too damn funny . . . oh, *I* see what you mean. Like *weird* funny, yeah, she *weird* funny all right."

The train rolled on, and Rags watched the white man, who had now turned his attention to the advertising panels, from which a defaced Miss Subways gazed out. "Where you headin'?"

"Uptown."

Rags laughed. "Well, shit, sure. Wheresabout uptown?"

The man looked at Rags, and, for an instant, the grimness of his face was frightening. "Nowhere special. Just riding."

"Where you live?"

"Here."

Rags shook his head as though he'd heard incorrectly. "You mean New York or *what*?"

"Just here."

"*Down* here?"

"Yes."

"The tunnels?"

"Yes."

"Bullshit. You ain't no skell."

"No what?"

"Skell. What we called live down here. You no skell.

Lowland Rider

You lookin' too *good* be a skell."

The man shrugged. Rags took it as an invitation, stepped across the aisle, and sat next to the man, who didn't move, except to open his mouth and breathe through it rather than through his nose.

"What's your name?"

The question seemed to take the stranger by surprise. He turned sharply and glared at Rags for a long time. Finally his face softened, and Rags felt the man was looking through him, toward something far away. "Jesse," he said at last, so softly that Rags could barely hear above the rattle of the car. "My name's Jesse."

"Jesse, huh? Hello, Jesse. I'm Rags." Rags grinned. "Bet you can't guess why I'm called that."

Jesse smiled back as he took in Rags's cloth-wrapped legs. "Bet I can. How come?"

"How come what?"

"How come you wear all those . . . those cloths?"

Rags's face twisted for a moment, but then the grin returned. "They *warm*, boy. Nothin' warmer'n you wrap a whole lotta shit around you like a mummy. Keep you *good* and warm."

"Why don't you just wear two pair of pants or something?"

"Hell, you can't find no *pants* down here. But you find *lotsa* rags."

"It's not all that cold, is it?"

Rags frowned. "Cold enough. Cold enough for me."

Jesse Gordon looked at Rags and wondered why he was lying. The early fall had been warm. The light turtleneck Jesse wore was more than sufficient, so the heat which surrounded Rags's body must have been stifling. The man's face was bright with sweat, and the smell coming off him was vile. Though there was no trace of dried urine or caked feces, two odors that seemed to predominate many of the stations, the stench of sweat, both fresh and long-dried, was so great that Jesse nearly gagged, until several minutes of proximity inured him to the smell, and he was able to examine the man boldly.

Rags was tall and wide, and Jesse suspected that much of his girth was due to the layers of cloth wrapped around him. The face, in contrast, was gaunt, deeply fissured black on black so that, from a distance, the sheened visage might resemble those African masks, carved of ebony, that Jesse's father had had in his shop before they were stolen in a burglary. Rags's head was tilted slightly to one side, whether from an unevenness in the multitextured collar of cloth that sheathed his neck or from a goiter Jesse could not tell. He guessed the man's age to be fifty. Despite the weight of years and experiences that Jesse could only imagine, there was a vitality about Rags, an inner fire that made the black man far more alive than all the other derelicts Jesse had seen in his short time below ground. The way in which he had confronted Baggie had impressed him as well. There had been an air of command in his tone that, no matter what his appearance or status, would brook no refusal. Whatever else he was, Jesse thought, this man was not a beggar. There was still pride in him.

There was something else as well—adaptation.

Lowland Rider

However long Rags had lived down here, it was far longer than the span of Jesse's own tenancy, and Jesse needed a mentor. There were, he well knew, techniques, tricks, procedures he must learn if he was to continue living below. In the few short weeks he had been in the tunnels, he had felt immersed in a quagmire of confusion. Like most New Yorkers, he knew only enough about the underground routes to get back and forth on frequently traveled byways. Everything beyond the Seventh Avenue local that took him to work, and the Lexington Avenue–Pelham Bay Park lines that went to his father's home in the Bronx, was a mystery. The hundreds of miles of track, the hundreds of stations that honeycombed subterranean New York City were nothing to him but brightly colored lines on a map, whose Plexiglass guard was most often veiled by fluorescent spray paint. The reality into which those parallel and intersecting lines translated was equally hidden to all but those who needed to travel them, to explore firsthand the dark lifeline, the web work of steel veins by which the city moved. In the mind of Jesse Gordon, as in the minds of most New Yorkers, those strange, interweaving lines were a source of fear. Even the lines with which one was aware had their unpleasantries, even their dangers. Might not those *unknown* routes then hold unheard of horrors, vicious deaths, predators more animal than human?

Jesse still believed in that predisposed idea, that nearly archetypal concept. There were certain lines he dared not ride, certain stations at which he would not yet get off, and when the necessity of transferring required him to step from the relative safety of the train into those strange burrows, he moved quickly, unhesitatingly, only his eyes showing the panic he was ashamed, in view of the purpose of his presence there, of feeling. Fear was still with him.

In the eyes of this large and odiferous black man, however, was no fear. The train, the tunnel, the entire network of catacombs were home to him. Jesse could feel it in the ease with which he sat beside him, the relaxed tone of his voice, all the qualities of self-possession which Jesse was so quick to notice, as they were so lacking in himself.

"How long have you been down here?" Jesse asked.

Rags shifted his body inside his cloth cocoon. "Long time. Years 'n years."

"You stay here all the time?"

"Most. One damn place bad as another. Somedays I go up above, get me some fresh air, maybe a washup at the shelter, little soup or somethin'. Mostly, I stay down here."

Jesse thought that perhaps he shouldn't ask, but did anyway. "Why?"

"I like it down here," Rags answered, perhaps too quickly. Then he sat silently, looking at his hands folded in his lap. After a time, he spoke again. "Here's where I feel safest."

"Down here?"

"Ain't so much crime's you'd think. Leastways it's what they say, and I think it's true. Lotta thievin', boys snatchin' purses and like that, but rapes and

Lowland Rider

murders and stuff, they say there ain't that much."

Jesse nodded. "You ever . . . see anything like that?"

A snort came from Rags, loud enough and sharp enough to make Jesse look up quickly and see a gobbet of mucus hanging from one of Rags's nostrils. The black man wiped it away with a ragged sleeve. "I seen things. And not too long ago neither. I seen that Enoch . . . talk about your devil, your evil . . ."

"Who? Enoch?"

"Never you mind. Don't gotta know about Enoch. Know too much, more'n you want."

The train howled to a stop. As it lurched, Jesse tensed and felt his stomach wrenched for what seemed the thousandth time that day. Rags, on the other hand, let himself roll with the motion of the train, like a wooden doll with a round, weighted bottom. He looked eminently relaxed. "You roll *with* it, not against it. It goes, you go. It stops, you stop. Otherwise you'll get a big mess of bruises."

Jesse smiled. "I *am* a big mess of bruises."

"They go 'way. You gotta remember, though. Go *with* it. That's the whole damn rule down here. Otherwise it spits you back up quick."

They rode on. Jesse tried to become aware of the motion of the car, pretending he was part of it. After a few moments he was swaying to its rhythms, which now felt more gentle, less violent.

"See there," Rags said. "You ridin' smoother already." The car hit a rough piece of track, and Rags's back slammed against the seat. "Shit . . ."

"Go with it, huh?" Jesse said, rubbing his sore spine with his knuckles.

"Sonovabitch. I shoulda been set for that one. I *remembered* that one."

"Wait a minute. You know the bumps in the lines?"

"Well, hell, not all of 'em. But this one damn sure. One I ride most."

"Why this one?"

"S'long. Got a lotta stops. Don't have to change trains so damn much. That's the ticket. That's what you want. Why you be gettin' off and walkin' down those damn tunnels you don't have to? You find the *long* ones, you ride them."

"Are there any that, uh, that you wouldn't ride?"

"I ridden 'em all. Each line shit somewhere on it, but one line be baddest. That's the Beast."

"The Beast?"

"New Lots."

"What?" asked Jesse, not understanding.

"Nostrand to New Lots Avenue. Out in Brooklyn. Everybody call it the Beast 'cause it so bad." The dark lines in Rags's forehead grew blacker as he frowned. "I don't ride it no more." His voice grew softer, and Jesse barely heard the last words ". . . leave that to Enoch."

It was the second time Rags had mentioned the mysterious Enoch, and Jesse's curiosity was aroused. "Who's this Enoch anyway?"

"Jes' a man," Rags said vehemently. "He's jes' a *man*, that's all he is, no more." But it sounded as though Rags was trying to convince himself of that.

Lowland Rider

"What's he do?"

"He don't do *nothin'*." Rags gave a bitter chuckle. "Nosir, he don't do *nothin'* hisself, jes' lets others do *for* him. He smart, but he jes' a *man*!" Rags banged a hammy fist onto his own thigh.

Suddenly Jesse felt uncomfortable. He realized that, although they had been talking like old comrades, he knew nothing about this big, strong black man by his side. He was alone in the last car of a subway train in the hours before dawn with a man who dressed in rags in the hottest weather, a man who stank of sweat and lived in tunnels, a man who, Jesse began to think, was most likely to be insane.

Just as quickly as that thought came to him, there came another—more complex and disjointed, illogical even, but sharp and strong just the same. *This is what you wanted*, it said, and added, *and are you not insane as well?*

"You play chess?"

Jesse looked up. Rags's face was still again, and his voice was calm. "Chess?"

"I found this." He held out a small black plastic box. On it, in gold, were the words, *Magna-Chess*. Snapping open the catch, Rags showed Jesse the interior—a red and black chessboard, and thirty-two small black and white plastic pieces with tiny black magnets affixed to their bases. "Guess it fell outa somebody's pocket. Never learned how to play, but I always wanted to."

Jesse clenched his teeth. He felt caught between laughing and running from the car, all the way through the train until he reached the motorman's compartment. Two madmen, speaking of chess. Of form, and structure, and strategies. It was funny and sad and absurd, and he thought of Donna and his father and Jennifer, and wondered why he was where he was, what he was really looking for, and if he could find it, and, most of all, if he wanted to find it.

He started to speak, but his throat was tight. He cleared it and said, "Yes. Yes, I play. I can teach you."

If you teach me.

They taught each other. Although they each had much to learn, Jesse had more. His decision to descend into the New York City subway system had been born of despair and revulsion. He had seen the act as a suicide sees the ocean in which he will drown himself, as a haven, an end, a comfort, something to which all thought can be yielded, all effort surrendered. What Jesse Gordon had not reckoned with was that, unlike a suicide, he had chosen to live, and living beneath the city, he quickly discovered, was the most exacting and painstaking way to live that he had ever known.

It was not merely riding, floating on waves until the sea eventually pulled you under; there was no sweet sleep at the line's end. That was where you rose from sleeping, and struggled again to stay above the waves, because beneath them, instead of rest, were sharks and smaller, fiercer fish, who bit your flesh with barbed teeth when you let yourself go under, so that

Lowland Rider

all you could do was stay afloat. Not *try* to stay afloat—there was no trying, for there could not be. You did it, and that was all.

JESSE GORDON'S JOURNAL: OCTOBER 6, 1986

I have found a friend here. It's absurd, ridiculous. If anyone had told me a month ago that my closest friend would be a black subway bum with an addled mind, I'd have called him crazy. Crazy or not, it's true. We're *both* crazy, *everyone's* crazy.

One thing is certain, though. If it wasn't for Rags—his name is Rags—I don't think I could survive the winter. I'm not sure I can even with him, but at least I've got a better chance. He is above all a *kind* man—dear, like a father at times in the way he treats me, and at other times like a child *I* must take care of. I'm certain there is something chronically wrong with his mind. He's extremely forgetful when it comes to general things like what month it is, but when it comes to the specifics of surviving underground, he is a master. Being with him, I almost feel like a student of Zen. His explanations are often as cryptic as those of some guru who speaks only in riddles, wanting his student, to figure out what the hell he's talking about.

Lowland Rider

I'm afraid I'm just as great a mystery to him. It's amazing that we're able to communicate at all.

Yesterday he asked me, "You hungry?"

I told him I was. I hadn't had a bite in twenty-four hours. I wondered if I should offer to buy him a sandwich. I had the money—about ten dollars in my pocket. But then I wondered what he ate—and how. More to the point, I knew that if I expected to stay here, live down here for any length of time, I had better learn the ways of the place. I still feel like a stranger, and I wonder if I will ever be able to feel at home the way Rags seems to. I asked him what he usually ate.

"Oh, what I find," he told me. "Sometimes I get some money, I buy me a whole hot dog or cheeseburger or somethin'."

"A *whole* one?"

"Yeah. Most times you can find a half or a few bites tossed away, you look hard."

My stomach churned at that. "You eat what other people throw away."

"Sure. Lotsa soft pretzels down the Brighton Beach line, but it don't take long to get sick of that shit. Fill you up, though. You ever see one of them things get wet? Puffs right up like a sponge."

"You ever steal any food?"

"Try not to, 'less I'm real hungry. Bible says thou shalt not steal."

Rags quotes the Bible quite a bit, something I found surprising at first, until he told me he had once been a preacher. I didn't ask him how he ended up like he has. When and if he wants me to know, I assume he'll tell me, and till then, it's none of my business. "Whatta you feel like?" he asked.

I said it didn't matter, that anything was fine, and he suggested we get on the Seventh Avenue line and head over to Penn Station, that the food was good there.

I didn't like it. It meant leaving the subway, going up into the station itself. "How'll we get back on the lines?" I asked him.

From somewhere in the folds of his swaddling, he brought out two tokens. "With these," he said, smiling at me. "I always got tokens, just like I always got pennies. Other stuff shines, and people pick it up, but not pennies. Even they *see* pennies, don't wanta pick 'em up. Not worth bendin' over for a penny. Is for me, though. And tokens. They're dark, not so shiny. See it, think it's old gum or dog shit or somethin'. Not me, though. I can tell a token fifty yards off. People *always* droppin' tokens."

My argument went up in flames, but I thought, after all, Penn Station is still underground. There is something important to me about not seeing daylight, and I knew I wouldn't unless I went out to where the old ticket windows used to be, and I would be careful not to do that.

Penn Station, like the subways themselves, contains a mixture of people—businessmen, travelers, and a few skells, but not many. I felt terribly out of place there, mostly because of Rags's presence. My own appearance might be called scruffy, but not yet shabby, while Rags is unmistakably a derelict. I recalled

Lowland Rider

I recalled that when I had taken trains out of Penn station I'd seen police rousting tramps and obvious psycho cases out of the terminal area and up onto the streets or down to the tracks below, and I asked Rags if we—while thinking *he*—wouldn't be bothered.

"Just keep movin'," he told me. "They see you goin' someplace, they hope it's out of their eyesight, so they leave you alone. Don't matter you move slow or fast, just so's you keep movin'."

We went up the stairs to the large, low-ceilinged room whose middle is taken up by the big call-board. Rags stationed us between the islands of seats where the passengers waited and the west stairways to the tracks. "We'll stand here, but you see a cop, you start movin'."

A few passed while we stood there, and when we saw them we moved, hugging the wall, going toward the subway entrance. They gave us the eye, but didn't say anything, and after they'd passed, we returned to our original location. After a while Rags nudged me, and I looked where he directed and saw a bearded man in his midthirties sitting on one of the benches. He was hurriedly eating a hot dog and watching the call-board as the train information rolled. His arm was looped through the strap of his leather shoulder bag, and he balanced a bag of french fries in his other hand. When he ate a french fry he did so gingerly, with an expression of distaste. "He's the one," Rags said. "Watch me."

Rags stood beside me until the call-board started to change again. Then he walked purposefully toward the trash can nearest the man, who, simultaneously with Rags, stood up and moved toward it as well, thrusting his half-eaten sandwich and barely touched french fries into the paper bag. Rags didn't say a word—just stood by the trash can and begged the man with his eyes. The man's face soured, but he thrust the food into Rags's hand and disappeared down a track entrance. Chuckling, Rags returned to me.

"You pick 'em out," he said, holding out the wet and stringy french fries. I ate a few and thanked him. "Pick out the ones eatin' on the run don't look like they're enjoyin' it anyways. Know damn well they ain't gonna finish. Then, when their train comes, get between them and the garbage and get a little old puppy dog look in your eyes. Easier for them to give it to you than to step around you to throw it away." He held up the packet of ketchup and I shook my head. He tore it open and squeezed the entire contents directly into his mouth, so that I could see what was left of his teeth. It wasn't much.

As he threw the empty packet into the trash, I saw his face change, grow very cold. There was fear in it too. "Come on," he said, and moved toward the subway entrance.

I caught up easily. "What's wrong?" I asked.

"Saw a man we don't wanta meet."

The name came to me quickly. "Enoch?"

"No, ain't Enoch. Montcalm."

We were going down the stairs by now, and I took the token Rags handed me. "Montcalm? Who's that?"

"TA cop."
"Just a cop?"
"Not just a cop. Montcalm knows me. Hates me. He's the one cop'd bust my ass sure."
"Why?"
"I know what he is."

CHAPTER 5

Bob Montcalm sucked in a bolt of smoke and blew it out again immediately. It had been the rag man, he was sure of it. Nobody dressed like that for fun. New York was fucked up all right, but wearing layers of rags hadn't become the newest fashion trend. Not yet anyway, he thought bitterly, watching the staircase where the black man had disappeared. Who had it been in the Oz books he'd read when he was a kid, the ones in his grandfather's apartment? That had been a rag man too, hadn't it?

No. The *Raggedy* Man, that was it. Montcalm bet nobody in Oz smelled like *his* rag man did. He would have gone after the old fart if he hadn't more important things to do.

Montcalm looked at the clock on the call-board and checked it against his watch. 2:38 P.M. Rodriguez had said 2:30, but Rodriguez was always late. Finally Montcalm spotted him, coming out of the newsstand with a *Post* tucked beneath his arm. Calmly, leisurely, the Latino walked through the crowded concourse,

Lowland Rider

looking neither right nor left, and headed toward the men's room on the lower level. Montcalm followed.

The rest room was nearly empty, but it didn't matter. When Montcalm entered, Rodriguez was already in one of the booths. Montcalm crouched and saw the angled points of the alligator shoes beneath the dirty metal door. Taking a comb from his pocket, Montcalm ran it through his thinning hair and studied his face in the mirror. It was not a handsome face. The eyes were deep set, and the shape of the nose revealed that it had been broken at least once. The chin was gray despite frequent shaving, and the lower lip hung pendulously, giving a sleepy, war-weary look.

Bob Montcalm was war-weary all right, but the impression of sleepiness was false. He was as alert to what was happening around him as any New York cop with twenty-five years of service, transit or street, and more alert than most. It was that alertness, that sense of being always on edge, that had brought him his first arrests, his first big successes, and to the attention of his superiors; had brought him to his own supervisory position. It had also brought him to people like Rodriguez. And Gina.

The toilet flushed, and Montcalm slid the comb back into his pocket and started to wash his hands. The booth door opened and Rodriguez appeared, glanced at Montcalm, and gave a short, nearly undetectable nod. Rodriguez washed his hands three sinks down from where Montcalm was standing, and walked out the door. Montcalm remained at the mirror a moment longer, looking at his own face with the expression of a vain man who has found one more gray hair. Then he turned and stepped into the booth Rodriguez had vacated.

The packet was where it was supposed to be, right behind the toilet bowl. Montcalm locked the booth door, sat on the seat, and opened the packet. He counted the bills, then put them into his inside coat pocket. The heroin was next. He opened one of the two Ziploc bags, touched his finger to the white powder, and tasted it. He spat the residue between his legs into the bowl, resealed the bag, put both of them into the outer pockets of his sport coat, made sure the pocket flaps were down, then buttoned his trench coat around him.

Leaving the rest room, he walked a circuitous route to a section of the terminal with lockers, waited until no one was in sight, then opened one of them. Inside was a locked briefcase. This he opened, and into it he put the currency he had received from Rodriguez. He fed the locker more coins, and closed the door tightly.

He took the Seventh Avenue-Broadway IRT to the 103rd Street station, and walked the two blocks to the apartment house where Gina lived. He walked with his hands in his pockets, without fear, knowing that his service revolver could deal with any spindly junkie desperate enough to try and mug him. The street seemed quiet, though, and by the time he got to the door he felt as relaxed as he could possibly expect to feel. She would be glad to see him, he knew. Why wouldn't she? He had what she wanted. He had *always* given her what she wanted.

He had to push the button four times before the

buzzer sounded at the lock. While he waited, he saw that two of the lobby mailboxes had been wrenched open and emptied, and thought that he should try to find Gina another apartment in a better building. The filth was moving south from above 110th Street. He hoped he could get her out before it was too late, get her out of it all.

The elevator was out of order again, so he trudged up the stairs to the fifth floor, where her door was ajar. Her thin hand hung on the frame like some white, sickly spider, and as she drew the door open for him, he was shocked anew at the hollowness of her face.

"Hi," he said, and kissed her cheek before she could draw away. She was wearing a worn, yellow bathrobe with bra and panties beneath, and she tugged the cord tighter, hiding her body from him. "Not glad to see me?"

"Sure. Sure I am." Her voice was outwardly calm, but underneath Montcalm could sense her relief, could tell how close she'd been to panic.

"You were pretty slow letting me in."

"I was sleeping."

Sure, Montcalm thought. And then you spent three minutes finding the buzzer.

"You bring it?"

"Yep." He took the packets from his pocket and set them on the battered coffee table. Gina snatched one up and opened it. "I got to, uh . . . I got to now."

Montcalm nodded. "Go ahead." She vanished into the kitchen, and Montcalm watched her go, still loving her, still wanting her. He looked around the room and grimaced. It was filthy. Piles of clothing lay here and there. An ironing board set up in the corner was gray with dust. Empty cans of Diet Coke sat everywhere, their silver tops dimmed with cigarette ash.

His head felt light, and he lowered it so that his chin touched his chest, and closed his eyes, trying to imagine how it never was, but might have been between them, if only they could have gotten away, out of New York, far from her old friends on 105th Street. She'd been beautiful the day he'd first met her, down there in the subway. There had been something in her face and voice that touched him, that let him see beneath the street-hardness she wore like a shield, something that had made her different. He could have busted her for possession. He had her dead to rights, had walked in the car just as she was about to snort a line. Anyone else, *anyone*, he would have busted in a second.

But instead he had showed her his shield, sat beside her, and spoke to her softly. "I won't bust you. Two conditions."

Her face had narrowed ferally. "What?"

"Toss the shit out the window. And let me buy you lunch."

She had given him a lopsided smile of mistrust, but lowered her window and let the white powder fly away.

"Now your evidence is gone. So why should I have lunch with you?"

"Because I'll buy you a good one, and because you'll really like me when you get to know me, and because if you don't I'll bust you anyway for solicitation."

She'd looked at him, unsure if she should take him seriously. Then she saw the laughter in his eyes, and laughed herself. "Don't know why, but all of a sudden I'm awful hungry."

He had fallen in love with her immediately, for reasons that he was never able to define, reasons having nothing to do with rationality, no definite plans as to how or why she would fit into his life. It had been enough that, after having been alone for twenty years, here she was, and it felt right, and he loved her and she loved him. Her background meant nothing to him, as his had been nothing to be proud of. Once she knew how he felt about drugs, she no longer spoke of her old acquaintances, no longer offered him joints or smoked them in front of him. He knew she smoked grass when he was not with her, but thought that when they got married she would give it up.

Marriage, however, had not ended her drug use. The only thing it *did* end was their relationship. She felt caged, she said, and the more she protested the more he did, perversely and inexplicably, to cage her. He knew, even as he did it, that it was the wrong course to take, and afterward he thought that he helped create a self-fulfilling prophecy. As much as he loved her and wanted to be happy with her, there was that part of him bred by the rough realities of the city that could not believe the fairy tale would come true. Had he been younger or she older, his expectations might have been greater, or hers less, so that the two sets might have merged into the fragile equilibrium on which most marriages survive and many flourish. As it was, they clashed incessantly, all the joy left behind in the days before they entered City Hall for their license.

Her friends began to reappear, as did the grass and the cocaine, and it wasn't long before he suspected her of sliding needles beneath her skin. When he learned that it was true, he was heartbroken, choked with guilt that his possessiveness had driven her to it. He still loved her, still saw those qualities that had initially drawn him to her, but before he was aware of it, she had become a junkie, her household expense money going for her more and more frequent doses.

When he stopped deluding himself and confronted her with what she was, there had been a scene. The next day when he came home, she was gone, her clothes with her. He wept most of the evening. Two days later, she called him. She was alone, couldn't find her friends anywhere, and needed junk.

Up to that time, Bob Montcalm had been an honest cop. There were addicts among his network of informants, but he had never tried to trade dope for information—it had been cash only. But this was different, he told himself. He had to get it. Just once. Just this once for Gina. And then, later, he could decide what to do. He wouldn't take her in, that much he knew. The thought of her screaming, strapped to a ward bed, was more than he could bear. The scandal of it all, of her being a cop's wife, had, to his credit, never occurred to him.

He found Willie at the 50th Street station, and pressed five twenties into his hand. "Get me horse," he said. "And get it fast."

Lowland Rider

Willie looked at the bills like he would a snake. "Jesus, Sergeant, whatta you . . . I can't do that . . ."

"You do it, you little fuck. You do it now, or I'll have you locked in a detox ward so fast you won't have time to puke. *One hour*."

Willie turned white, and scurried up to the street. In forty-five minutes he was back, holding a small bag of potato chips which he handed to Montcalm. "In there," he said nervously. "And change too."

Montcalm had pressed the bag, snapping the chips inside until his fingers felt a padded roundness that did not break. "Good. Forget about this, Willie. Just forget all about it."

"You bet, Sergeant."

He'd gone to the address Gina had given him, the one on 103rd Street where he now sat. It had been the first time he'd seen her need a fix, and it wasn't pretty. She had injected right in front of him, and he had watched closely, unable to look away, finally amazed at the way she became, in a few short minutes, another person, relaxed, lighthearted, almost affectionate once more.

It was the same way she came back into the room now, her hair combed, her face smiling at him, her robe rearranged, so that it gaped in the front with an air of casual yet calculated sexuality. She came to the couch, leaned over, and kissed him, warmly but close-mouthed, on the lips. "You're a good man, Bobby boy," she whispered.

"Yeah," he grunted, sounding more gruff than he felt.

"Want a drink?"

"Sure."

She went into the kitchen and came back with a rocks glass half full of bourbon. He took a large swallow as she sat beside him, and rested her head on his shoulder so that her dark hair touched his cheek. It smelled of stale perfume, wilted roses. "You are good to me, Bob."

"Sure," he repeated, wishing that he was either not there or could be there with her always. They sat like that for a long time, not moving, until at last he took another swallow of his drink. "How's the money?"

"I could use a little more. If you can spare it."

"How much?"

"Two . . . three hundred?"

"All right." He edged away from her, took out his wallet, and handed her fifteen twenties. "You've got to eat more. You look thin."

She squeezed his fingers as she took the bills. "You're cute. You worry about me too much."

"You're still my wife. I love you, Gina."

Her expression changed subtly. Sadness and a trace of panic touched her eyes, and she shook her head. "You're crazy."

"Yeah. You're lucky I am."

"You know you can have a divorce."

"I don't want it. I want you."

"We've been through this—"

"I know, every time I come. Every time I bring you this . . . this *shit*." She stood up and started to cross the room, but he followed her and stopped her, his hands on her shoulders pulling her back against him, her hair in his face so that he spoke through it, as through some dark, fine web. "I can help you. Nobody else, just me. I *swear* there'd have to be nobody else, just you and me, Gina. Together we could do it. It could be like it was before, I *know* it could, but you got to trust me. You're gonna wind up dead, you keep this up. Jesus, it's been almost a year, a *year*, Gina."

She trembled, and started to move away from him, then gave up. "I know of . . ." she said breathily, ". . . of *lots* of people been on it for . . . for *years*—"

"But not you . . ."

". . . and they're *fine* . . . there's nothing wrong with them, just that—"

"Just that they're *junkies*!" He swung her around and held her chin so that she had to look at him. "Goddam zombie *junkies*, Gina! And it's only because I've taken care of you that you're not like them. You want that? You want to be like them?"

"No . . ."

"What would you do? What would you do if it weren't for me?"

"I . . . don't know."

"Goddam right you don't know. I get you your *junk*, I get you your *money* . . . what the hell would you do . . ."

He trailed off impotently, and sank back down on the couch. Gina remained standing, her back to him. "Maybe . . . maybe I'd trick."

Shaking with sudden rage, he looked up at her. "Don't say that. Don't even think it. I ever hear you say anything like that again, that's the end of it, Gina. Just get that out of your head right now."

"I'm sorry, Bob. I won't. I didn't mean it." She sat

beside him. "Would you . . . do you want to make it with me?"

He wanted to. But pride held him back, pride and the overwhelming feeling that he must not love her until she was free again, and, contradictorily, his again. The time would come. He would make it come. "No. Not now."

"You never want to."

"Do you? Honestly?"

She shook her head. "I just never feel like it."

"You got a lover, Gina. Smack's your lover. It's all you need, isn't it?"

He didn't expect her to answer, and she didn't.

"I'm going," he said, standing up and moving to the door, trying to remember what it had been like the last time they'd made love, a year ago, the last time he'd made love to any woman.

"Bob?" Her voice stopped him at the door. "You'll come back?" She sounded like a little girl, alone and afraid.

"What do you think?"

"Yes."

"I'll come back. Someday I'll come back and take you out of here."

He closed the door so he wouldn't have to say any more, and went down the stairs thinking of his dream, the dream of having enough money to take Gina away from the city, far out into the country, maybe northeastern Pennsylvania, where his mother and father had taken him on vacation when he was young. He would buy a house high up on some mountain, with no one else around, and he would take Gina there, and he would help her to stop, and hold her when she wanted to scream, and quiet her and take care of her until she was herself again, the real Gina he had loved, and she would love him again, and it would be all right. They would be away and safe. They would escape.

The dream had haunted him ever since he had realized the depth of Gina's addiction. He knew it could come true—but not on his salary alone. The trick was to find a way to keep Gina supplied with drugs while building up enough cash to move from the city. He could not take another job, so the only alternative was to develop a second source of income from his present one.

Bob Montcalm, although he had never been a crooked cop, knew that they existed, and felt sure that a few of his colleagues on the transit police force were not above picking up a little extra cash when it could be done with minimal risk. Through Willie, who finally became convinced of his sincerity, Montcalm contacted Rodriguez, and made a deal. For certain considerations that Montcalm made on the tracks and stations within his jurisdiction, he was to receive small amounts of heroin and larger amounts of cash. These considerations included informing Rodriguez as to which stations were under surveillance by narcotics agents, the establishment of "safe" stations and trains where exchanges could be made without fear of arrest, and anything else Montcalm could do to make life easier for Rodriguez. Montcalm never tried to find out who was behind Rodriguez, nor did he wish to know. It was enough that once every two weeks he collected the cash and Gina's heroin. Montcalm insisted that he receive the material outside of the subway lines. Too many people knew him below, police and criminals alike.

So twice a month Montcalm made his deliveries to Gina, and twice a month he tucked away cash in a locker at Penn Station, fifty yards away from the locker in which Jesse Gordon kept his money. There was already fourteen thousand in Montcalm's locker. He felt uneasy about keeping so much money in a public place, but he felt more uneasy about keeping it in a bank or his apartment, where it could be traced in an investigation. When there was enough, then he would take Gina away. They would leave the city behind, and he would never see Rodriguez, or a subway station, or a packet of heroin again.

CHAPTER 6

Something was wrong. Something was very, very wrong, thought Manuel Alvarez as he sat back, trying to make himself relax on the hard plastic seat. The rush had hit the way it always had before, the sweet warmth surging through him, the world suddenly friendly again. But now something was, dammit, *wrong*. He didn't feel good, and he'd always felt good before, always for a nice long time. But this time he felt slow and lazy, like his legs were made of iron. He was sure he'd done everything right, just the way he always had, just the way his brother Juan had shown him when he'd taken his first jolt. And the stuff was good, he was sure it was. He'd always been able to trust King's shit before, so why would it be different now?

But why the fuck did he feel so *bad*?

He looked at the Seiko he'd ripped off the week before, and saw that it had only been fifteen minutes since he'd slipped the needle into his vein, since the warmth had hit him in the toilet of the 125th Street station. He'd just wanted to ride then, lie back and let the train cruise him for a while, maybe later find Juan and his friends and rip off some Krylon and do a little bombing. He'd expected to stay warm for hours. So why was he so cold? And why were the ads so blurry, the letters so hard to read? Why was the car empty all of a sudden, and what were those noises, those badass moans and groans, why did his head hurt so much, why did his gut ache?

Why the hell was he lying on the floor?

And why was it getting so dark? All except for that dude, that dude who was bending over him, and looking into his face, that gorgeous, beautiful dude whose face was glowing brighter and brighter, until it seemed that all the pain in Manuel Alvarez's body was just burned away, and it wasn't cold any more, but warm again, wonderfully warm, as though it were the best and longest trip he'd ever taken, the ultimate score, the high that would last forever and ever.

Enoch stood up. There was dirty snow on the floor where he had knelt over the body of the dying boy, but the knees of Enoch's pants were unstained, white, and shining. A smile formed gently on his soft mouth as he gazed down at the stiffening body.

The train came to a harsh stop, throwing forward the passengers in the cars ahead, but Enoch only swayed like a reed in the breeze, as if the car in which he was now the only living being were under some special dispensation, some glamour, some enchantment. The doors clattered open and he stepped out, moving against the herd plunging toward the street, seeking instead the opposite way, the darkness, into which the whiteness of his visage was slowly lost to sight, like a lantern vanishing into the depths of a cave.

P A R T 3

Then did there appear to him
A figure robed in black.
It had nae mouth, nor ear, nor chin,
And een a nose did lack.

But eyen it had that blazed at him,
More fierce than tongue can tell,
And such a voice, as hollow as
The deepest pits of Hell.

"Yea Gordon," quoth the spectre strange,
"Now hearken unto me.
If thou'lt nae be Life's messenger,
Then Death's shalt thou noo be . . ."

—*Jamie Gordon, the Lowland Rider*

JESSE GORDON'S JOURNAL: DECEMBER 10, 1986

. . . one of the surprising things is that it is hardly ever dark down here. When you think of the tunnels you immediately think of blackness, and yet, in all the weeks I've been down here, I haven't been in total darkness for more than a few seconds at a time, when the trains momentarily lose their interior power. This world is lit by neon, and I'm slowly learning to function within it. Food seems to be the only area in which I'm not a real skell, for all the skells I've seen suffer from malnutrition of one kind or another, and I won't do that to myself. I try to eat a well-balanced diet. There are fruit and vegetable stands down here, and sometimes I buy a trip to the salad bar at a subterranean restaurant. There are places where you can pick up a decent sandwich pretty cheap. On the whole, I eat about the equivalent of one large meal a day. At this rate, the money should last quite a few years. Rags doesn't know I have it, and I'll continue to keep him in the dark. Every once in a while I pretend to find some money, and then I treat him to a cheeseburger. I should give him more for all he's taught me. Still, a lot of things I had to figure out on my own, and now I have it pretty well down to a science.

I wash—my body and my underwear—every three days. Undershirt, shorts, and socks get the sink treatment with soap from the receptacles. I dry them under the electric hand dryers. Every few weeks I wash sweaters and jeans the same way, dry them as best I can under a dryer, then carry them around with me until they air-dry enough for me to put them in the locker. Rags thinks I'm crazy. The other day he asked me what I do it for. "So I don't smell so bad," I answered.

"Meanin' I do?"

"It's your choice."

He looked angry and embarrassed, and I was sorry I'd said it. "I ain't tryin' to impress anybody," he said. "Who *you* tryin' to impress?"

I didn't tell him that I couldn't eat at a salad bar smelling like a sewer, so I just shrugged and mumbled something about liking to feel clean, and let it go at that. I don't like to argue with Rags. He's been a tremendous help. Without him, it would have taken me months to figure out which lines I could ride on the longest, to learn which cops were willing to overlook skells, which stations I could sleep in safely. Appearances are important too. If you don't want to be victimized, look poor, and just a little mean, so it's not worth anyone's while to hassle you. But when a cop comes around, you lose that hardness and look harmless instead—gentle as a kitten—simple and sleepy and not too swift, so that the worst they'll do is tell you to move along, no loitering, which you do, being very careful never to argue with them. "Most of 'em's nice," Rags told me, "but now and then you get some prick who gets his kicks outa beatin' on skells. Like Montcalm."

"The guy at Penn Station?"

"Yeah. Real mean bastard. Been around for years. I remember him when I first come down here. He was just a nobody then. Now he a sergeant."

"Hates skells, huh?"

"Back then he'd jes' as soon kill you's look at you. Course he never did, but he kicked and beat on a good many, includin' me. That was when he was straight, too."

"You mean he's crooked?"

"As a dog's hind leg. Into drugs, and that's the worst."

"How do you know that?"

"Through the grapevine."

"Grapevine?"

"There's more than jes' us down here. Word gets round about things like that."

Montcalm. Someone to watch for, though I don't even know what he looks like. I've been back to Penn Station every day to renew my locker, so I may have passed him a dozen times. I may have even sat next to him on a train and never knew it, though I doubt that, if he's really as hard on skells as Rags makes out. He could probably tell I was one. Maybe the smell isn't there—though I come close on the third day—but the look is. And the attitude. I *feel* like a skell now. I have to admit that I'm almost comfortable down here. Or maybe comfortable isn't the word. Maybe it's *resigned*. Resigned to my fate.

Every now and then I wonder if they're looking for me. They must know I'm still alive. They'd hardly think the boy's body was my own, and who else could have closed out my bank account? Are they looking for me? Does anyone care? Am I wanted for murder? I think about these things, but they really don't worry me. I read discarded newspapers occasionally, but so far I haven't come across anything about myself, not even in the *Post*. When I first came down I was too depressed—*depressed*. What an understatement. I was too *devastated* to even think about checking any newspapers, so I probably missed it. It doesn't matter. No one will be looking for me down here, and even if they were, my beard is fully grown in. It makes me look very different—far heavier than before, and somehow crueler, which is only fitting. That poor boy.

My poor wife and daughter.

There is no God.

CHAPTER 7

Jesse Gordon and Rags stood in front of the dirt-caked mirrors of the 157th Street station men's room and shared half a pumpernickel bagel. Strands of lint clung like webs to the grainy surface, but Jesse picked them off, flicked them away, and chewed reflectively. "Don't have any cream cheese, do you?" he asked Rags.

Rags chuckled. "You sure crazy. Next you be askin' for that lox stuff. What is that anyway?"

"Salted fish."

"Jew food."

"So are bagels." Jesse swallowed the last bite and washed his hands at the sink. "Haven't seen you for a few days. Where you been keeping yourself?"

"South mostly. Down to Coney and Brighton Beach." Rags let a few drops of water touch his hands, and patted his face with them. "Whyn't you never come down with me? Get you up above. Sun's shinin', weather's nice and warm, trees gettin' green. Don't you miss all that?"

"No. I prefer it down here."

The two of them walked out of the men's room and sat on a bench near the end of the platform. "Can't talk you into it."

"Nope. No thanks, Rags."

"You don't know what you're missin', Jesse. I just set back and wait, and when that train come out of the tunnel into the warm sun, it's like bein' born all over again. And how you gettin' on?"

"Getting by okay. One day's pretty much like another."

"That's the nice part, ain't it? No surprises. Leastways not *too* many." Rags patted the bundle of cloth along his left side.

"Still there, are they?" Jesse asked smiling.

"Yeah. I keep checkin', though." He tilted his head even further than usual and looked at Jesse. In his collar of rags, his head resembled a black marble egg gone crooked on its base. "Wanta see 'em?"

Jesse was about to nod, but instead he asked a question. "What's wrong with your neck, Rags?"

For a moment Rags's face quivered like jelly. "My neck?"

"Why do you hold your head to the side like that?"

"It's . . . nothin'."

"No, Rags. It's something. Pull your scarves away."

"Jesse . . ."

"Come on, Rags," Jesse urged gently. "Let me see."

Rags sighed deeply, pressed his head further to the left, and tugged down on the mass of cloth. Jesse saw what looked like a smooth and ovoid piece of coal, three inches long, jutting nearly an inch from the right side of Rags's neck.

Lowland Rider

"Does it hurt?" Jesse asked.

"Naw, not at all."

"Have you seen a doctor about it?"

"Oh, sure," Rags chuckled, covering the tumor quickly, as embarrassed as if he'd been showing his privates. "Sure, we got Blue Cross down here."

"I'm not kidding, Rags," Jesse said. "That's nothing to fool with."

"Who'm I gonna see down here, Jesse? There ain't no doctors down here."

"Up above, Rags. Go to a hospital. They'll look at it, it won't cost anything."

Rags shook his head angrily. "What good'd it do? I couldn't afford no operation or nothin'."

"There are always ways around that, Rags. But you've got to have it looked at. If something like that was malignant . . ." Jesse left the rest unspoken.

"Malignant. Like a cancer?"

"Don't tell me you haven't thought of that."

"A cancer," Rags said again, and then shook the thought from him like a dog shaking off water. "You want a book or don't you?" His hand went inside the labyrinth of fabric, made it heave like a cat beneath a blanket, then reappeared, clutching two books, one of them small and bound in black leather, the other larger, bound in a light gray cloth. A few traces still remained of the orange ink that had adorned the spine. "Which?" Rags asked, offering both.

"See a doctor, Rags. Promise."

"All right, damn it, I'll see a doctor, now hush up about all that. *Which?*"

"I guess I feel like a ballad today," answered Jesse,

taking the gray book and opening it at random. An old black woman stepped around the corner and eyed them nervously, a large basket purse hanging at the end of one arm. Jesse flashed a smile, hoping to relax her, and looked down at the book. The woman edged past them and moved rapidly away.

"Lady's scared," Rags whispered.

Jesse nodded and flipped through the book. The pages were so damp that they felt like cloth, as if Rags's essence had penetrated the hard covers and transmuted the paper. He stopped at a ballad of Robin Hood and read it. When he finished, he turned to Rags, who was painfully intent upon his Bible. Jesse waited until he looked up, then handed back the volume. "Have you read all of these?"

Rags pumped his head up and down. "You bet. More'n once, too, like the Bible. I forget 'em by the next time I read 'em, though, so I don't get bored. Which reminds me—you sure your name ain't *Jamie* Gordon?"

Jesse laughed. "No, why?"

"I was ridin' and readin' the other day and I found this one I forgot about. Lemme see now . . ." Rags paged through the book for a few minutes. While he did, Jesse noticed a stocky white boy in denim enter the platform area. He looked around, gave Jesse and Rags a quick glance of appraisal and a smirk of dismissal, then moved slowly toward the woman. Her eyes were fixed on the dark hole of the tracks. She did not see him. "Here we go," Rags said. "Look here."

He set the book on Jesse's lap. It was open to a

Lowland Rider

ballad entitled, *Jamie Gordon, the Lowland Rider*. Jesse started to read:

> Oh there was a rider daring,
> Yes, there was a rider bold . . .

Jesse became lost in the poem, adrift in a story so similar to his own that tears came to his eyes, and a shuddering gasp escaped him. "Hey," said Rags. "Jesse, what's the . . ."

The words were cut off by an echoing shriek. The two men looked up and saw the denim-clad boy wrestling with the black woman at the platform's edge. The boy held a knife with which he was trying to cut the handle of the woman's bag, which she was pressing to her side with surprising ferocity. He grunted as he sawed away, the bag in one hand.

Jesse jumped to his feet and started to move toward the struggle, but Rags put a heavy hand on his shoulder. "*No way*," he whispered harshly. "Come *on*," and he turned and headed for the exit. Jesse took a step toward Rags, then looked back to where the man and woman were still fighting. The man was kicking the woman in the legs now, and she staggered to stay upright. Her screams were growing weaker, but she still hung on to the purse.

"*Jesse!*" It was Rags who called his name, but for a moment it seemed to Jesse Gordon as though the woman, whom he had never seen before, had called on him for help.

Jesse!

He heard it again, and knew that it was not Rags, not even the woman, but someone else, a voice that ordered him to do what he had been about to do on his own before Rags had tried to stop him. He started to run.

The boy had reached the end of his patience. If he could not slash the purse off a live arm, he would wrench it off a dead one. His arm shot behind him like a bow being drawn, and plunged forward, intending to tear through the old brown cloth coat, to cut and weaken and kill, if need be, the old woman who was being so absurdly uncooperative.

The knife never touched her. Something grabbed his arm and twisted him around as easily as if he were a child, and suddenly he was facing the younger of the two bums he'd seen sitting on the platform. In the dark frame of hair and beard, the man's eyes were alive with fury, like some Biblical avenger, and the fist that drove the boy to the concrete landed with the impact of a trip-hammer.

When he shook his head to clear his vision, he still felt his knife in his hand. Beside him the old woman was panting with exhaustion and terror, clinging to her ratty purse like a lifeline, and above him stood the crazy bum, fists clenched at his sides. "Bastard!" the boy spat out, and came up fast, his knife held low, aiming for the gut. The bum jerked away, his fists went up, and thundered down on the back of the boy's head. The boy sank down again, his face striking the concrete, his nose breaking with a sharp snap that echoed for a moment until it was muffled by the boy's howl of pain.

He twisted again, and brought himself to a sitting position, the knife held in front of him, the blood from his nose darkening his jean jacket. "That's it, man," he said brokenly. "I'm gonna kill you now."

He lifted himself carefully to his feet. Except for the brutal pain in his nose, he was unhurt, and the street coolness that had betrayed him by its absence had returned. No more quick, angry, unplanned thrusts. He had the knife, so he would back this turkey up and wait for his moment. No use being stupid.

The bum's eyes grew wary, but the boy could detect no fear in them as he backed him toward the wall. The boy held himself low, moved on the balls of his feet, ignored the blood that dripped down over his mouth and chin, ignored everything except the sonovabitch he intended to gut. The bum was getting closer to the bench. Soon, the boy knew, the back of his legs would strike it, unsteadying him for just a moment, just long enough.

Two more steps, then one, and the bum bumped the bench, rocked on his heels, and the boy pounced.

At that same second something grabbed him at his groin and his neck. Unable to scream out his pain, he felt himself being lifted into the air, and through a red haze saw the dirty, vaulted arch of the station ceiling move past him and turn dark. Then he was flying, weightless, through the air for what seemed like minutes, but what was actually just long enough for him to realize how stupid it all was, because the old bitch probably had nothing anyway. With that in mind, he landed on the third rail.

"*Now* come on!" Rags shouted, running toward the exit with his rolling gait, like a garment center rack come to life. Jesse stood spellbound, held by the sight of the boy's body jerking convulsively, the sound of muffled crackling, like sparks heard underwater, the smell that was already creeping up from the bed of the tracks, the smell of burning cloth, charred flesh.

"Jesse! Goddammit!"

He whipped his head to the left and saw Rags at the end of the platform, beckoning to him, waving his burly arms. Jesse looked down at the woman. She was looking at him. There was pain in her face, and apprehension, as if she thought a new attacker might now replace the first.

"You all right?" Jesse asked, and her expression went blank for a moment before she nodded dumbly. Jesse turned then, and ran down the platform to Rags. Together they made their way through tunnels and down ramps until they found themselves on a downtown express. They chose the seat, just big enough for two, by the door. Rags was panting, and his face shone with sweat.

"Oh man. Oh man, Jesse, you really done it now." Rags wiped his forehead with a piece of blue cloth he'd drawn from his pocket.

Jesse said nothing. He only sat, knees apart, his hands between them, gazing down at the floor. His whole body was trembling.

"*Damn*, don't do that again. *Please*."

Lowland Rider

"I had to," he said in a low, cracking voice.

"No, you *didn't* have to!" Rags turned to him, his face angry. "You don't *mess* with things, Jesse. Not down here. You just stay the hell away from trouble 'cause if you don't you gonna be *in* it. Dumbest thing in the world you mess in somethin' like that . . ." He trailed off into mumbling, and they rode for a time in silence, the heavy bass rumble and higher *click-clack* of the steel wheels on the track the only sound.

"Thanks, Rags."

"F'what?"

"For messing with things. You saved my life." Jesse had stopped shaking. He gave Rags a thin smile.

"Yeah. Prob'ly."

"Thought you said you shouldn't mess with things."

"Well, hell, I wasn't 'bout to let that boy kill you."

"So you killed him instead."

Rags's face became more pouched than before. "What you say?"

"You killed him."

"I *killed* him?" he said unbelievingly.

"He hit the third rail, Rags. Landed right on it."

"I didn't . . . I didn't *see*, I was runnin'. Soon's I threw him, I was runnin' . . ."

Jesse was amazed. At first he could not believe that Rags did not know what he had done, but the older man's dismay was so heartfelt, his shock so real, that Jesse knew he was not feigning. There was no artifice in Rags. Suddenly the man's shoulders began to heave up and down, and Jesse saw that he was crying.

"I didn't wanta kill nobody . . ."

He put an arm around the big man, and patted his shoulder. "It's all right. He would've . . . killed the old lady, would've killed me . . ."

"I ain't never killed nobody, Jesse . . ."

"It's done, Rags. He didn't deserve any better."

Rags snuffled through the next stop, then said, "Oh, Jesus, you think that lady'll tell about us? What we look like? She seen us both . . ." His eyes widened. "And I called you Jesse! She heard me call you Jesse!"

Jesse shook his head. "She was too upset. I don't think she even knew what was going on." It was a lie, and he knew it. The old lady had been totally aware of what had happened. "Besides, we saved her. Why would she report us?"

"Oh, I hope she don't," Rags moaned.

So do I, Jesse thought, then considered what it would mean. They would have to hide, but weren't they already hidden? How much more deeply buried could they be?

The hell with it all. The boy had gotten what he'd deserved. He had tried to prey on the weak, had been given a chance to run, but had chosen to try and kill instead, and had received a killer's justice. No tears for him, Jesse thought.

They rode through half the night with a minimum of talk, and played several games of chess, which boosted Rags's spirits. By the time they transferred to the Canarsie line, he was smiling again. "I got to hand it to you, Jesse. I been ridin' a good many years and that's the first time I ever seen anybody do anything like that." He scowled momentarily. "Now wait. I *did* see one poor fool try to stop a snatchin' coupla years ago, but as I recall it was his wife or girlfriend or somethin'. Besides, he got cut up pretty bad, so's you could say that didn't really count. People don't do much to help other people. Not down here. Not very often up there either."

"That's probably smartest."

"Don't mean it's right. Now I was gonna just walk away from that shit tonight till you butted in. I woulda felt bad, sure, but I woulda felt a whole lot worse gettin' cut up. Can't blame people not wantin' to get cut up. I *been* cut up, and it ain't no fun. But hell, you just jumped in there like . . . like that Jamie Gordon guy, a-fightin' and swingin' your old sword . . . yeah, maybe you oughta *get* a sword. Scare the shit outa these punks. Yessir, be callin' *you* the Lowland Rider you keep that crap up."

Jesse got on the train ahead of Rags and took a seat. His face had gone hard at Rags's first mention of the ballad, and the black man noticed it.

"What's the matter? I say somethin'?"

"No, Rags. Only maybe that name fits me too well."

"Lowland Rider? That why you acted so funny when you read it?"

Jesse looked around the car. There was only one other passenger, a Hasidic student at the other end of the car, seemingly involved in a Hebrew newspaper. He looked back at Rags. Though weary with years, the man's face was open and honest. "I'm going to tell you something, Rags. Secrets. Just between you and me."

"Who would I tell?"

Then Jesse told him about Donna and Jennifer, about the gang and what they had done, and what

Jesse had done to one of them. When he finished there were tears in his eyes, not at the pain of the memory, but the relief of being able to tell the story, and seeing his own horror mirrored in another person's eyes, even if that sympathetic listener was among the lowest of men. To Jesse, he was both father and priest and the small amount of God in which he still believed, and when he was through he felt better than he had in months.

"Dear God, Jesse," Rags said, putting a comforting hand on Jesse's knee, "that's a sad story, true enough. I didn't know before why you'd come on down here, but now I think I see. Least I see better. Terrible thing to carry around with you. I'm real sorry."

"I hate them when I see them, Rags."

Rags nodded. "You mean spics."

"No, not spics. I mean anybody who preys on anybody else. Anyone who turns something good into something rotten. I hate them because I'm one of them myself."

"Can't be, Jesse. You're a good man."

"I should've been better."

Rags swallowed heavily. "So should everybody, what's that prove?"

"I killed a boy who was trying to help me, Rags. That doesn't die easy."

"We're all human, Jesse. You wasn't in your right mind. You shouldn't blame yourself." Rags whispered the next words earnestly, as if trying to convince both of them of their truth. "Only God's perfect."

Jesse sat lost in thought. "God . . ." he whispered once, then was silent. After a time the train ground to

Lowland Rider

a halt and he looked up. "Where are we?"

"14th Street."

"Let's get off. I found a five yesterday," Jesse said, getting to his feet. "I'll stand you a hot dog, okay?"

"Yeah, sure." Rags followed Jesse out of the car and through the labyrinth. Within minutes they were chewing hot dogs, washing down the meat and buns with coffee. When they were finished, they found a bench and began to play chess. A few moves into the game Rags spoke quietly. "Jesse?"

"Hmm?"

"What I said about you gettin' a sword and all. I was jes' jokin', y'know?"

Jesse looked up from the board. There was no humor in his face, only sadness, deep and lurking. "I know," he said.

Coolly and methodically, he won the game.

JESSE GORDON'S JOURNAL:
MAY 17, 1987

I try to do what I can. The opportunities occur infrequently, but more often than you would expect them to. If I let my imagination roam, it would not be difficult to conclude that I am drawn to these things. Or drawing them. As though my experiences imbued me with some electromagnetic force that pulls me to where these things are happening, where this evil is taking place.

That sounds too melodramatic—*evil*. As though this is some moral swamp which nurtures sin. Yet maybe it's not too far off the mark.

And it's not too far off because I don't want it to be. That's one positive thing about the underground— you can make it whatever you like. It reeks with symbolism, with countless opportunities for microcosmic role-playing. It lets me take fifteen-year-old punks and turn them into criminal masterminds, lets me take the tunnels and make them halls of Hell. It lets Rags take this man Enoch and turn him into the

Devil himself, Satan ruling the underworld, pulling the strings that make all the puppets dance to the tune of evil.

Enigmas within enigmas. Webs within webs.

Here's one I like: tunnels within tunnels. And no light at the end of any of them.

Enough writing. My fingers hurt, and so does my head.

CHAPTER 8

May, she thought, was not the best month to do research on the subways. The place was a madhouse any time of the year, and the unseasonably high temperatures only made things worse. People seemed edgier, and the crazies, who in cooler weather were merely amusing, were now bathed in sweat, poised on the brink of violence. Or so it seemed to Claudia Dorner.

Claudia was no stranger to subways. She had ridden them for twelve years, since she had first moved to Manhattan when she was twenty-two. Her outlook then had been as fresh and new as her looks and her MBA from Penn. She had taken a position with an investment firm, which she found, despite her degree, bored her. To alleviate this boredom, she had two passionate yet unproductive love affairs, began to write, and finally got married to Steve Fuller, an accountant in her firm.

She sold her first article, a humorous guide to executive fashion, to *Working Woman*, about the same

Lowland Rider

time she got a divorce from Steve, who she discovered was cheating on her after five years of marriage. Figuring that she had more of a talent for satire than for holding men, she concentrated on satire, and wrote and sold so much of it so frequently that eventually guilt replaced the pleasure in her success, shunting it aside with the unforgiving question of why, with all her obvious talent, she had not yet produced anything *serious*.

The only thing that oppressed her more than this nagging question was the subway ride she took every day from her Eighty-fourth Street apartment to her office on Wall Street. Although she could afford a cab, she felt that the twelve dollar a day fare was a type of blackmail, an unnamed predator upon the fear and discomfort she felt so intensely on the trains, and she quite simply would not be so manipulated. So she rode the lines that gradually got worse and worse, and her freshness withdrew, deeper in, masked by the white bisque that serves as flesh on so many New Yorkers, until one day her fear and her desire met in the realization that here was her subject, here was something *serious*, something inconceivable and alien that was somehow also rich in meaning. Once the idea took root, she became obsessive about it, and quickly produced a proposal which she presented to Julia McWilliams, the articles editor at *Manhattan Magazine*, to whom she had sold several New York pieces. Julia had been intrigued by the idea as well.

"The subways," she told Claudia, "have always caused that ambivalence, that love-hate relationship, in New Yorkers. I mean, they're as much a part of the city as cable cars are of San Francisco, but everybody *likes* cable cars. I don't know of one poor bastard who'd admit to actually liking the subway."

"Is it a go then?"

Julia paused for a long while. "You really think you can get these people to talk to you?"

"I can try."

"You'll go escorted."

"I wasn't planning to."

"Christ, Claudia. Even Paul Theroux went with cops. The piece in the *Times* he did a few years back?"

Claudia narrowed her lips, shook her head. "Do you think anyone down there would talk to me if I was with a cop? I read the article too, and Theroux didn't interview any skells."

"So what are you planning to do, pack a gun?"

"I thought about it." And she had, but decided not to. She didn't know weapons, and the thought was strong that when someone takes out a weapon, it usually gets used. "I'll be all right."

Finally Julia nodded. "Okay then. But up your life insurance, toots. I'll tell you that *I* wouldn't do it."

They talked money then, and the next day Claudia went down with a tape recorder and a note pad. Julia insisted on assigning a photographer, a bearded veteran named Wynn who looked like a retired fullback. Claudia quickly learned that it was a mistake. When she got close enough to a skell to talk, they invariably looked at her, then at Wynn standing a yard away like some strap-enwrapped mountain of muscle, and scurried quickly away. Although she was reluctant to lose the protection that Wynn provided, she knew there would be no story as long as he was around. After repeated urging, Julia agreed to drop Wynn from the piece, use artwork, and leave Claudia on her own.

Even then, Claudia was unsuccessful at establishing any rapport between herself and the skells. Her first conversation with an elderly gentleman, wearing coveralls and a yellow T-shirt that had once been white, was transcribed from her tape recorder as follows:

CLAUDIA: Hello.
MAN: Hey.
CLAUDIA: Do you mind if I talk to you?
MAN: Hey.
CLAUDIA: Do you mind?
MAN: Got a quarter?
CLAUDIA: Yes, here you are.
MAN: Got a quarter?
CLAUDIA: Yes. I just gave you one. There, see?
MAN: Got a quarter?
CLAUDIA: It's in your hand. Your hand.
MAN: Quarter.
CLAUDIA: Yes. What's your name?
MAN: I don't know.

And there the conversation stopped. The old man stood up and left the car.

There was another conversation, with another old man:

CLAUDIA: Hello.
MAN: Hello.
CLAUDIA: What's your name?
MAN: Bob. What's yours?
CLAUDIA: Claudia.
MAN: Will you marry me?
CLAUDIA: Marry you? This is awfully sudden.
MAN: You're all alike. All bitches.

As with his predecessor, the man stood and left the car.

Later that same day, Claudia approached a middle-aged woman sweating inside a heavy cloth coat, who, as soon as Claudia spoke to her, began screaming. "Shut up! Shut up!" the woman cried. "You won't give it to me! You got it, but you won't give it to me!" On this occasion, Claudia was the one to retreat from the car.

It did not take her long to rethink her premise. She had supposed that there were people who came down into the subways for logical reasons, or at least for reasons that she could sympathize with, if not fully understand. She had thought of the subway as a symbol, that perhaps she could answer mysteries, illuminate the mystique, crude and cruel, that hung, veillike, from the cold walls of these tunnels. Instead she had found only an asylum, and the theory that, instead of people being made mad by the life below, they had come down here already insane.

Now she sat trembling in spite of the warmth, and felt the fear and discomfort creeping back. Into her

Lowland Rider

mind came the urge to resign herself to the fact that she would not understand, that this place and its people would be, to her, eternally alien. Just as she was about to stand and walk into the sunlight, Jesse Gordon entered the car.

She did not recognize him at first. His hair was long, with dark tendrils curling over his collar, and his black beard had grown in fully, covering his throat to the hollow of his neck, and riding up his face to the top of his cheekbones so that his eyes seemed hidden behind a mask. Rags was with him, bundled in cloths, and Claudia marked the pair of them as skells.

Talk to them, she thought, but hesitated. If she had been alone with them, she would have obeyed her impulse and forgotten the subway and her piece, and sought the fresh air. But the presence of other passengers gave her courage, so she waited until the train began to move, then stood and made her way to where the men sat talking quietly. She grasped the hanger in front of them and looked down. "Excuse me . . ."

The younger man looked up first, and she saw his eyes and the contours of his face beneath the beard, and she remembered those eyes looking down at her in candlelight, that face sheened with satiny sweat . . .

"Jesse . . ."

His expression was perfectly blank. Then the furrow between his eyes deepened, and she knew he remembered too, remembered his ex-lover from the time they had both been single, careless, and, perhaps just a little, in love. "I'm sorry, I don't think I . . ."

"Claudia. Claudia Dorner, Jesse."

He gave a grim smile that admitted he was found out, then nodded. "Hello, Claudia. I didn't think anyone would recognize me."

"My God, it *is* you. What are you . . . doing down here? I mean, I mean they're *looking* for you."

"Then I suppose I'm hiding down here." He turned to the black man next to him. "Rags, this is Claudia. Claudia, Rags."

Rags and Claudia looked at each other without speaking, both of them wary.

"Say hello, Rags. Miss Dorner is the first to have found me. I guess that merits some recognition."

"'Lo," Rags said, and looked at Jesse, fear in his rheumy eyes. "I gotta be goin'. Things to do."

He shuffled off into the next car, as Jesse looked after him. "There goes my best friend," he said. "And he was lying. He has nothing to do. Nothing at all except to get another train." He sighed deeply. "So. What are you going to do now?"

"Do?"

"You said they're looking for me. Are you going to tell them you found me?"

"I . . . don't know. I hadn't thought about it."

"You'd better." He turned toward her, resting his thigh and knee on the seat. "What do they want me for?"

"For questioning, I think. I mean . . ." She laughed uncomfortably. "After what happened. Your . . . wife and daughter—I was so sorry to hear—and that man they found."

"Rhoads?" Jesse asked quietly.

Lowland Rider

"Yes, him. But the other one. The Spanish man. No one knows what really happened. No one knows where you went."

He nodded. "I went down here."

She frowned as if she did not understand. "You're . . . living down here now."

"Yes."

"I don't . . . why, Jesse?"

He leaned back, looked up at the ceiling. A moment passed before he spoke. "What happened. Because of it. They were . . . killed. I wasn't. Maybe I should've been. Maybe not. I don't know. But this seems, somehow, like the right place to be."

She nodded. "Inexplicable."

"That's the word."

"And you're staying?"

"I am."

The door at the front end of the car opened, and a transit policeman walked in. He paused as he neared Claudia and Jesse, pursed his lips, and made it plain by his expression that he thought the well-dressed Claudia should not be sitting so near such a disreputable character as the heavily bearded skell at her side. But Claudia disarmed him with a smile, which he gave back grudgingly, and he walked out the rear door.

"What did that mean?" Jesse asked.

"Sorry?"

"Did that mean you're not going to turn me in?"

"Is there any reason I should?"

"In God's blind eyes, no."

"Then I won't. On one condition."

"Which is?"

She interlaced her fingers as if praying, tried to appear sincere, even though she knew that what she was making was a deal, and looked full into Jesse Gordon's eyes. "Let me ride the trains with you."

He frowned, and his eyes squeezed nearly shut in concentration. "What?"

She told him then about the story she wanted to write, about her fascination with the lines and the people who rode them, about her desire to turn over the rocks and uncover the mysteries of the skells. When she finished, he laughed softly.

"There aren't any mysteries. Not one thing or two or three, at any rate. They're down here because they want to be, or because there's nowhere else to go. If you're looking for something you can say in one sentence, or one paragraph, or even one article to sum it all up, you won't find it. If there are ten thousand skells, there are ten thousand reasons."

"I'd like to find some of them."

"And you want me to help you."

"Yes."

"And you'll turn me in if I don't."

Claudia opened her mouth to speak, then closed it again. "No," she said finally. "I won't turn you in." She looked at Jesse with as much hardness as she could show. "But I hope you'll help me out of gratitude."

"Oh yes," Jesse said, nodding. "I've got a lot to be grateful for."

Lowland Rider

He smiled at her. It was a crooked smile, the smile, she thought, of a man whose mind is not right. *But why would he be down here otherwise?*

CHAPTER 9

Duke Sinclair's thigh ached. He'd been chasing a couple of graffiti artists who'd pulled out cans of Krylon right in front of him and started bombing the outside of a car at the Chambers Street station. He was wearing what he called his Superpimp getup—black/white shoes, tight dark jeans, a green satin jacket, shades, and a white felt broad-brimmed hat with a peacock feather band—so naturally the kids figured he was one of them or at least sympathetic. But as soon as the first burst of Day-Glo paint shot from the nozzle, he'd yelled, "Police! You're under arrest!"

Now *that* had dog-hearted them. They'd frozen for an instant, looking so scared that he would have sworn they weren't going to kick up a fuss, but he was wrong. He'd walked toward them, one hand in his pocket, as though his gun were in there, instead of behind his back, tucked into his waistband. "Okay, fellas, let's just . . ."

That was when they moved. One leapt for him, aiming the spray paint at his face, but Sinclair threw up an arm and caught the wetness on his sleeve instead. When he looked back up, the boy who had sprayed him was twenty feet down the platform, the other twice as far. Sinclair started to run after them. He reached behind him for his gun, then stopped himself. *All I need. Bag me a motherfucking graffiti writer, it's all over.* But at least he could bluff.

"Halt!" he cried. "Stop or I'll shoot!"

Bullshit. Bombers weren't good enough to excuse a warning shot. Especially not down here. He had only once heard a shot fired in the five years he had spent in the transit police, and he never wanted to hear one again. His ears had rung for a week.

"Goddammit! You fucking *hold* it!" Sinclair was gaining, and he thought he could at least catch the one in the rear before he hit the street. They were through the exit now, and the boy was only a few yards in front of him, heading for the steps to Chambers Street. Then, on the stairs, the boy turned and hurled the can of Krylon as fiercely as he could at Sinclair.

The policeman threw himself to the side, but the can struck his leg and clattered off down the steps. Sinclair yelped and staggered, and when he looked back up he saw the boy disappearing around the side of the street level kiosk. "Shit!" Sinclair snarled, ignoring the sharp ache in his thigh and pulling himself up the last few steps.

The street was as empty as a 4:00 A.M. station, the boys nowhere to be seen. He heard footsteps echoing somewhere, but could not pinpoint their location. He was as angry at himself as at them. Stupid bastards. He probably wouldn't have chased them if they'd just started to run, but that damn kid had to spray him first. A hundred dollar jacket shot to shit. He'd twisted his ankle, and his thigh hurt like hell where the kid had dinged it, and all he had to show for it was a spray can of Day-Glo orange Krylon. He could almost hear Montcalm laughing at him now.

Montcalm. Sinclair gingerly pulled back his sleeve and looked at his watch. At least the paint hadn't gotten it. Forty-five minutes until he had to meet the man, and it would take him that long to get over to 34th Street. Hell, even if he *had* nabbed those kids he couldn't have booked them. Montcalm hated for him to be late, no matter what the reason. Sinclair sighed. A crap day all-around.

Montcalm was waiting for him, naturally. He was sitting at the bar of the Oyster Bar as if he owned the place, frowning when he spotted Sinclair. "You're late," he said. "And you're limping." Disgust wrinkled his mouth. "What's that shit on your arm?"

He told Montcalm what had happened, and when Montcalm laughed Sinclair felt self-satisfied with his prediction, angry, and a bit relieved. It was better to have Montcalm laughing.

"You want a drink?" Montcalm offered.

"I'm on duty."

"Fuck it, I'm your boss. Beer over here!" He turned back to Sinclair. "Want you to do something for me."

"Sure."

"There's gonna be a little dealing on the Fulton Street line the next two, three days. Not exactly sure when—nobody is—but it's arranged that it'll be on your time." The beer came, and Sinclair sucked off the

Lowland Rider

foam and took a short swallow. Montcalm waited until the bartender moved away before he continued. "You see anything going down from now till Tuesday, look the other way. After that, bust 'em up, because they won't be our people."

"Got it."

"Not all you got." Montcalm reached out with his right hand, and Sinclair grasped it and shook it, palming the wad of bills the bigger man had given him. "Two hundred," Montcalm said, smiling.

"That's, uh . . . less than I usually . . ."

The smile froze and broke. "Yeah, well, it's less than I usually get too. Times are tough. But there'll be more. These deals go the way they're supposed to, we'll have a nice bonus, okay?"

Sinclair nodded. "Okay. Sure."

"One more thing. Our friends are getting a little pissed at the . . . freedom with which the competition's doing business in their territory. *Our* territory. And that means *your* territory."

"I can only bust 'em if I see 'em."

"Then keep your eyes open, Duke. The narcotics boys rule everywhere else, so down here it's up to *us* to make sure it all stays clean. That's our job, right?"

"Right."

"Except for a few exceptions." Montcalm stood up and put three singles on the bar. "That'll take care of it. Finish your beer. I gotta go."

Left alone, Sinclair looked at the multicolored bottles on the bar and at his own black face reflected in the mirror behind them. He noticed he was scowling, and hoped he had not been doing so when

Montcalm was there. He'd been wrong to kick about the two hundred. Montcalm wasn't the type to be swayed by complaints. Next time he'd be likely to give even less just to teach Sinclair a lesson. Yeah, a crappy day all around.

Sinclair wondered if Montcalm was starting to suspect the other deals he'd gotten into, and hoped he wasn't. That was all he needed—for Montcalm to learn that he'd been playing both sides against the middle. But what the hell, it wasn't like he was doing anything wrong, cheating the dealers by turning a blind eye to the other dealers. Not that it mattered anyway—if he took them off the street or out of the tunnels, it'd be barely a day before somebody else took their place. Like cleaning out maggots from a dead elephant. A thankless job, so why fight it? Get the thieves and the rapists, the slashers and the hoods, but fuck the dealers. Besides, they paid him well. He'd made five thousand tax-free dollars from Montcalm last year, and half again that from the guys he did business with on his own. More could keep coming in, as long as he played it cool. Maybe he'd ask Travis to do some deals up above for a while, just long enough to mellow out Montcalm's people. He wouldn't get any payoffs, but he wouldn't get any hassles either. After all, he was a cop.

CHAPTER

10

How can blood be so hot?

Baggie always asked herself that after a killing. In winter, when the stations were cold, the warmth felt good on her hands, and once the bastards had stopped moving, once they couldn't bite with their animal teeth or scratch with the animal claws their rough, horny, prying hands had become, she would sometimes, if her fingers were very cold, let the blood flow over them and warm them. Once they were warm, and once the blood started to dry so that her fingers looked coated with flaking rust, she washed them off so that no one would notice the blood on her hands and take the sons of bitches away from her. One time, when there had been no bathroom or water fountain nearby, she had licked the dry scaliness off her fingers. It had not tasted bad, and, in a way, she had enjoyed it, sucking her fingers until they were clean, until her flesh was pale again.

But in the summer, on nights like this, when she sweated beneath her clothes, and every movement slid wet cloth against wet skin so that she felt taut and slippery, when the moisture made her dress adhere to the hair beneath her arms, and press itself up between her buttocks so that the cloth seemed to seek entrance like some filthy man she had not yet killed, on these nights she tried to keep the blood from touching her. It burned on summer nights. When it got against her, she could see it steam, and when she washed it off, some red marks stayed, just like a burn, like the mark on her breast from the coat hanger one night years before.

It was on her now, and she rubbed at it fiercely, feeling it eat into her. The sweat in her dress diluted it, made it only a pink smear that grew lighter and lighter, and then disappeared. She sighed in relief, then drew the bag nearer and looked into it. She thought she recognized the bastard. One of those Marines, that's who it was. That nigger marine that night at the Ansonia. Well, it served him fucking right, after what he'd done to her. He had hurt her like they all hurt her, but she'd get back at them, she had time. They always came. They always smelled it, just like they'd claimed they could smell her cunt, like it was sending out a message, like she was some animal. Some bitch in heat.

Only she wasn't an animal. She'd never wanted them. They'd smelled what they wanted to smell, the sonsabitches, seen what they'd wanted to see, taken what they'd wanted to take. But she'd pay them back. She had time to pay back all of them. All of them.

She looked up from the bag and saw God standing before her.

God was dressed all in white, a pure, cool, bright

Lowland Rider

white that nearly blinded her, but that made her feel at peace with herself and everything around her. She thought, as she looked into his beautiful face, that she had seen him years before, just catching a glimpse of that same face through the glass of the car in which they'd found the dead man. She thought it had been him, but she wasn't sure.

What she *was* sure of, though, was that she loved him. He was not, she could tell, a man like other men. There was something beyond sex in him, something divine.

"My God," she whispered. "Oh my God."

"My name is Enoch," he said gently, smiling at her.

"I saw you . . . once, years ago." Her voice cracked.

"Yes."

"You . . . look the same."

"I do not change."

She felt choked, as though a great bolus that might have been her heart was swelling, growing in her throat. "What can I do . . ."

"Do?"

"To . . . *serve* you. Anything. Anything."

"Would you kill for me?" His smile did not fade.

"Yes." She took the handles of the shopping bag and slid it in front of him.

"No." He shook his head. "Not your creatures. Not your bastards. Others. Before they disguise themselves. While they are still in their true form."

"Yes. Oh yes."

He rested his long-fingered hand on her hair. It felt cool and soothing. "Do you know what it means to kill men?"

The curtains parted for a moment, the power of her god's presence destroying the illusions she had nurtured, the lies she had lived, so that she saw herself as a killer of animals, soulless things, creatures of no importance or worth, and a great sorrow at the waste of her life overcame her. "No. I don't know."

"You will."

"Yes. For you."

"Would you die for me?"

"Oh *yes*," she answered so that the word echoed in the empty station. "I would, my Lord."

"Live now. And serve me." His face lost its smile, and was transfigured by a look of such deep and abiding love for her that she wished with all her heart to die at that moment, in the fear that she would never know such joy again. "Serve me, my darling little Sunny. My Sunny girl."

It was a name no one had called her in half a century, the name her mother had called her before The Fall. *My Sunny. My Sunny little girl.* And she saw daffodils yellow as the sun clutched in her hand, smelled the sharp sweet smell of high grass after rain, heard the songs of robins, felt her mother's caresses upon her hair, knew that somewhere all was as it had been, and that Mother still loved her, still waited for her Sunny.

"Don't cry. It's all true. It's all there. All the love."

But she couldn't stop. She cried and cried, the tears of decades cascading over her cheeks, falling from her whiskered chin in a tattoo of droplets, one after another, caught in the hollow of her Lord's hand.

When she could see once more, when the haze that

had smeared her vision was cleared, she looked up and found herself alone. Although she could still feel the cooling touch of his hand, he was not there. The station was empty of even the sound of a train rattling somewhere far off. She was alone, filled with a love more thrilling and more violent than her hate.

"Enoch," she moaned, feeling his name in her mouth, feeling the goodness and rightness of it.

"*Enoch.*" It was a prayer, a litany, a love song all in one word, beginning with an outward breath, opened by the humming *N*, ceasing abruptly, like a command from God.

"*Enoch!*" And the joy drowned her as she worshipped him, adored him, and shivered with the excitement of what she would do for him.

For him, she would savage the city.

CHAPTER 11

"Aw shit, man," said Rags, peering through the graffiti-smeared glass that covered the subway map. "Son of a whore."

"What is it?"

"You know where we goin'?"

Jesse nodded. "Bergen Street, right?"

"Wrong. They messin' with the tracks again. We goin' out on the shithole Fulton Street line."

"Oh well . . ."

"Oh well my ass. Can't get turned around till we get to Broadway–East New York, and then we gotta get over to Eastern Parkway station. *Damn*. What shit."

"What's wrong with it?"

"Montcalm's line, for one."

"The skell hater."

"Right."

Jesse shrugged. "Well, we're stuck on it. Just have to keep a low profile."

Rags's face crinkled. "Huh?"

"Lay low. Pretend we're not here."

"Yeah, sure. Montcalm or his boys get on here, all

Lowland Rider

the pretendin' in the world don't stop us from gettin' whomped."

Jesse laughed and sat back on the bench, stretching his legs out in front of him. Rags joined him, but sat erect, looking at the rear door of the car, then at the front, and back again incessantly, as if at some subterranean tennis match. "You gonna see that girl again?" he asked after a while.

"Yeah."

"Shouldn't."

"Why not?"

"She ain't one of us, Jesse. She's just snoopy, nosin' around, what the hell she wanta know anyway?"

"I guess what makes us tick, Rags."

"None of her damn business. She jes' better stay out of *my* face, I tell you that."

Jesse laughed. "Or what, Rags? You gonna mess her up?"

Rags gave a series of unhappy grunts. "Well, maybe. I just ain't gonna say."

"You wouldn't hurt a fly," said Jesse, shaking his head.

"You forgettin', Jesse?" Rags asked, his mouth grim. "You forgettin' I killed a boy?"

"That wasn't killing, Rags. You did the world a service."

"She makes me nervous, that's all. Knows who you are, *where* you are, knows what you done . . ."

"She won't turn me in. She needs me." Even as he said it, Jesse wondered if it was really true. He had sensed something in Claudia, a desire beyond mere curiosity. He felt almost as though she were still attracted to him, though their affair had ended twelve years before.

When he had first seen her at the agency Christmas party to which she'd been invited, he had been so struck by her that he asked a mutual friend to introduce him. They had chatted, made a movie date, and had become lovers within a month. The relationship, though passionate in the bedroom, was lukewarm elsewhere, and by April had run its course. When Jesse married Donna eighteen months later, he was pleased to hear that Claudia had gotten married as well. Though he had thought of her occasionally over the years, he had not seen her until she sat down next to him on the subway. He found himself wondering if he would have evaded her, had he seen her before she recognized him, and decided that he would have.

The train slowed, and he heard Rags swear beside him.

"What is it?"

"Come on, into the next car." Jesse followed his friend, then looked behind him through several windows to catch a glimpse of a dark blue uniform and the slight flash of a badge. "Sonovabitch," Rags muttered. "He gonna follow us straight on through. Jes' keep walkin', Jesse."

But as quickly as they moved, the transit cop moved faster, until he was less than two cars behind. "We get off?" Jesse asked.

"Not yet, not yet, jes' keep walkin'."

Suddenly, the pair of doors they were next to began to close. "*Now*," said Rags, squeezing through, Jesse

Lowland Rider

right behind. On the platform, he kept walking toward the rear of the train as all the doors clattered shut and the cars began to move. Rags stopped and heaved a deep breath. "That does it," he said. "Cop's on his way to the next station."

"How'd you see him?"

"Outside. Angled way down. Made out the way he moved. Nothin' moves like a cop."

"We've been on the same cars with cops, Rags."

"Not on this line we ain't."

"Where are we anyway?"

"Utica Avenue station. No Man's Land."

"What do we do?"

"Sit our asses down and wait." Rags plopped down on a bench and Jesse joined him. The station was silent. After twenty minutes they had seen no one, and no other train had come. Then, from far off, they heard footsteps echoing through the tunnel, and saw two men come around the corner. They were as thick-bodied as trees, and their skin had the flat, lusterless brown of the Chicano who never sees sunlight. The larger of the pair carried a child's red plaid book bag in a meaty hand. Despite the heat, they both wore jackets.

When they saw Rags and Jesse, they didn't slow, but walked past them, not even turning to look. At the end of the platform they stopped and stood, not talking.

Soon two more men appeared. They were blacks, and though they were thinner, the tightness of their muscles made them appear no less strong. They too wore jackets, and one of them had a brown parcel whose end boldly protruded from his pocket.

"Oh, fuck me," whispered Rags.

"What?"

"Fuckin' drug deal. Exchange."

"Those guys?" Jesse whispered back, and Rags nodded. "In front of us? Of strangers?"

"We ain't nobody. Even if we was, this's all been taken care of. It's a clean place for these bastards."

"You mean no cops."

"That's right. Thanks to our friend, Montcalm. He sets it all up, the transit cops ain't here to see nothin'."

"Son of a bitch," Jesse said, more in awe at the smoothness of the operation than in anger. "What are they dealing?"

"Smack, prob'ly. Maybe this new shit, this crack stuff. Somethin' high-priced. No grass, that's too small potatoes."

Jesse eyed Rags. "How do you know all this?"

"I know. Let's get outa here." Rags stood up.

"Why?"

"*Why?*" Rags's voice squeaked. "You just look down the tracks at those boys and tell *me* why."

The four men had stopped talking quietly, and were looking up the platform at Rags and Jesse.

"You think we make them nervous?"

"Jesse, don't be an asshole. Let's *go*."

"Where would we go? You said this is a bad neighborhood."

"Jesse . . ."

Jesse reeled to his feet, staggered, and clutched at Rags. "Whatta fuck," he slurred, "whatta fuck *they* care?" His voice was loud enough for the men to hear, and all four of them tensed. "*Tired!*" Jesse whined,

"Jes' wanna siddown, f'crissake..." and with a moan he fell back onto the bench, his head rolling for several seconds with the impact.

The men watched for a second longer, then laughed, and directed their attention back to each other.

"What the game?" Rags asked.

"I just want to watch, Rags. Maybe go into business."

"*What*?"

"The dope business, Rags."

"You gonna get into the *dead* business, boy! You thinking of messing with them?"

"The cops won't."

Rags stared stonily at Jesse. "You dead and you don't know it. You mess with them, you look at them sideways, and you a dead man."

"I already am. Dead and in hell. That's why it doesn't matter, Rags. Why I'm not scared. They can't do any worse than what's been done. Now. Which ones'll have the dope?"

"What you tryin' to prove?"

"Which ones?"

"The spics will. The parcel. Money's in the bag."

"What are the spics carrying?"

"Huh?"

"You think they have guns?"

Rags snorted angrily. "How the fuck I know?"

"Sons of bitches."

"Come on, Jesse..."

"Which one, you think?" Jesse's words were sharp. "If just one had a gun, which one would it be?"

"Shit, I don't know..."

"The shorter one, I bet. The little man."

"Yeah, fuck, sure, the little man, sure. Jesse . . ."

Jesse looked at Rags with clear, cold eyes. "Get out, Rags. Get up the stairs. I'm going to make some trouble here. You stay out of it."

Rags didn't argue. He merely shook his massive head, muttered, "Fuckin' crazy . . ." and went toward the stairs from which the Chicanos had come. He looked back once, and disappeared around the corner.

Alone on the bench, Jesse sat and watched the four men at the other end of the platform. Though three of them were talking and examining the contents of the packages, the shorter Chicano was looking down the platform at Jesse. Jesse coughed wetly, spat on the concrete, lowered his head so that it fell between his knees, and did not look back up until he heard footsteps once more. The blacks had vanished around the far corner, and the Chicanos were moving toward Jesse and the stairs beyond him. Jesse coughed again, closing off his throat so that air exploded from his nostrils with a burst of noise that made the smaller man stiffen and slow, then pick up his pace when he noticed that the larger man had paid Jesse no mind.

"Hey," Jesse croaked when the pair was ten feet away. "You guys . . ." He pushed himself to his feet and stumbled sideways, blocking their way. The smaller man said something in Spanish, and put his left hand on Jesse's chest to shove him out of the way.

Jesse grabbed the wrist and hurled the unprepared and off-balance man directly against the dirty tile wall, where his head hit with a loud crack. In an instant, Jesse had ripped open the man's jacket and

Lowland Rider

run his hands over the torso from armpit to waist, where he felt the hard butt of a pistol.

If the big man had not been momentarily stunned by the unexpectedness and ferocity of the attack on his partner, he could easily have brought down Jesse with his own pistol. But he barely had time to yank the .38 from his waistband and begin to aim before the gun in Jesse's hand exploded, sending a bullet into the big man's cheek. His head snapped back, his arms flew up, and his pistol sailed down into the chasm of the tracks.

Jesse's ears felt as if they'd been hammered, and it took all his will to aim and fire again. The second bullet caught the big man, still standing, in the chest. He fell at last, flat on his back, his bleeding head on the yellow warning line at the platform's edge.

Whirling, Jesse thrust the pistol toward the man from whom he had taken it, who was still lying on his stomach where he had fallen. He was beginning to move, placing his hands against the concrete beneath him to push himself up. He froze when he saw his gun in Jesse's hand.

"Give it here," Jesse said, his voice shaking.

Blood trickled down into the man's eyes, but he blinked it away savagely, glared at Jesse, and spat out a burst of Spanish.

"You know what I want," Jesse said more harshly. "Give it." He held the gun straight out in front of him, pointing directly at the man's face.

The man rolled over on his side and spread his arms apart. "Got nothing, man. *He* got it." He pointed to the dead man at the edge of the platform.

Keeping the pistol trained on the living man, Jesse went to the dead one and patted down the body. The packet was in a lined, zippered pocket in the back of the man's jacket, and Jesse, working with one hand, had to rip the cloth to get it out. He tore the tape and pushed back the paper.

There were two long, flat bags of black plastic, inside of which he could feel fine powder. Far down the tracks he heard the approaching roar of a train. It helped him decide what to do.

Jesse pressed the packets under his left arm. "Get up," he told the Chicano, "and come over here." The man got to his feet and, with effort, joined Jesse at the side of the tracks. The sound of the train was growing louder.

"Push him off."

"*What?*"

"He's dead. It doesn't hurt when you're dead. Do it."

The man tried to push the body with his feet, but it was too heavy, and he had to get on his knees, drag the body so that it was parallel to the tracks, and roll it off. Jesse did not hear it land. The din of the train was too great.

"Take these," Jesse said, handing the packets to the man. "When the train comes, throw them at the front of it."

The man's eyes widened and his mouth gaped. Jesse had to laugh. "You *crazy*, man! Don't you know what this shit *is?*"

"Dream dust," Jesse answered. "Let the train dream. Throw it. And aim well."

Lowland Rider

The light of the train was now visible in the tunnel, and soon the bright, white eye rounded the corner and bore down on them. It was a through express, and would not stop.

"Get ready . . ." he told the man. " . . . set . . . *now*!"

With a sob, the man hurled the packets into the face of the onrushing train. Jesse imagined he heard a pop, and then two white bombs exploded through which the train roared unperturbed, like a plane through a cloud. The fine white powder made sudden traceries in the air that the train pushed to either side, and there was an ever so slight hiccup in the rhythm of the wheels as they passed over and tore up the dead man, but that was all. The sound died away, and, except for a few barely distinguishable wisps of pale residue on the platform, there was no indication that drugs had ever soiled Utica Avenue station.

"You just made a big mistake, man," the Chicano said, trembling.

"Everyone does. When they're born."

"You gonna kill me?"

He looked at the man for a long time. "No. I don't have to."

"They're not gonna let this go. We'll find out who you are, man."

Jesse nodded. "When you do, let me know."

The man frowned, and the sound of another train came from far off. "Stay there," Jesse told the man. "Right there until the train leaves."

The train, a local, slowed as it appeared, and the doors slammed open. Three people got off further up the platform, and Jesse stepped into the nearest car. He stood just inside the door, the gun, unseen by the few other passengers, hanging at his side. The Chicano stood glaring, unable to move, and the doors closed. The train began to move, and the Chicano, now protected by the door, shrieked curses at Jesse, who heard them only as a slight whine above the clatter of the wheels and the lurching of the car, like a wasp on the other side of a closed and locked window.

CHAPTER 12

Montcalm's face was pasty in the light of the fluorescents. He could feel sweat on his upper lip, and he covered his teeth with his lips and sucked downward to dry it. Montcalm didn't like to sweat, and he didn't like the man who stood at the sink next to his own.

Rodriguez wasn't sweating at all. In spite of the heat and the tight-fitting black suit he wore, his skin was as dry as sand, each lock of dark hair powdered into place. "And I tell you," he was saying, "it had to be your man."

"And *I'm* telling *you* it *wasn't*." Montcalm held his hand beneath the tap and splashed cold water onto his face.

"I pay you good, Roberto. Why you wanna double-cross me?"

"*Jesus*, Tony! Use your head! I mean . . ." He lowered his voice, squeezed his hands into fists to keep his temper in check. "If it'd been my boys, we wouldn't've gone after the shit, we'd have gone after the *money*. If it *was* us, which it wasn't."

"You get stuff. I give you stuff."

"Then why wipe it? If I wanted it, why throw it into a fucking train? It doesn't make any sense!"

Rodriguez's face grew very stern. "Somebody pressing you, Bob?"

"Huh?"

"Pressing. Sniffing around. Checking you out. You going chicken on me? Getting religion?"

"Hell, no! There haven't been any leaks, nobody's asked me nothin'."

"You're not trying to scare me off, discourage me? Because if you were, this would be the way. A way that would give you all these excuses, these alibis."

"I swear to God, Tony, I had *nothing* to do with this."

"You don't want my business, Bob? You don't want the money? Or the smack? You could just tell me. You didn't have to blow away ten grand street value of good dope."

"I *didn't*."

An old man with a battered, plaid suitcase walked into the men's room. Both Rodriguez and Montcalm glared at him with such hostility that he turned immediately and shambled out.

"I want your money, Tony," Montcalm continued. "I want your business. I wouldn't fuck it up for anything. So why blame me? I mean, you got competition, don't you?"

The suggestion enraged Rodriguez, and he shook a long, dark finger at Montcalm. "I got *no* competition, asshole! Not over there. Nobody messes with me there, so don't go telling me it's some fucking competition, all right? Now you listen to me, Bob. Maybe you're on the level, and I'll give you the benefit of the doubt, although I don't often do that. But you better make damn sure this doesn't happen again. You're the law down there, and when I make arrangements with the law I expect it to protect me, just like any other citizen. So you—or one of the boys on your payroll— you find this guy and you stop him. Waste his ass. And you either bring me his balls in a bag, or I'm gonna take my business somewhere else."

"But, Tony, it might've just been some crazy . . ."

"You're fucking right, pal. Crazy is the word. You find him, and you kill him. If he ain't your own man, then it's no sweat. If he is and you been jivin' me, then you're fucked. Because you're gonna have to kill one of your own. And I don't think the rest of your boys will like that a whole lot . . ."

"Tony . . ."

"But whatever happens, I'll find out, won't I? You find this motherfucker and you *kill* him, Bob. And till you do, all bets are off. No more money, no more dope."

Montcalm could feel the blood rush to his cheeks. "Look, you can't just cut me off like that . . ."

"I like dealing on your line, Bob. It's nice and safe. It used to be. You're gonna have to prove to me it still is. Get him. Then we'll talk some more. But unless you can tell me you got him, just stay the fuck away from me."

Rodriguez pivoted and walked quickly out of the men's room. Montcalm remained, leaning with both hands on the white porcelain, a sick lump in his throat. He thought of Gina, of the money in the locker that he would have to start spending to feed her habit, of the way people went higher and then slipped back, until it became harder and harder to climb any more, and he thought finally of that goddammed sonovabitch who fucked it all up, that sonovabitch who he would find, and stop, and kill.

CHAPTER 13

Butch Devlin hated to scrub tile. Actually, it wasn't the tile that he hated as much as the grout in between. Hell, the tile itself wiped clean as a whistle, and stayed smooth and cool on a hot summer day like this. Of course he couldn't know that it was a hot summer day. He never knew what the weather was like until he went home. But it had been a hot summer morning when he came in, so odds were damned good that it would be a hot summer day when he got off at five.

Despite the air-conditioning that kept Penn Station at a constant comfortable temperature, Devlin yanked his handkerchief out of his hip pocket and smeared it across his damp forehead. It didn't make sense that such a little job could make you sweat so much. Or maybe it wasn't the job, he thought. Maybe it was the crack.

The thought made him edgy, and he stuck out his lower lip and rubbed the small, wiry brush into the can of cleaning compound. As he scrubbed on his hands and knees, he remembered with a combination of pleasure and guilt how he had first smoked the stuff. Mike, one of the black janitors, had introduced him to it. Devlin didn't often hang out with the blacks, but Mike was different—cheerful, friendly, not at all sullen like the rest of them Devlin worked with, the ones who made it a point to ignore him in the locker room. Mike was about Devlin's age—midthirties—but acted like an older man, deferential to the whites. If there was mockery behind the easy smiles, it was well hidden. Devlin had never seen it.

He and Mike had talked about drugs one day during lunch break, and Devlin mentioned that he smoked grass occasionally. "Grass is okay," Mike nodded. "But you ever smoke crack?"

Devlin had heard of it, and had the impression that it was dangerous, something like angel dust.

"Naw, man," Mike responded to Devlin's concern. "Ain't a thing like that shit. It's just cocaine, only you smoke it instead of snort it."

"Cocaine's too rich for me."

"Ten bucks too rich? Come on, Butch."

"Ten bucks? *You* come on. How can coke sell so cheap?"

Mike shrugged. "Hey, I don't question gifts from God, man. All I know is that it makes grass feel like Winstons."

Devlin thought for a moment, remembering the one time he had smoked grass that had been laced with opium, not realizing the presence of the additive until he had come down from his first toke, a whiff of magic that had sent him into what seemed like a half hour's romp through the most colorful and vivid landscape

Lowland Rider

he had ever dreamed of. "Good shit, huh?"

"Dynamite. You wanta try it?"

They met after their shift was over, grabbed a burger, and took a train up to 155th Street. Devlin was nervous about going so far uptown, but Mike only laughed. "Hell, Butch, we ain't goin' to Harlem, we're goin' to Washington Heights! There're white guys up there, don't worry."

Mike led Devlin to a run-down apartment house, where they went around to a back stairway and down to cellar level. Mike knocked and after a minute a small panel slid back, showing a pair of white eyes set in a black face. Mike smiled at the eyes, and the door opened. Mike and Devlin went in, and Mike led the way down a long corridor past the doorman, who, Devlin noticed, had a holstered revolver in full view.

"Hey, Mike," he whispered, "what the hell is this? Prohibition or something?"

"Nah, they just like to make sure the customers don't have to worry about bein' interrupted. No sweat."

Devlin followed Mike to the end of the corridor, where he knocked again, and again the door was opened by a man wearing a holster and pistol. The man smiled and beckoned them in, murmuring "Howya, Mike?" The room was large, with several more doors opening off it. It was thickly carpeted, and comfortable looking chairs and sofas were placed in clumps centering around a smaller forest of green glass water pipes. Several people were sitting in these islands of comfort, smoking from the pipes. Lights from the floor lamps glowed dimly in the thin mist, soft music played, and a sharp, indefinable odor filled the air.

"Step right up, Butch," Mike instructed, walking to the far wall. He took out a ten dollar bill, put it into a drawer that slid out from the wall, and closed the drawer. In five seconds the drawer slid open, and Mike took from it a small vial that contained some yellow-white pellets. He held it up so that Devlin could see. "The automat of dreams," he whispered, grinning. "Do it."

"Ten, right?" Devlin asked. Mike nodded, and Devlin took two fives from his wallet, put them in the drawer, and slid it shut. When it reopened, he took his vial and joined Mike.

Two hours later he had spent three hundred dollars. He had never smoked any grass that could compare with the crack. Even hash, which he had bought once or twice, was not its equal. He spent his money and didn't care about spending it, until he realized he had none left.

"Then the party's over," Mike grinned, making a gesture with his hands like a genie granting a final wish. "Let's go."

The next night after work, Mike asked Butch if he wanted to go back to the base house again. He wanted to all right, but he had no more cash. He'd purposely stayed away from the bank during his lunch hour, figuring that if he didn't have it, he wouldn't spend it. "No thanks," he told Mike. "I'm tapped out."

"Well, look," Mike told him. "I got fifty bucks. It won't last long, but we could get a couple good hits out of it."

"No man, I don't want you paying for my dope."

"Hey, consider it a loan. You can pay me the twenty-five when you got it."

Twenty-five dollars didn't seem like much, and Mike really seemed to want Devlin's company, so he agreed to go with him. When they got there, Devlin found that he was right, twenty-five bucks wasn't much. In fact it wasn't nearly enough. So he cashed in his watch for three more vials.

It went like that for a number of weeks, until Devlin grew slowly addicted to crack. He denied that fact to himself, of course, and was finally forced to deny the drug to himself as well, as his savings account was depleted within a month. His options were simple— either stop smoking crack, or start stealing.

Butch Devlin was not a thief. He'd been brought up Irish Catholic, and the one time that he'd taken a comic book from a drug store without paying for it, he had felt guilty and told his father, who, in the time-honored tradition, took him back to the drugstore and made him confess, give back the comic book, and work for the druggist two hours after school for a week, suffering the druggist's suspicious glares and searches when Devlin went home each night. He had never taken a thing since. It was not in him to steal.

So he crouched on the floor, scrubbing the grout between the tiles, wishing that the floor was one flat slab of concrete that he could merely mop and be done with it. Payday was three days away, and he wondered if he could hold out that long.

Before too long he had finished in the men's room, and went out into the alcove where the rental lockers stood. The room was long and narrow, and he decided to start at the far end, from where he could see some of the passengers walking to their trains. It was summer, after all, and a lot of the women in the city seemed to like to show off what they had in the chest department. Butch Devlin always appreciated that. He scrubbed, one eye on his work, the other on the opening into the terminal. Unfortunately, the scenery was dull, and in a half hour of rubbing and scrubbing, he had seen only one girl in a halter top, the kind of girl whose belly dictated against such exposure.

Devlin was thinking of crack of a different sort when the bearded man came into the locker area. He was tall and gaunt, and dressed in jeans and a T-shirt. He smelled vaguely of sweat, not as strongly as some of the people who, Devlin suspected, lived out of lockers. He had a key in his hand, but stopped when he saw Devlin looking at him.

Devlin stopped too. The man's eyes were *hot*—that was the only way that Devlin could think of them. They burned, as though the man had a fever, and Devlin felt as if they seared right through his own eyes and into his head. It was a nasty feeling, and Devlin looked away quickly, turned around, and went back to his job. Junkie, probably, he thought angrily, surprised at the effect the man's presence had on him. Working in the rest rooms of Penn Station, he had seen every kind of human sludge imaginable. Funny, then, that this man made him feel so insecure, almost frightened.

Devlin finished digging out a particularly tough

Lowland Rider

deposit of something he didn't care to identify, and turned to put more cleaning compound on his brush. The bearded man, he saw, had opened the locker, and was removing something from a leather bag. In the glimpse he had of it, Devlin could easily see that it was money, and that, though the man took only a few bills, there was a large wad that went back into the bag.

The man's head turned in Devlin's direction, and he jerked his gaze back to the floor before the man could tell for sure that he was being spied upon. Devlin heard the sound of a zipper, then coins dropping into metal, and the slam of the locker door. He did not wish to meet the heat of that glare again, so he kept his head down as the man walked past him and out into the terminal.

When the footsteps died away, Devlin stood up and walked over to locker number 4602, where the man had been standing, and thought about what was inside.

Money.

That much was sure. He had seen it. The pile of bills had been at least an inch thick, and that bag was big. There was no telling how many packets might be inside it. Hundreds? Maybe even thousands? More? Maybe the man wasn't a junkie at all—maybe he was a *dealer*. Yeah, that was it—he was a dealer, and this was where he stashed his money. Oh Jesus, oh Jesus, how the hell much money was *in* there anyway? Enough to buy one helluva lot of crack, that was damn sure. And to take it from that guy, from that *drug dealer*, well, hell, that wasn't like stealing, was it? No, that was just like getting some of his own back, that was all. Shit, that guy probably sold heroin to school kids, when you came right down to it. And if he hadn't yet, he sure enough would, unless somebody put him out of business.

Now how the hell, Butch Devlin thought, do you get into one of those fucking *lockers*?

CHAPTER 14

"This is it," Jesse told her. "This is the Beast. Not much to see, is it?" They were riding the eastern spur of the Number 2 IRT line, heading out to New Lots Avenue.

Claudia made a sound that was almost a chuckle if there hadn't been so much unease in it. "We've only started, after all. Is it really that bad?"

"You're the one who told *me* about it. That article."

"Well, it said it was the worst. The scariest."

Jesse finally turned to look at her. She was dressed in a pair of Pumas, designer jeans, a red-checked blouse, and a Mets cap. She carried no purse, just a note pad, into which she occasionally scribbled. "The scariest. That's what you're after? Thrills? A fun house ride?"

"I'm after people. I just thought that the more interesting ones might be on a line that's a little . . . well, *looser*."

"Loose." Jesse nodded. "You'll get loose." He leaned back and closed his eyes.

Eventually the train slowed, the clatter of wheels on

rails became less urgent, and Claudia stood up. "Let's get off," she said.

"Get off? I thought you wanted to ride this to the end?"

"I do," she said, moving toward the door so that Jesse had to rise and follow. "But I want to get off at some of the stations too."

"You know someone on Utica Avenue?"

She smiled. "No, but maybe I'll get lucky."

Maybe you'll get killed, Jesse thought savagely, as a wave of rage swept through him, so unexpected that it startled him. His emotions toward Claudia had been perplexingly ambivalent. There were times when he wanted to hold her, not in a sexual sense, but simply for warmth, to feel a woman in his arms again, and then there were times when he wanted to do nothing less than smash her head against the walls. Her presence freed him when he did not want to be free, reminded him of his humanity when he needed to be inhuman to survive.

"It's nine o'clock at night," he told her as he followed her onto the platform. "You're safer on the train than on the platform. Let's stay on the train."

"You're with me," she answered so simply and smugly that he felt furious again.

"I'm not Superman. I can't be responsible for your safety."

"I'm not asking you to be. I just want you to come with me. I'm a fast runner, I wore my sneakers."

Jesus, he thought, sneakers. Like she was talking about a Sunday afternoon jog through Central Park. She looked as though she jogged, tan and healthy. He couldn't see an extra pound of flesh on her anywhere. Desire rose in him for a moment, but he bit it back. There was no room in his life for desire.

The doors shut behind them. A few other people had gotten off the train, and were now moving toward the stairs. Down the platform Jesse saw two men sitting on a bench. The one closest to them was leaning back, his arms stretched over the back. The other one was leaning forward to look around his seatmate. They were dressed shabbily, and Jesse felt sure they were skells. Plain muggers would have looked better. There was something else too—they looked at home, like Rags, like Baggie, like *me*, Jesse thought.

"Who are they?" Claudia asked easily, as if she expected him to know every sleazy denizen of the tunnels.

"I haven't been introduced," Jesse said quietly, wishing another train would come.

"Are they skells, do you think?"

"I think."

"Let's talk to them."

She didn't understand. She was playing fucking games. "You don't want to talk to them," he told her.

"That's what I came down here for, isn't it?"

"Claudia, they don't look friendly. The fact is they look mean. Now there are a lot of *old* skells, harmless, not dangerous at all—but they aren't on *this* line."

"Jesse, I want a cross section. Sure, I want to talk to some of the old ones, but it's the young ones that fascinate me—they're still able to talk sensibly about things. They haven't—"

He finished it for her. "Gone crazy yet."

She smiled sheepishly. "I didn't mean—"

"It's all right." He looked up the platform at the two men. "So what's going to be the topic of discussion with our two friends there?"

"I just want to talk to them, that's all." She didn't know what the hell she wanted.

Jesse and Claudia walked toward them. The nearest one was bald in a patchwork way. There were still tufts of hair sprouting here and there, but the general effect was that of a defoliated forest. He was also the bigger of the pair, paunchy but muscular. Even sitting down he looked tall. The other man was small and weasellike, his face crossed with scars. As Jesse and Claudia got nearer, the men began to put their backs up, and their faces got meaner and uglier. But when they saw the man and woman more clearly, Jesse thought the hostility seemed to go out of them. The meanness and ugliness of their souls were still there, but now they seemed cowed, like mad dogs not quite mad enough not to recognize a man with a whip. There was energy there, and violence, but it was held in.

Claudia sensed it too, and her voice shook when she talked to them. "Hello. Do you . . . live down here? In the subways?"

In spite of what seemed to be their fear, they looked at each other and turned back to her with a smirk. "Why, you want to rent a fucking room?" said the weasel-faced man. Jesse thought about telling him to watch his mouth, but didn't. This was their place—

Lowland Rider

and his. The woman was the invader, and if she wanted to communicate with them it had to be on their terms. He wasn't going to help her. They had not been close for many years, and he owed her nothing. All he would do would be to keep her from getting hurt. Or try to.

"No, I just want to talk to you."

"Tell them why," Jesse said.

Startled, she turned to him. "What?"

"Tell them why you want to talk to them."

"I . . ." She looked back at the men, who were both eyeing Jesse suspiciously. "I'm writing an article. A magazine piece. On the people who live down here."

"Yeah?" the bald man said.

"Yes. I want to know . . . why the people who are here . . . are here."

The smaller man twisted his mouth in what was supposed to be a smile. His teeth were green. "Rent control," he said.

"I'm . . . sorry?"

"What do you wanna hear? My life story?"

"If you want to tell it to me."

"I don't. And neither does he," the small man said, gesturing to his companion. "Now why don't you leave us the hell alone. We ain't done nothing wrong."

Jesse thought it seemed strange. The man was talking to Jesse almost as if he were a transit cop. "What's wrong?" he said, addressing the man for the first time.

"Nothing's wrong, and I don't want no trouble," the smaller man said.

175

"What makes you think we're trouble?"

"'Cause I know you."

Jesse's gut felt cold. "You know me?"

"You're that guy. We heard what you look like."

"That guy," Jesse repeated, feeling stupid and scared, wondering how they knew who Jesse Gordon was.

"That . . ." The bald man paused before he said it. "That guy who's been fuckin' around down here."

"The one who messed that deal," the other man explained. "You're him, ain't you?"

"What else have you heard about . . . this guy?" Jesse asked.

"That he done some other things," the weasel-faced man said. "That he messed some people over." He narrowed his eyes. "That he made himself some enemies."

"Where did you hear all this?"

"People."

People. It was true enough. Jesse wondered if they'd heard about him making the heroin disappear, or the mugger Rags had killed, or the other things he'd done in the few weeks since. It didn't matter. What mattered was that they had heard of him through the network. The skells knew. And since Jesse always wore the same clothes, they knew what he looked like.

He didn't ask the two men any more. Claudia looked at him oddly, then tried to break through the wall they'd put up, but it was no use, and before long Jesse and Claudia were back on the train heading toward New Lots.

"Tell me about it," she said when they were alone again.

"About what?"

"About what they said, what else?"

"It's nothing."

"Those two didn't think it was nothing."

"It's just . . . something I've been doing."

"What? What have you been doing?"

He felt like he was ten years old. "I've been . . . helping people."

"I don't get it."

"Helping. When people get . . . in trouble."

"You mean like in crimes? Like stopping things?"

"Yes, yes . . ." He didn't think he'd ever felt so embarrassed.

"Like . . . like *Death Wish*? Like Goetz?"

"No, not . . . well, sort of . . ."

"You . . . you *kill* people?"

"No, not if I don't have to, no, no, not at all, no, I don't kill people." Which was a lie. He had.

"You'll be killed," she said flatly, and he wondered if what he had told her had numbed her somehow.

"No. I'm careful." He smiled thinly. "But if I do die," he went on, "it doesn't matter much, does it?"

"Yes, it matters. It matters to me." She put a hand on his arm. "You're a good man, Jesse. What happened to you, to your family, it was awful. But you've let it bury you down here. You've done nothing wrong. You can come back up, be who you were before, be Jesse Gordon. You don't have to be this person they're talking about, you don't have to prove anything . . ."

"I'm not trying to prove anything."

"You are . . ."

"I don't want to talk about it, all right? You wanted to ride the Beast, you're riding it." He stared hard at her. "So just enjoy the trip. Ask your questions to the people. But don't ask them to me." He shook his head. "Not yet."

CHAPTER 15

Gladys H. Mitchell stared at the man and listened. It was two in the morning at the Rector Street station of the IRT line, and everything was quiet. The man was drunk, that much she was sure of. She had smelled the whisky on his breath as he walked past her when he came into the station, and he had tottered as he moved. Oh, he was drunk all right. She had seen enough drunken men, rubbed enough of their limp cocks to recognize a drunk when she saw one. He sat down on a bench at the end of the platform, no doubt to wait for his train, or to wait for a train that he thought was his.

This station saw very few trains this time of the night, and the first reason Baggie was here was that no one would chase her away. The second reason was that if no one was there to chase her away, no one would be there to stop her from doing what she had to do to serve Enoch.

"Enoch." She whispered his name, and it seemed as though the station, the tunnel, the whole network of lines trembled with the majesty of it. She loved him as

she had never loved anything before, not even the days in the sunshine when she was her mother's Sunny girl. For even then, even at that young age, she knew those days would pass away. But Enoch—Enoch would go on and on forever and ever, World Without End, Amen. He would not die, nor would he age, as had she, his worshipper. She knew that he was God.

And she would do what her God had asked her to. She would kill men, she would know what it was like to kill men, as those men had killed her, over and over again, with their great, sharp cocks, their devil's tails whipping her insides, and now she would kill *them*, yes she would, and she would scrape *their* insides now with that knife, that long and shining knife with the button she caressed even now, rubbing her thumb over it, the smoothest thing on earth and under it, but no devil's tail, oh no, not her sweet knife—no, her knife was God's tongue, *that's* what her knife was, and it would sing to her the songs of blood, and she would sing them back to her God, back to Enoch.

The station was quiet. The man was alone, all alone. And for the first time in so many years, perhaps the first time ever, Gladys H. Mitchell felt power.

She stood, and left her bags—actually left them there behind her, something she had not done since she had filled the first one years before—and started to walk toward the drunken man, who sat unaware, his head hanging almost between his knees, moving slowly back and forth like some hairy, ovoid pendulum.

But it was not a pendulum that Gladys H. Mitchell saw. It was something else dangling between the man's

Lowland Rider

thighs, something she had seen too many times between too many thighs, something that her knife, her sweet, holy knife, was made to slash and cut, to let the breeders breed no more.

She would cut off his balls, and offer them to God.

"That big one," she said harshly, seeing only the back of the man's head, covered with coarse hair, swaying back and forth, back and forth, "I'll cut off that *big* one..."

She pressed the smooth button and the blade sprang out, the Tongue of God, ready to sing its anthem. She drew closer, raised her arm above her head...

And God's eye shone out of the tunnel, blinding her, God's voice roared against the filthy walls, and the train, God's mailed fist, came thrusting into the tunnel, filling it up from wall-to-wall. The man's head came wavering up at the sound of it, and he saw the woman, the arm, the knife, saw and stared as the train slowed and stopped.

Gladys H. Mitchell fixed him with a glare that sobered him instantly, and he moaned and threw himself away from her, off the end of the bench, falling hard onto the concrete. The doors of the train opened.

And Gladys H. Mitchell stepped on, holding her clean and shining knife.

She continued to glare at the man until the doors shut and the train rattled north toward Cortlandt Street. Then she fell onto her knees in the empty car and wailed. "Forgive me, my God, oh, forgive me, my Lord Enoch..." She had not killed the man, and prayed fervently that she was not damned for her cowardice. The train had frightened her. There could have been people on it who would have seen her sacrifice the man, and then she might have been caught, and then she would have been taken up above and locked away. Being locked up would have been bad enough, but crueler still would be her absence from the place where Enoch walked. That was the one thing that she could never bear, now that she had basked in his glory.

"Oh, forgive me . . ." she blubbered for several minutes, before she remembered that in her flight from the Rector Street station, she had left her bags containing everything she owned except her knife. Her first reaction was to plan to get off at the next station and go back. But when she thought about it, she decided that what was in her bags did not matter any more. She still had her knife, and she had her love for Enoch, and that was all she needed now.

Nevertheless, she got off at Cortlandt Street and rummaged through the garbage cans on the platform until she found a discarded shopping bag and a bit of a hot dog. Putting the meat in the bag, she went down to the end of the platform and waited. In another hour a small rat came up over the edge of the tracks, paused, moved toward the bag, paused, moved, paused, over and over again until it was within a few inches of the open mouth of the bag.

From the time the rat had appeared until the time it stood at the portal was fourteen minutes, but they had been the longest fourteen minutes of Baggie's life. She had begun to sweat copiously when the animal appeared, and bit the inside of her cheek to keep from trembling. When the animal was halfway between the track and the bag, she urinated from excitement, and the smell made the rat take an even longer pause before moving again. By the time it was at the bag, her mouth was filled with blood, and she could contain herself no longer. The animal's eyes were hidden from hers now, and she raised the knife and threw herself downward.

She had not waited long enough. Had she maintained her former patience, she would have caught the animal through its torso. As it was, the knife ripped through the mouth of the bag and glanced off the skull of the startled beast, which had only just begun to put its head inside. It gave a brief, sharp screech, turned, and ran back over the lip of the platform.

Baggie gave a howl of rage and frustration, and flung herself after the fleeing creature, but she was far too slow and too old, tripping and tumbling to the edge, where only a savage effort kept her from falling onto the tracks below. Furious, she lay there, impotently drawing the knife in long scratches over the concrete, thinking over and over again that animals were no longer enough, would never again be enough, thinking how true it was that a single glimpse of heaven made the earth hell for ever after.

CHAPTER 16

Jesse Gordon rode and thought and watched. He rode alone most of the time, joining Rags for an occasional ride and a game of chess. But Rags seemed uneasy around him now, as if Jesse were carrying a sign around his neck that begged for trouble.

He met Claudia only once since their trip together on the Beast. She brought him a brown, crew neck sweater that she fished self-consciously from a Barney's bag. "I thought maybe you could use it," she told him. "Those black ones you wear are pretty thin."

He didn't take it when she held it out to him. "I don't need it," he said. "I've got a jacket if I get cold."

"But I bought it just for you . . ."

"Thank you. I appreciate the gesture. But I don't want you to bring me anything."

She smiled and shrugged to hide her embarrassment. "Okay, I'll just keep it. I love men's sweaters anyway. They're so nice and roomy . . ." Later, when she bought a soft pretzel and offered him one, he shook his head. But when she started to throw hers away after eating only half of it, he stopped her. "Wait. I'll eat it."

She looked at him, puzzled. "I just asked if you wanted one and you said no."

"I didn't want you to buy me one," he told her. "But I'll eat what you throw away."

"What's the difference?"

"There's a difference," he said, taking the pretzel from her hand and biting into it.

Claudia gave a little laugh and shook her head. "I don't understand you, Jesse."

He swallowed before he answered. "Maybe you're not supposed to."

They traveled the safer and more comfortable Washington Heights line early on a Sunday morning, and Claudia spoke to and actually got some rational responses from several skells. An older man confessed to her with tears in his eyes that he had been in prison for twenty years, and when he had been released he had found that the world had changed so much that he didn't know how to live in it anymore, and had gone below into the tunnels, where he had remained for the past four years.

Another skell, a woman, told Claudia that she had come down below because she hated the sun. When Claudia asked her why, she answered that the sun had killed her child and made her blind. Claudia remarked that the woman did not seem blind, but the woman answered very calmly that no matter what things seemed, she was indeed blind, even though she could see Claudia and everything else in the subway car. When Claudia asked how the sun had killed her child, the woman said that it had given her daughter cancer and sucked her life away. Skin cancer? Claudia asked, but the woman said no, that it was deeper than that, and then very politely excused herself and walked into the next car.

Jesse had no idea if what Claudia was getting from these bizarre conversations was useful to her, but when they parted, with plans to meet two weeks later, she hugged her note pad to her chest like a purse filled with money. Only once had she mentioned his vigilantism, but when he made it clear that he would not talk about it, she did not speak of it again.

Now he rode on the Sixth Avenue IND on a hot Tuesday afternoon, watching the people sitting across from him—a young and expressionless Puerto Rican couple holding hands, two older white men in business suits, a black man wearing a jogging suit and a Walkman. The door to the car ahead opened, and Bob Montcalm walked in.

Jesse knew it was him immediately, though he wore no uniform and displayed no badge of office. Rags had described him often enough, and there was no mistaking the air of propriety that accompanied the man as he moved through the car with the rough grace that came from years of riding. He walked as though he owned the car, and so, Jesse thought, he did. He was the power here. Others may have had guns and knives, and prowled through the tunnels in numbers, but Bob Montcalm was the power.

He stopped beside Jesse, who looked up at his fissured face under the thinning hair. Montcalm was

Lowland Rider

not a tall man, but to Jesse he looked big and burly, like a man used to fighting, and Jesse was reminded of his own comparatively short time underground. He wondered for a moment if he could beat this Montcalm in a fight, and knew in a flash of self-realization that he could, and easily. Montcalm had the bulk, but Jesse had the will.

"Mind if I sit down?" Montcalm asked, nodding to the seat beside Jesse.

Jesse slowly looked around the car. "There are lots of other seats. You sure you want to sit beside me?"

Montcalm nodded. "Yeah. Even though you stink a little." That was a lie, something to get under Jesse's skin, which he had washed thoroughly not less than three hours before in the 49th Street station men's room.

"Sit down then," Jesse said.

Montcalm sat, leaving a foot of space between them. Jesse noticed that Montcalm was looking him up and down, but the visual frisk didn't last long—it was obvious that there was no room in Jesse's T-shirt for a weapon, and the pockets of the jeans were snug against his thighs. Montcalm sat back and sighed, then gave a twisted smile of exasperation. "You've been causing me trouble."

Jesse didn't answer right away. He only sat and watched the man, noticing how the lines around the eyes twitched, while the rest of the face struggled to hold steady, look firm. The man was close to rage. "I don't know how," Jesse said finally.

"You been getting into things that don't concern you."

"How do you know that? How do you even know who I am?"

Montcalm nodded shortly. "I know who you are."

"What's my name?"

"I don't know your name. But I know who you are."

Jesse nodded back without smiling. "There's a difference."

"Fuck this shit," Montcalm said. "I'm not getting in any pissing contest with you, pal. I've just got one thing to say, and that's this—get the fuck out of here. You get off this line and out of these tunnels, so I don't ever see your face again, and I don't ever hear of anybody else seeing it either." The face was getting red now.

"Why?" Jesse asked quietly.

Montcalm gave a half-laugh of disbelief. "You asshole. Don't fuck with me."

"No, why, really? I mean, who do you think I am? What do you think I've done? For all I know, you could be some maniac who wanders around the subway trying to scare people."

Montcalm shook his head. "*You're* who I want to scare."

"You sure you've got the right guy?"

"Yeah, I'm sure. I got a lot of friends down here. They tell me what I want to know."

"And you think I made you unhappy somehow?"

"That's right."

"Then why don't you arrest me, Sergeant Montcalm?"

Something flared in Montcalm's eyes, but he smothered it and grinned instead. "I told you you were the right guy."

"If I am, arrest me," Jesse said calmly, turning away from Montcalm and looking across the aisle at the dark reflections of Montcalm and himself.

"Smart guy," Montcalm said. "Real smart, aren't you?"

"Arrest me," Jesse repeated. "Then you could arrest Rodriguez too. And then maybe yourself. We could all go to prison together."

Bob Montcalm felt his stomach turn over. Rodriguez? he thought. How the hell did he know about Rodriguez? "Who the fuck is Rodriguez?" he said, hearing his voice shake.

"Rodriguez is your pimp," the man answered, still looking across the aisle. "Rodriguez is the man who pays you money to be a whore."

"What do you know?" Montcalm asked cautiously. "What do you know about Rodriguez?"

"Rodriguez gives you money, he gives you dope. You protect his people."

"Where . . . how do you know that?"

"I know. You have your ways of finding out things. I have mine."

Montcalm was scared of this man. He was scared of his knowledge and he was scared of his eyes. He had such dead eyes. How could he threaten a man who was already dead? But he had to. He thought of Gina and he knew he had no choice. "Do you know that if you don't get out of here, if you don't stay out of my business, you're dead."

"I'm already dead."

It was bravado, Montcalm felt almost certain of it. But there was something in the man's voice, a flatness he'd never heard from anyone before, that gave him the shivers. "I'm not fucking around. You'll be dead."

The man turned and looked into Montcalm's eyes. "And you'll kill me?"

Montcalm wouldn't. He couldn't. He had never killed anyone in his life, and believed himself to be incapable of it. Fifteen years before he had come close and had declined. He was uniformed then, patrolling the Pelham Bay Parkway line a few hours after rush hour on a Wednesday evening. He had rounded a corner and seen two men wrenching a briefcase away from a portly, middle-aged man. One of the men was slashing at the fat man's arm with a knife while the other was pulling at the briefcase. The victim was blubbering and howling, and Montcalm could see that nothing short of unconsciousness was going to make the man give up his treasure. Montcalm had started to run toward them, and had just drawn his gun when he saw the man with the knife raise it over his head.

Montcalm instantly knew the mugger's intent. He was going to stab the man either in the chest, the face, or the neck. Montcalm also knew that the only way to stop him was to bring up his gun and fire.

But he didn't. And the mugger stabbed the man in the neck, severing his jugular vein so that he bled to death while Montcalm held the two men at gunpoint until both medical and police assistance came. If they would have tried to escape, he would have had to let

Lowland Rider

them go. He knew that if he had not shot the man before, then he would not shoot him if he tried to escape. He wondered if he could shoot someone to save his own life, and decided that he probably could, but hoped that he would never have to make that choice.

In the fifteen years that followed, he had been lucky. Although he made his share of arrests, he had never had to kill a man, and since he knew his weakness, he developed a hard and frightening facade, a look that said *I would as easily kill you as hold you here. Please try to run. Go ahead, try it.* The look worked. No one ever had. No one, he thought, until now.

"You'll kill me? You'll do it yourself?" the man with the dead eyes repeated.

"That's right," said Montcalm, looking as hard as he knew how.

"I don't think so," said the nameless man who was fucking up his life so royally. "I don't think you'll do that."

"I will and I can. Don't you know who the hell I am down here?"

"The big man?"

"Yeah. That's right."

The stranger shook his head. "*A* big man, maybe. But not *the* big man."

Montcalm's eyes narrowed. "Who then? You?"

"Not me, and not Rodriguez."

"I don't know what the fuck you're talking about. I'm the law down here, friend. Me."

"Uh-huh." The man nodded agreement and got to his feet as the train pulled into a station. "You have anything else to say to me?"

"I've said all I have to." He looked up with hard eyes as the man nodded again.

"Uh-huh."

"Remember it. I don't want to see you again."

The doors opened and the man stepped off. When he was gone and the train was moving again, Montcalm sat back against the hard seat, devitalized by the confrontation with the man with the dead eyes, devitalized and beaten. The man would not leave the subways, for some reason of his own that Montcalm could not even guess at. There was no possibility that the man was a plant, a cop set to trap Montcalm. No, the guy was not a cop. He had skell written all over him. But how in hell could a skell have so goddam much self-confidence? How could a skell be so unafraid of Bob Montcalm, the big man of the line?

The big man . . .

And what the hell was *that* all about? About there being somebody *else* who was the big man? Who the hell was the big man if not Bob Montcalm?

Who in hell . . .?

CHAPTER 17

Who in hell was this Enoch, Frank Zito wondered fearfully. And what the hell did he want with an *eye*, for crissakes?

Frank Zito had the eye in his pocket. It was wrapped in a piece of Saran Wrap that he had taken from his mother's kitchen drawer. But the eye was not from a person he had killed, since Frank Zito had never killed anyone. Rather it had been dug, not too delicately, from the head of an elderly vagrant whose body Frank Zito had found hunched over in an alley two blocks from where he lived. The indelicacy was due to the fact that Frank Zito had done the job with a dull pocket knife in semidarkness.

Still, he had the eye now, and could feel its fluid softness press against his pants pocket as he walked beside his friend Harry toward an abandoned spur of the Concourse line. He and Harry had gotten off at the 161st Street station, had waited until there was no one else on the platform, and then jumped down onto the tracks. Walking on the tracks always scared Frank Zito, even at three in the morning when the trains ran less frequently. "Don't worry so much," Harry had told him. "There are those whadyacallems, those things you can get into when a train goes by, got 'em for the guys that work the tracks. We'll hear 'em comin'."

Frank Zito wondered why he had ever let Harry talk him into this. Frank had heard the stories all right, about this guy who dressed all in white and lived down in the tunnels like a skell, but who *wasn't* a skell, this guy everybody called Enoch and talked about like he was Jesus—God forgive him for even *thinkin'* that—this guy who would actually *give* you shit, like money and jewelry and stuff, if you brought him things he wanted, eyes and fingers and shit like that.

"He gotta be crazy," Frank Zito had told Harry when Harry explained it to him.

"Uh-uh," Harry said. "You see him, you know he ain't crazy."

"You done it?"

"Yeah. Look." Harry held out a diamond. It was small, but it looked real as hell, and Frank Zito reached out a hand to touch it. "Uh-uh," Harry said, closing his fingers and putting the stone back into his pocket.

"He give you *that*? This Enoch?"

"Yeah."

Frank Zito frowned. "What you give him?"

A smile curled Harry's lips. "Teeth."

"Teeth?"

"Yeah. From this guy. Little guy. I worked him over, took his wallet, knocked out some teeth. They were lyin' there after he ran away."

"You gave this weirdo some *teeth* and he gave you that stone?"

"He ain't a weirdo, don't call him that."

"Well, what the fuck am I supposed to call him, the tooth fairy?"

Harry jabbed a finger into Frank's chest, and the force behind it reminded Frank that Harry outweighed him by fifty pounds. "No shit, Zito. You don't talk about him like that. You wouldn't if you seen him."

"Okay, hey, I'm sorry, all right? It's just hard to believe that some dude'd give you a rock like that for some fucking *teeth*."

"I said he did, didn't I?"

"Yeah, yeah."

"So you want in on this?"

At first Frank Zito didn't want anything to do with it. Frank didn't like to get in fights. But the more he thought about the diamond Harry had shown him, the more he thought about making this Enoch character an offering of his own. Shit, there were plenty of people around the Bronx who'd kill somebody for a handful of change, let alone a fucking diamond. And it wasn't morality that kept Frank Zito from mugging or killing people as much as it was the fear that he might get killed himself by a prospective victim, or at least get caught, go to prison, and get his young and pretty ass drilled for ten years. Frank had never been a junkie, never been desperate for money, so the possible rewards had never been worth the risk.

But a *diamond*. And just for some *teeth*.

So one night Frank Zito had gone prowling for a

victim. If he had to kill them he had to kill them. But if he could just knock out some teeth that was better, and maybe he'd be able to pick up a wallet or a purse in the bargain. Instead he'd been lucky, and tripped over the old bum lying dead in the alley. Frank decided to take some teeth, but when he pried open the man's jaw he found that there weren't any to take.

He decided to cut off a finger, but quickly learned that bone, even brittle with age, was much harder than he had thought it would be. What the fuck else was there? he wondered. Hair? No, hair was nothing. He wouldn't get a piece of coal for a bunch of hair—that Enoch guy would laugh at him and tell him to go back to the barber shop. An ear? He tugged at his own ear and felt the tough cartilage clinging to the skull. Maybe, maybe. But something easier, something softer . . .

What the hell. The eye.

The thought made him queasy, but after all it wasn't much worse than pulling teeth out of that stinking mouth, was it? Sure, it would be messy, but it would wash off. Everything would wash off.

So he did it, felt proud of himself when he didn't vomit, and carried it home inside a discarded bag from McDonald's. When his mother asked him about it, he told her it was french fries, and was relieved when she didn't ask him for some. That night, after she was asleep, he wrapped it in Saran Wrap and put it at the back of the drawer beneath his underwear. The refrigerator would have been better, but he didn't want to take a chance on his mother spotting it behind a six-pack. The next day he saw Harry and told him

Lowland Rider

that he had something for Enoch. Harry said there would be an offering held early Sunday morning, and that he would meet him at the local subway station at midnight.

For three days the eye sat in the underwear drawer, and when Frank Zito took it out on Saturday night he saw that its thick yellow color had changed to a sickly gray spotted with patches of black, and that it had grown much, much softer. He wrapped it in several more thicknesses of Saran Wrap, and put it in his pocket.

Neither he nor Harry talked much on their way to the offering, and when they walked down the tunnel, they didn't speak a word. Instead they listened to the sound of muffled footsteps that seemed to be all around them, although they saw no one else in the thin beam of Harry's flashlight. Finally Frank glimpsed some light ahead, and heard the murmur of voices. As they rounded the last curve, the light grew brighter, and they walked off the track onto a side spur that had been closed off to trains forty years earlier, and came into a chamber fifty feet long by twenty wide, lit by flashlights and several Coleman lanterns.

There were not as many people there as Frank Zito had thought there would be, and it made him uncomfortable. He had hoped that there might be a hundred or more, though that seemed unlikely. Actually, there were less than twenty, and he felt vulnerably conspicuous in the small group. Some of them were as young as he and Harry, while others wore the sagging clothes and skin of old age. But all of them, Frank Zito was alarmed to see, had a small parcel, some of them dripping onto the gravel floor, and a touch of fire in their eyes that he found it impossible to emulate. He would have turned and gone away had it not been for his fear of Harry, and the irrational but deeply felt fear that the others, the strangers with the bright eyes, would not let him leave. So he stayed and watched, facing a flat, black wall.

After ten minutes Frank Zito turned to Harry and whispered, "When's he show up?"

Harry didn't answer. Instead his eyes went wide, and when Frank looked back at the wall where Harry was looking, he saw that the man he took to be Enoch was there, as if he'd just materialized in front of them. There was a soft smile on his face, and he held his hands out in front of him and a little to each side, like some of the pictures of Jesus that Frank had seen in Sunday school papers when he was a kid. He looked a little, Frank Zito thought, like a nigger and a little like a slant, but a little like a white guy too, and Frank was surprised at the beauty of the combination. This Enoch (for who else could it be?) *was* beautiful, and Frank Zito, who had never harbored a homosexual thought in his young life, recognized him as such and felt excited by the thought. His hand that held the wrapped jelly trembled, and he felt a smile break out upon his own face in response to Enoch's. It seemed as though Enoch were looking right at him, and he felt, not unpleasantly, the hair on the back of his neck tingle.

"Have you brought me offerings?" Enoch said, and the words, gentle and strangely unisexual, poured like honey into Frank Zito's ears. A man in his forties stepped up first, carrying a Pick 'n Pay shopping bag. He set it at Enoch's feet, reached in with both hands, and from it drew something dark and dripping. It was some kind of internal organ. Frank Zito supposed rather calmly that it could have been a heart, since it was small and he remembered from high school health that your heart was the size of a fist.

To his surprise, Frank Zito was neither shocked nor repulsed by the act. It seemed the most natural and gracious thing in the world for this man to bring Enoch this gift. But what did surprise Frank was what happened to the gift when the man held it out to Enoch.

Enoch was dressed in white, all white from his shoulders to his trouser cuffs, and Frank Zito tensed in expectation of the way that whiteness would be stained with that dark and dreadful fluid that dripped like red molasses over the supplicant's hands. But Enoch held his own hands out farther, did not change expression as the man placed the bleeding organ into them, and drew his hands into his body, until the heart, if that was what it was, covered Enoch's own heart, hidden by his long-fingered hands. Then Enoch brought his hands out again, and the organ was gone. Not a vestige of red remained on Enoch's garments. Instead he held a pale blue stone whose facets threw the lantern light about the chamber like fireflies.

The man bowed and took the stone, and Frank Zito wondered if what he thought had happened had truly happened, or if this Enoch only made him *think* it had happened. Sleight-of-hand was one thing, but to slip a dripping chunk of meat into the front of your shirt without leaving a single stain? He watched more closely as the next person stood before the immaculate Enoch. It was a boy still in his teens, who bowed and held out something that could only have been a tongue. Frank could see the budded surface from where he stood. It was still pink, and oozed moistness where it had been crudely hacked from its root. Again Enoch took the organ, pressed it to his breast, and transformed it into a gem, which he presented to the boy, who bowed again and backed away.

And so the ceremony continued, with the celebrants coming one at a time before Enoch, making their gifts, taking their rewards. Only one person stepped forward without an offering, an old woman who Frank Zito thought looked half-mad. He heard her clearly as she fell to her hands and knees before Enoch.

"Oh, master," she sniveled, "I have nothing for you, nothing. I was afraid, so afraid. I almost had him, he was almost mine, but the lights came, and I . . . I was *afraid . . .*"

"My girl," Enoch answered her. "My Sunny girl, you must not be afraid when you do my will. You are in my service now, and not the service of this world or those who dwell herein. Have no fear, for you serve me."

The tired face, wet with tears, looked up. "You forgive me then?"

"I forgive you, for you come to me with the truth. But I say to you, do not come before me again without making to me an offering. You cannot enter my kingdom and enjoy its treasures without bearing the key, the key made by your own hands. To come before

Lowland Rider

me again without the key would be death. And to die would be to lose the kingdom."

The crone could not answer him. She only sobbed, backing away on her hands and knees until she finally rose and staggered off into the darkness of the tunnel, out of the sight of the others.

Then Frank Zito felt Enoch's eyes upon him, and heard the unspoken command that those eyes made— *Come to me.* And Frank Zito was afraid, more afraid than he had ever been before, for he knew that what he brought to Enoch, that gray and rotting thing that Enoch called the key, had not been made by his own hands. What Enoch wanted was murder and violence, not a fleshy souvenir of a tawdry but natural death. The old woman had been spared because, although she brought no key, she at least brought the truth. But Frank Zito brought only a lie, a key that he had not forged, only stolen. He knew that he should tell the truth immediately, beg for forgiveness as the old woman had done. But he could not. Not when those calm and peaceful Jesus-eyes of Enoch's looked into his so warmly, trustfully.

Masterfully.

Enoch smiled at him, and he walked forward, trying not to nervously squeeze that soft pouch of Saran Wrap too hard, trying to keep the lie off of his face, out of his mind, pretending that he had picked this pulpy fruit himself from living flesh, with his own arm, of his own will, lying to himself as fervently as he could.

He unwrapped the gift with shaking fingers, held its gelatinous softness in his palm, let the wrapping fall to his feet, and tipped his hand so that the dull and slimy orb fell into the pool of Enoch's hands with a faint, wet sound that seemed horribly loud in the silence. For now the chamber was even quieter than before. It was as if everyone had stopped the breath in their lungs, the blood through the veins. It was the deepest silence Frank Zito had ever not heard.

Enoch cupped his hands so that Frank could not see the grayish-brown eye, then folded them together flatly, like the picture of the praying hands in Frank's mother's bedroom. Frank winced, expecting to see dark matter seep from between Enoch's fingers, but instead something else came through the cracks.

Light.

It was a white, burning light, and in its nearly blinding glare Frank Zito could see that Enoch had for the first time lost his smile, leaving not an expressionless human face, but a blank void into which Frank was afraid he would fall and fall forever. Then, slowly, the face appeared again, the smile returned, and Enoch opened his light-filled hands, turning the palms toward Frank Zito.

A human eye, white and healthy and alive with intelligence, glared out at Frank Zito from each of Enoch's palms.

"They see the truth," Enoch said tenderly. "You bring no gift, but lies. The kingdom and its treasures is not for such as you."

Enoch's eyes, full of love, and the eyes in his palms, full of hate, held Frank Zito. He drowned in them, all fear gone, only a disappointment and a sorrow so great that he did not even feel it when the others fell upon him and tore him apart with their knives and nails and hands.

And while Frank Zito died, Jesse Gordon, riding past, saw the glow of the flashlights and lanterns from the abandoned spur, wondered what made the light in the dark tunnel, and felt a pain very deep inside him.

CHAPTER 18

"What is it?" asked Claudia.

"I . . . nothing."

Jesse slumped back in his seat as if he'd just been struck, and Claudia looked at him carefully. He'd been losing weight, she thought, in just the few weeks that she'd been with him. But it didn't appear to be a loss due to malnutrition or disease. On the contrary, it seemed to be a purposeful loss to achieve a rangy gauntness, the tightness and leanness of form for which an athlete would strive before a particularly important encounter. Still, the way he fell back in the seat like that made her even more curious about him than she already was.

He looked up at her. "Aren't you tired?"

"No. I took a nap this evening. *Yesterday* evening," she corrected, and looked at her watch. It read 4:00 A.M.

"You're not getting much tonight."

Claudia shrugged. "Atmosphere."

"Atmosphere," Jesse repeated sardonically. "We haven't spoken to a soul."

"It's all right."

"What's the point of it? It just wastes your time. And mine."

She smiled at him. "You have somewhere special to go?"

"There's always somewhere to go. Even down here." He turned and looked out the window again.

"If I'm keeping you from something—"

"I said I'd help you get your story, so I will. But I'm not helping much tonight." He looked at her, and she read reproof in his glance. "Of course that's not altogether my fault. I didn't suggest this line. *You* wanted to ride this one."

That was true. Jesse had suggested the IND Queens line, long and eccentrically peopled in the early morning hours, but Claudia had asked for a ride on the Concourse line, which Jesse had previously described to her as often dull, sometimes dangerous, but seldom strange.

"Atmosphere aside," he went on, "just what are you getting out of this? I mean, what can this have to do with your story?"

"You'd be surprised," she told him, and he looked at her narrowly. She reminded herself to shut up, not to say too much, to pretend to be more interested in the other people in the car, despite the fact that they were a man who was obviously coming home from a late shift, a couple who had had a night on the town and were now dozing, heads together, and a black kid in a jogging suit who Claudia guessed was a runner for a crack dealer, coming home from a tough night's work. But she wasn't interested in them. Nor was she interested in skells. Skells were no longer Claudia Dorner's subject. That function had fallen to Jesse Gordon.

She had already written eighteen pages about him—a compilation of what the news stories had told her, an account of her own meeting with him, physical description, and a character analysis based on both her present knowledge of him and her memories of the time they had been lovers. She'd also scanned the newspapers for incidents that might be connected to Jesse's cryptic comment about "helping" people, and had come across three incidents in past months of apparent murder victims being found in the subways, at different times and in different stations and trains. As she read between the lines, she imagined that there could have been a pattern, that the descriptions of the victims made it clear that they might as easily have been predators who had been caught in the act, though none of the papers, not even the *Post*, had suggested that still another vigilante might be abroad.

Jesse Gordon fascinated her, personally and professionally. He was her story, no one else. After he told her that there was a story for every skell in the tunnels, she knew that he was right, and that to classify them all would be impossible. Better then to concentrate on one, whose story was as dramatic and tragic as any other could possibly be. One who she already knew, who posed no threat of violence to her, and who would actually be her protector, one who did not reek of sweat and urine, who, though aloof and mysterious and a little frightening, was clean and not unattractive.

Lowland Rider

One who she was drawn to despite her attempts to deny it.

He seemed to her the last of the romantic figures. He had lost everything precious to him, and had buried himself to atone for a self-declared sin that most men in the same situation would have committed gladly, and not thought about twice. There was something in his eyes and face that puzzled and mesmerized her. He held her interest unequivocally, and she thought that she might even love him once again, not with that first, basic sexual love she had felt for him years before, but with a deeper, more mature love born of mutual loss. He was her subject, she thought romantically. As surely as Johnson was Boswell's, or "La Gioconda" was da Vinci's, he was her subject. And he must not know it.

"I haven't seen you for a few days, Jesse," she said to him as offhandedly as she knew how. "What have you been doing with yourself?"

"I've been riding," he told her, and looked out the window again.

"What you said before about . . . helping people? Have you been doing any more of that?"

He didn't answer for a long time, then said softly, "What can I do for anyone?"

"But what you told me before—"

"Forget that."

"I can't." He looked at her. "I mean, what you told me—I've been thinking about it. I think it's good."

Jesse looked away. "Thanks."

She watched him, but he did not look back at her. The train slowed to a stop at a station. She didn't know what station it was. She didn't care. "You won't tell me about it?"

"Why should I?"

"Because you might want to talk about it. Do you talk to Rags about it?"

"Rags doesn't want to hear about it. It frightens Rags. It should frighten you too."

"It doesn't though."

"It did before. You told me I should stop, come back up."

"I'm still frightened for you. But you don't have to stop, not if you're doing good." She took a deep breath, wishing that he would look at her when he spoke. "But I think you should come back up."

"Why? To clear my name?" His tone was dull, far away, as if he were talking only to himself, arguing with an inner voice rather than with Claudia.

"Maybe. If you want to."

"No one up there can clear my name. No one there can change what I did. Besides," he went on dreamily, "what would I do up there? What good could I do? Down here I can. More than up there. Down here I can . . ." He was quiet for a while, and the train started up again. She barely heard his next words—". . . keep the balance."

"The balance?" she repeated, not sure whether he heard her or not. But he nodded.

"Sometimes I think that's why I came. I can't believe, I've tried but I can't, that it was all for nothing, that they died for no reason. Maybe it was to bring me down here. I don't know."

Now his voice was full of pain, of hard thoughts

Lowland Rider

only now spoken, not as much to her as to himself, and she hesitated to do anything for fear of breaking the spell that let him speak, though she wanted with all her heart to touch him, to ease his agony.

He turned to her, and a smile came over his face. It was not a light smile. It was a smile that scared her, the smile on a skull.

"Are you getting enough now?" he said.

It caught her. "Enough? I . . . I don't know what you—"

"You know just what I mean. I've figured it out, haven't I? Why you wanted to come on this line, where nothing happens. You don't want to talk to skells anymore, do you? You want to talk to me. I'm your story."

"No, I . . ."

"You're lying, Claudia. I can catch lies now, I'm a lot better at it than I used to be. This whole place is full of lies. You see them on every face. I see one on yours now."

She saw no point in continuing the masquerade. "All right, Jesse, it's true. I *am* more interested in you than in these others—how can you expect me not to be? You may be the only good man to have come down here, to do what you're doing. There's a story in that."

"I could keep you from telling it, you know."

Despite his words, she did not feel afraid of him. "How?"

"I could kill you. Unsolved murders down here every day."

"You wouldn't do that. I know you too well to believe that."

"I've killed people. Down here."

"And I believe that too. But you wouldn't kill me."

He glared at her for a long time, but finally it was he who turned away. "No," he said. "You're right. I wouldn't do that."

"Who have you killed, Jesse?" she asked quietly.

"I've killed killers," he answered. "And I've stolen from thieves."

"Why?"

"Why?" he echoed. "Because someone has to. Because if I don't kill them, they'll kill other people."

"Do you mean that you stop them—kill them—while they're in the act?"

"Of course!" He sounded furious that she should consider any other possibility. "Do you think I just go looking for people who *look* like criminals? You think I examine bumps on their heads? Hell, no! You *see* it down here, you see it all the time. Most people look away, walk away. I don't anymore."

"But I still don't see why—"

"Because it's why I'm *here*! Why what happened happened!" The older man woke up and looked dully at Jesse. The couple stirred, but kept their eyes closed. The young man in the jogging suit kept his cool, and didn't allow himself to look at Jesse and Claudia. "I'm not saying it was divine guidance," Jesse went on. "How the hell can I believe in a God who'd kill my wife and child just to drag me down here to play cops and robbers? But it was *me* who guided myself down here, because there has to be a goddammed, fucking *reason* for it, don't you see that?"

Claudia thought before she answered, and in the

time it took Jesse slumped back again, his eyes staring at the ceiling. "I think maybe I do," she said, and when she looked at him again, his eyes were filled with tears.

"There has to be a *reason*," he said again.

"Don't send me away," she asked him, and heard her own voice breaking.

"You can't ride with me. Not all the time."

"Just sometimes," she said. "But talk to me. Tell me things."

"Not everything. I don't *know* everything."

"All right."

"And don't write it," he told her, his expression suddenly firm again, "until I'm dead."

"You won't die. You'll come back up."

"I don't know." She thought he looked now like a little boy afraid to close his eyes in the dark. "I don't know."

"I love you, Jesse." She didn't plan to say it. It slipped out as naturally and truthfully as her hand slipped over his.

When he looked at her, she saw horror in his eyes. He spoke a single word that made her draw her hand away, a word as heavy as lead, as cold as iron.

"Don't."

She never saw him cry again.

CHAPTER 19

The cottage was everything that New York City was not. It was open, it was clean, it was full of sunshine and fresh air, surrounded by flowers and trees, and there was nothing, thought Bob Montcalm, that could not happen there. He could be happy, Gina could be free, they could love each other again.

He passed the sheaf of photographs back across the desktop to the realtor, a prissy man in his fifties, who took them with a flourish. "A beautiful property, isn't it?"

"It's very nice," Montcalm agreed. "How long's it been on the market?"

"Oh, that's the amazing part. Nearly a year now. I didn't expect that, not at all. I thought it would go very quickly."

"So what's the problem, the price?"

"Not to *my* way of thinking. Seven acres of land, state forest all around, three bedrooms, for only a hundred and ten thousand."

A hundred and ten thousand, Montcalm thought. Jesus. "So what is it then?"

"The location apparently. It's just a bit further out than most people seem to like. It was originally built as a hunting lodge, but when the owner retired he had it remodeled to live in year-round, and he did until his death."

"Far away from town then?"

"My, yes. Of a town of any size, at least." The realtor took a road atlas from the shelf behind him and opened it to a map of eastern Pennsylvania. "Now here's the Delaware State Forest and here's Peck's Pond, which apparently is tiny-tiny. The cottage is three miles away from the village, so it is *very* isolated. A wonderful retirement home, but I don't believe there are many job possibilities there. What, uh, *is* your line of work, Mr. Montcalm?"

"Transit police."

"Oh my, well, there certainly wouldn't be much opportunity for professional growth at Peck's Pond, would there?"

"I'm thinking of taking an early retirement."

"Ah, well, that would be all right then. You're not very old, are you?"

"Old enough. I've been with the city twenty-five years."

"And you can retire then, eh? Well, that's very nice. Would you like to see the property?"

"I can't get away just now. Maybe in a few weeks."

"Of course I can't guarantee that it will be available much longer."

"I'll have to take the risk. One thing though . . ."

"Yes?"

"Is there any chance that the property would be

available as a rental?"

"Oh no, Mr. Montcalm. In fact, if you're looking for someplace isolated and rural, you'd have a very difficult time finding a rental property. We don't handle rentals at all, you see. Besides, with mortgage rates what they are right now, it's the perfect time to buy, isn't it?"

Montcalm knew nothing about real estate, and was tired of pretending he did. "What kind of down payment would a place like this take?"

"Well, with a place like this you wouldn't want to go into it with less than twenty percent—twenty-two thousand dollars. And then you've got brokerage fees, and insurance, of course—homeowners and mortgage . . ."

The list droned on of things that Montcalm had never thought about. It occurred to him that he would need a car as well, something he'd never owned in his life. He'd never had the need for one. The tunnels had taken him everywhere he'd needed to go.

The cost of everything was overwhelming, and he tried to figure it out as he headed uptown—twenty-two for the down payment, figure two more for insurance, another two grand for the broker's fee, at least five for a car, another two for appliances, a grand to move the shit out of his apartment, and probably a whole lot more for stuff he'd never even thought of. That was thirty-four thousand all told.

He had twelve thousand in his various savings accounts and CD's, and another fourteen from Rodriguez in the locker at Penn Station. That was twenty-six grand. Christ, he was already eight thou-

Lowland Rider

sand in the hole. Even if he was able to borrow it, that meant he'd have to pay it back plus the monthly mortgage payment which sure as hell wouldn't be tiny-tiny, in the fag realtor's words. There was no way he could do it on his pension.

There were several alternatives. The first was to find a cheaper place to buy, which was not too likely without going into the area himself and beating the bushes, if he could find the time. The second was to hold off for a while and pray to God that Gina wouldn't OD before he was able to rack up a larger pile from his dealings with Rodriguez. Maybe, if he handled it right, he could move from protection into distribution. After all, that was where the real money was. And he hadn't been caught yet, not even suspected by anyone who really mattered. But the only way to expand was to resolve this problem with Rodriguez right away. And the only way to do that was to find out who the hell this prick on the trains was and stop him from fucking up anything else.

The mug books were a long shot, but he figured the best way to deal with this bastard was to find out who he was. So he went to the transit police headquarters on Gold Street in Brooklyn and started running the man's description through the computer.

It took only seventeen minutes for Jesse Gordon's face to come up on the terminal.

The photograph had obviously been cropped from a family portrait. Montcalm could see the edge of someone's shoulder to the man's left. He read the report quickly. The man, Jesse Gordon, was wanted for questioning in the deaths of his wife and child, a state assessor named Peter Rhoads, and a young man named Carlos Alvarez. From the description of the case, Montcalm came to the same conclusion that the police had—that a gang had done most of the dirty work, that Gordon might or might not have killed Alvarez, and that afterward he'd suffered a kind of temporary insanity that had driven him into hiding, a withdrawal from reality, as the police psychologist on the case had put it.

Into hiding. But not out of the city, as the psychologist suspected in her report. No, that was where Montcalm and the psychologist differed. Not out. Down.

And something else—the temporary insanity thing? How crazy could a guy be to go to the bank and take out all his money before "withdrawing from reality"? Crazy like a fox, maybe. Fifty thousand dollars could buy you a lot of years as a skell. No rent to pay, no utilitics, hell, the city would take care of that. How much of that fifty thousand dollars, Montcalm wondered, had Jesse Gordon already spent? And how much was left?

A lot. One helluva lot. So if there was some way of getting not only Jesse Gordon, but his money as well . . .

It would be enough. He'd have to struggle, have to get some dummy job out in the boonies to give them enough money to live on. But even if Gordon had only half of it left, it would be enough. He could do it for Gina, for the two of them.

But first he had to find Gordon again, and that would be a problem if Montcalm had succeeded in

Lowland Rider

scaring him out of the city. Then Montcalm remembered Gordon's eyes, and knew that he would still be on the lines. There was something about Gordon that wasn't going to scare. He would stay, and so would his money.

Montcalm rode the trains to 103rd Street and walked over to Gina's building. He pushed the button several times, but got no answer, so he took out his key and unlocked the outer door. As he trudged up the steps he heard rapid footfalls from above, and when he stepped onto the third floor landing he saw a thin white man with long hair and a wispy beard coming down the stairs. The man had a Morris the Cat backpack slung over one shoulder, and was moving fast, too fast for Montcalm's peace of mind. He moved to the middle of the landing so that the bearded man could not get by him without pushing him, and when he did, Montcalm grabbed him by an arm and pressed him back against the railing.

"In a hurry?"

The man looked angrily at Montcalm. "What the fuck business is it of yours, man?"

Montcalm flashed his badge with his free hand. "You live here? 'Cause if you don't, I got more questions."

"Yeah . . . yeah, I live here."

"Where here?"

"Uh, eighth floor."

"Building only has seven floors, asshole. You live on the roof?" It was a lie. The building had ten floors, but Montcalm figured the guy probably never looked up when he came into a building.

The man's face softened to the look of a school kid caught in a lie, but then hardened again. "Okay, I don't live here. So what? I mean, you got a warrant for me or something?"

"Who were you visiting?"

"None of your goddam *business*, man!"

"I decide that."

"Hey, I don't care who the fuck you are, you got no right to hassle me like this, you don't know me—"

"What's in the bag?"

"It's *my* bag!"

"I don't doubt that. I just want to know what's in it."

The man tried to break away, but Montcalm held him, grabbed his other arm, and twisted him around so that his head and shoulders hung past the railing over the stairs ten feet below. Pressing the man's chest onto the railing, Montcalm wrenched the bag off his shoulder and pulled the snaps apart. "You can't *do* this!" the man grunted. "Illegal search! You can't make this stick!"

The Baggies and glass tubes inside told Montcalm everything he needed to know. "No, but I can make *you* stick."

"Wh . . . what?"

"I can make you stick to the stairs when I throw you over."

"Hey, wait a min—"

"Where were you just now? Where were you coming from?"

"No, man, no! This is coercion, you can't make me—"

Lowland Rider

Montcalm, furious, pushed the man further so that his belly now pressed on the railing. "*Where?*"

"Bob . . . Bobby?"

Montcalm looked up and saw Gina, dressed in shorts and a halter top, standing at the end of the landing. "Let him go. Please."

Montcalm shook the man like a rat. "What did you *sell* her?"

"I . . ."

"He didn't sell me anything, Bob. Honest to God, we were just talking, just a visit, that's all."

"Did you *touch* her?" Montcalm raged, pushing the man further until his weight alone would have taken him over had Montcalm suddenly let go.

The man seemed to know now that this was more than just a suspicious cop. This was a jealous and righteously pissed off husband who was only too willing to tip him over the edge. "No, man, not at all . . . just talkin', y'know? No drugs, no nothin', really, I *swear*, man!"

Gina took a few more steps toward the men. "Really, Bob, he's telling the truth. Please let him go."

Montcalm eyed her closely. She looked pale, but not stoned. Sweat shone on her body, but he believed it was from the heat rather than from drugs or lovemaking. He knew how she felt about lovemaking.

"Please, man . . ." Montcalm looked down at the shivering man and knew he could not throw him over the side. A moment ago, gripped by his fury, he might have. But not now. Not with Gina standing there, looking at him with her dead-alive eyes that were still so beautiful.

He pulled the man back and shoved the backpack into his arms. "Get out of here," Montcalm told him. "And don't let me find you in here again."

"Right, man," the dealer said, bowing obsequiously as he backed away, then hitting the stairs and running down them three at a time.

When Montcalm could no longer hear his footsteps, he turned back to Gina. "I'm getting you out of here," he said.

She shook her head, not understanding. "Out . . . now?"

"Soon. I'm getting you out of here and getting you clean."

They went back to the apartment and he gave her the money and the heroin he had bought. "It's not like the other stuff," he said. "It may not be as good, I don't know, so be careful."

Willie had gotten it for him, and Montcalm had paid dearly for it. Rodriguez was cut off as a source of supply until Montcalm could get rid of Gordon, but he didn't tell Gina that, just as he had never told her about working with Rodriguez, about any of the things he had done because he loved her so much.

He stayed with her for a half hour. They sat on the couch and watched a game show, and Gina didn't shoot up while he was there. When he left, he kissed her and told her again, "Soon, I promise," and she kissed him back and told him that she would not see Matt, the bearded man with the drugs, again, not even to talk to.

On his way back to the subway, Montcalm checked his wallet, and found that he had only fifteen dollars

Lowland Rider

left. The bank was closed this late in the afternoon, so he decided to go down to Penn Station and take some cash out of his locker. There would be enough to replenish it when he found out where Gordon hid his money. Enough to replenish it and to give him and Gina a chance at a whole new life.

He rode the sixty-nine blocks with a smile on his face, thinking of that new life, thinking of Gina in the country, with sunlight on her hair and the stench of the city a dimly forgotten memory. He didn't play his usual game of watching the other people on the car, marking them for what they were—good, bad, or indifferent. In spite of the run-in with Matt, in spite of the work that lay ahead to root out Gordon and his money, Bob Montcalm felt good, as if things were going to finally go well for him.

He got off the train at Penn Station with a light, boyish step, and threaded his way through the tunnels until he arrived at the alcove with the locker where he kept his money. He moved it frequently from locker to locker, just in case they were ever inspected, a threat for which he had never seen any evidence. And if inspectors ever did open it, what would they find but a locked briefcase on which they would lock the door again?

He read the number on the key—9273—and put it into the corresponding lock, then opened the locker, unlocked his briefcase, and took two hundred dollars in twenties from it. He locked it again, dropped fifty cents into the slot, closed the door, and took the key. Smiling, he walked out of the alcove into the commotion of the station and headed up toward the street, thinking that he deserved a good dinner.

When he was gone, Jesse Gordon stepped from around the corner, walked up to the lockers, and shook the handle of locker number 9273. Then he opened the door of the locker numbered 9277, fed two quarters into the slot, closed the door, and took the key, which he dropped into his pocket, where its rough edge pressed against his thigh, an irritant impossible to ignore.

He left the alcove, and took a stairway down.

CHAPTER

20

Jesse Gordon found Rags scrounging through a garbage can in the 59th Street station. When Jesse called his name, Rags came up holding a half-eaten Kentucky Fried Chicken breast. His face broke into a picket-fence smile, and he walked toward Jesse, chuckling and nodding. He was glad to see Jesse well, and glad to see him alive at all.

"Where the hell you been at, Jesse? I ain't seen you now for what, a couple weeks?"

"Not that long, Rags."

"You stayin' outa trouble?"

"I'm afraid not."

Rags nodded. "I know. I been hearin' about you, about what you been doin'. You're doin' some good, Jesse, but I think you gonna pay for it sooner'r later. You, uh, want some chicken?" He held out the breast. Its color was good. It had not been thrown away too long before.

"No thanks, Rags."

"Gettin' picky?"

"Just not hungry."

"You look like you could use some fattenin' up. You feelin' okay?"

"I'm fine, Rags. But I need your help for something."

Sweet God, what now? Rags thought, remembering the last time he had helped Jesse, helped him by killing a boy. That had stayed with Rags. He had never done anything like it before, and he woke up from his sleeps sweating beyond the heat, beyond the rags swathed around his body. The dream never varied—he would be sitting on some unidentified platform, he would hear a cry and look up, and there would be Jesse, bent back over the edge by someone whose face he could not see, and Rags would stand up, move through dream-mush toward the man harming Jesse, pick him up (he was light as air) and throw him onto the tracks, and as the man flew through the air he turned so that Rags could see his face, and instead of the boy, it was Enoch, and he was smiling, his face glowing with light, even as the oncoming express struck him in midair, turning him into a cloud of white flame.

One time Rags woke up screaming, just as a transit cop was passing through the car on which he rode. The cop had questioned him, but seemed satisfied that Rags was neither drunk nor stoned, and only told him to get off at the next station. A tougher one might have arrested him, but probably not. Still, he had paid a price for the first time he'd helped Jesse Gordon.

"I don't know, Jesse . . ."

"You don't have to actually *do* anything, Rags. Just be a lookout for me."

"A lookout," Rags said flatly. "Lookin' out for what, Jesse?"

"For cops, for Montcalm."

"Montcalm?"

"I've found out where he keeps his money, Rags. The money he gets from Rodriguez. His drug money."

Rags shook his head. "You over your head, Jesse. You way over your head. You mess with them once, you maybe get away with it. But you keep doin' it, they not gonna turn their backs. They gonna kill you, that's all. I ain't ready to die yet."

"When will you be, Rags?" At first Rags didn't think he heard Jesse correctly, and cocked his head and gave a puzzled look. "When *will* you be ready to die?"

"What you mean?"

"I mean I'm ready now. So I'm not afraid. Oh, a little, maybe, of the pain. And of the mystery. But not enough to stop me. That's what I've learned. Not to be afraid. I haven't done both yet, but I don't believe that dying can be as bad as living."

Rags nodded slowly. "You right." More loudly he added, "I *know* you right, Jesse. You come down here because you do somethin' bad, least you think you do. But you don't do nothin'. No sir, you don't do nothin' like I do." Tears filled his eyes. "You wanta know why I come down here? You want me to tell you? I tell you, then you see if you still want me to help you, look out for you. But not here. Can't tell you here, not with all these people, no sir . . ."

They boarded a downtown train, found a car with

only a few passengers in it, and sat in the unoccupied end.

"I told you I was a preacher, and I was. Congregational Baptist, down in North Carolina, little town near Asheville. Never had no seminary learning. My daddy was a preacher and so I took it up. I was a good one too. Until what happened happened. I was married, but my wife and I had no kids for a long time. Then, when I was forty or so and she was 'bout thirty-five, she got pregnant. She was pretty well along when one of the families in the congregation, their house caught fire. The mother and father were caught in a upstairs bedroom and they burned to death, but the firemen got out their little girl, girl eight years old. My wife and I, we took her in, it was our responsibility as the preacher and his wife. The first night she stayed with us, my wife got sick and started bleedin' from down there, and I took her to the hospital in Asheville. Wasn't nothin' I could do, the doctors said, and they thought she'd be all right and not lose the baby, so I went back home, where I'd left the little girl. When I got back . . ."

Rags took a deep, shuddering breath, and hugged himself hard to keep from shaking.

"When I got back she was sittin' there in my wife's rocker, lookin' so sweet and pretty and scared, and I was scared too, scared that somethin' would happen to my wife and I'd be all alone. And I wanted to comfort that little girl who'd just lost her mommy and daddy, and I wanted comfort too. So I held her and cuddled her and sang hymns to her, and while I was doin' that I started to think about other things, bad

Lowland Rider

things, and I knew they were wrong, and I sang more hymns and I prayed inside to God to keep me from doin' what I wanted to do. But it wasn't any use. I . . . I done things with her. I didn't hurt her, I wouldn'ta hurt her. But I done things I shouldn't, things that I can't even speak of." A sob racked Rags's body. "Oh God, she was so little, and she trusted me so much, and believed the things I told her . . ."

He clasped his hands at the back of his neck and pulled down, as if he wanted to tear off his head. "I *musta* hurt her, she was so little. But she didn't cry, not at all. After she went to sleep I thought about what I'd done. And I thought about killin' myself, but I was scared to. Y'see, I never knew that I felt that way, I'd never had the chance before, and it scared me somethin' awful, like lookin' in the mirror and seein' a monster starin' back at you. And I worried the little girl might say somethin' to somebody, my wife might find out and other people'd know too, and it wouldn't mean just not bein' a preacher anymore, but goin' to jail if I didn't get hung first. But then I wondered what if she *didn't* say nothin', and maybe she wouldn't. And I thought about my little baby comin' along, and I thought about what if it was a little girl. And I couldn't bear that thought, 'cause I had to think about what I might do to *her*, and when I thought about that I went outside and I threw up, hard. And I knew I had to go away, go somewhere where I wouldn't be tempted never again. But I couldn't jes' go away and leave my wife there in the hospital, not knowin' what might happen to her. So I waited through that night, not sleepin' at all. Next mornin' I called up the hospital."

227

Rags broke off, cleared his throat, wiped his eyes with a dirty sleeve. "She was dead, Jesse. My wife was dead. Died toward morning. I knew it was my fault, knew it was God's punishment on me, knew how he couldn't let me have a daughter of my own, so he took her, and took my wife too, so as to punish me.

"Now there was nothin' to keep me there, nothin' at all. I took enough money to get me here, and got on the bus to New York City. I come down here, and here I been ever since."

Jesse looked at him without expression. "And the rags . . ."

"Just wanted to wrap this poor body up, keep it covered away. Keep it *always* covered away."

"God, Rags. God, I'm sorry."

"No more than me. Now you know, Jesse. You know why I ain't ready to die yet. 'Cause when I do, I go to hell."

"No, Rags. *This* is hell. When you die, you leave it."

"I can't believe that, Jesse. That goes against everything I ever believed."

"You believe good works save souls, Rags?"

"I . . . I don't know. Maybe they can."

"I'm doing good works, Rags. I'm taking away bad money from a bad man. You help me, who knows? Maybe God will smile on you, maybe forgive you."

"I don't know life works that way, Jesse."

"I don't know either, Rags. I'm just making this up as I go along. But it's worked so far. You wouldn't be doing harm, Rags. You'd be doing good. We can give it to people who need it. And I'll tell you one thing I do know. When you finally do die, Rags, you won't go to

Lowland Rider

hell. That I know for a fact. Just believe in me. And help me. You'll feel better. Maybe you can even take off those rags."

The train shook them both. Rags looked at Jesse, tears cutting trails through the dirt on his face. "I won't take off my rags, Jesse. But I'll help you. Maybe I been scared of goin' to hell for too long. Been scared of too many things too long. But you tell me what to do. I'll help you now."

Jesse gave Rags forty dollars, which Rags took to a hardware store on Eighth Avenue. There he bought a cold chisel, a hammer, and a pair of compound leverage shears, which he brought back to Jesse, along with the change, in a shopping bag. He didn't ask Jesse where he had gotten forty dollars, although he wondered about it. Forty dollars was a huge amount of money to Rags, weeks worth of watching the concrete, of accumulating nickels and pennies and dimes. But Jesse had simply handed him two twenty dollar bills and told him what to buy, as if it were the most natural thing in the world, and Rags did what he was asked. He gave Jesse the bag, and stood awkwardly while Jesse examined the contents.

"You really gonna do this, Jesse?"

"*We* are, Rags."

"What if he catches us?"

"We run. We're both very good at that. But he won't catch us. Now we've got to wait for a while. Meet me back here at four o'clock tomorrow morning. We'll do it then."

Rags rode and tried to sleep, but couldn't. It was as though he needed to practice watchfulness in preparation for what the morning would hold. He found himself thinking about Jesse Gordon, about what made him tick, what drove him. Jesse had changed so much from the wary, frightened man he had first met months before. He had come down into these tunnels to escape what had happened up above, to get away from the death of his family and the killing he had done himself. But instead he had come down here and begun to do more killing. Rags tried to sort it out in his mind, to get it to where it made sense to him.

Jesse was obsessed, that was the word. He was obsessed with Montcalm, and obsessed with Enoch. Obsessed, like that sea captain, named after King Ahab in the Bible, was obsessed with that whale, Moby Dick. Rags had found that book on a train and read it, though he skipped a lot of it. He guessed it was pretty much the same thing. That captain had lost his leg, and Jesse had lost his family. But where Ahab had the whale to go after, Jesse could only go after bad folks in general. It made sense, he supposed—as much sense as anything like that could.

Rags sighed and tried to stop thinking about it, then closed his eyes and tried to go to sleep. But the thought of Jesse kept coming back to him, and the lump on his neck started to hurt again. It had been hurting on and off for a couple of weeks now, and though Rags knew that he should follow Jesse's advice and see a doctor at a free clinic, he was afraid to, afraid that the doctor would tell him that it was a cancer and that it couldn't be cured. Rags had once heard that when tumors started to hurt, then it was too late to do anything about them. He didn't want to

Lowland Rider

know that it was a cancer. He didn't want to hear that he was going to die, despite what Jesse had told him about not going to hell. The pain, and the fear of the pain, did not let him sleep.

At four o'clock, when he rounded the corner where he had last seen Jesse, Jesse was still there, standing as though he had never moved from the spot, holding the shopping bag in his right hand. He led Rags through a maze of tunnels and rooms into an alcove where a wall of lockers stood at the far end. "I've watched security," Jesse told him. "They come around every twenty-five minutes. It's more than enough time to get in and get the money."

"You gonna be loud?"

"Just at first. I've got to break through from inside my locker to Montcalm's with the chisel. From then on, no noise. Now stand over there, right at the entrance."

"What if somebody comes?"

"Then I throw the tools in my locker, drop in some quarters, shut the door, and walk out. I've got plenty of quarters."

"How the hell you cut through that steel?"

"These are compound leverage shears. They use them on planes. Once I get a hole made, they'll cut through it like butter. Okay. Start watching."

Rags watched what was happening outside, but he watched Jesse too, as he placed the chisel an inch from the bottom of the inner wall of his locker and struck it with the hammer. A hollow crash came from the unsupported metal, making Rags wince. Another crash followed, and a third. It seemed to Rags that the clamor must echo through the halls and stairs, up into the very office of station security. "Jesse!" he hissed. "Jesus, man!"

A fourth crash sounded, and an instant later a metallic squeal grated on Rags's ears. "I'm through," Jesse said. "No more banging."

Rags watched him wiggle the tip of the shears through the hole he had made and begin to cut a circle through the steel. "How long this gonna take?"

"Be patient, Rags. Good things take time."

"Yeah, time. Like ten to twenty years for breakin' into that thing."

Jesse's only response was the *snip snip snip* of his shears as they made their way through the steel. "Damn," whispered Rags to himself. "Damn, damn, *damn . . .*"

Finally Rags heard the grinding of wrenched metal, a final, triumphant *snip*, and a clatter as the pie-shaped piece of steel fell to the bottom of Jesse's locker. He saw Jesse's arm disappear into the hole he had made, and heard a clunking sound as Jesse maneuvered whatever was on the other side. In another few seconds, Rags saw the end of a briefcase emerge through the hole, and Jesse angled it around, bringing it out the door of his own locker. He put the case into the shopping bag and dropped the hammer in beside it. Then he put the shears and chisel inside the locker, put more quarters in the slot, closed the door, and threw the locker key into a waste can. "This way we'll be sure," he told Rags, "that Montcalm gets the surprise."

They opened the locked briefcase with the claw of

Lowland Rider

the hammer in an empty car on the downtown Sixth Avenue train. It was full of envelopes stuffed with money—mostly twenty dollar bills. "Damn, Jesse!" Rags hissed. "There must be hundreds here."

"Thousand, Rags. Thousands, at least."

They counted nearly fourteen thousand dollars. "What you gonna do with this?"

"You want some?" Jesse asked him.

Rags licked his lips. "Could buy a good meal for a change. I could go for that."

"Take what you want then. But not more than you can spend in a day. After all, you don't want to be caught with stolen money on you, do you?"

Rags laughed uncomfortably, but took two twenty dollar bills. "What you gonna do with the rest?"

"Give it away," said Jesse. "I don't want to be caught with it either. I'll give it back to the people it came from."

"What? You mean them dopers, the junkies?"

"No. The people the junkies got it from in the first place. Redistribute the wealth, Rags. Do I sound like a communist?"

"I don't know what you sound like, Jesse Gordon. You sound crazy is all."

Jesse smiled, dumped the contents of the briefcase into the shopping bag, and slid the empty briefcase under the seat. "Go get yourself a good meal, Rags. I'd join you, but I've got some money to give away."

Father Richard Mulcahy was returning to his parish in Gramercy from a visit to a parishioner who was dying of cancer in Lenox Hill Hospital. The priest was weary and depressed, and had just closed his eyes to try and steal a brief nap when he became aware of someone standing next to him. He opened his eyes and saw a young man in T-shirt and jeans, carrying a large shopping bag. Father Mulcahy tensed as the man reached inside it, then relaxed as he saw that the stranger held nothing more threatening than a thick, white envelope, which he held out to the priest.

"Here, Father. For the church."

Mulcahy didn't understand. In his fourteen years as a priest, he'd never had anyone come up and give him anything on the subway. "I'm sorry? I . . ."

"Take it, Father. At least I know you're straight." The man dropped the envelope into the priest's lap, and walked into the next car.

Father Mulcahy opened the envelope and saw that it was stuffed with twenty dollar bills. The first thing he did was to look about sharply to see who might have noticed the gift; the second was to thank God; the third was to get off at the next stop and take a cab, more expensive but more secure, the rest of the way to his parish house.

Rennie Russell was blind and old and poor, and sold pencils out of a coffee can in the 50th Street station. When he heard footsteps coming toward him, he called out "Buy a pencil, fifty cents," and heard the sound of one being lifted from the can. He held out his hand, but instead of two quarters he felt someone press a wad of paper into his palm.

"They're all twenties," a voice said. "Don't let anyone tell you any different."

Lowland Rider

"Hey, what—" But the footsteps clicked away. Rennie fingered the paper. It had the limp, raggy feel of money, and was the right size too. He counted it, and found there were twenty-five bills. If the man was telling the truth, that meant there were five hundred dollars here. He'd take it to the bank. They wouldn't cheat him at the bank.

Five hundred dollars, he thought in amazement. For a *pencil*. That man must've had a story he wanted to write down real bad . . .

Jeanette Lewis's baby was sick. She was riding home from the doctor's office, holding her son in one arm and the doctor's bill with the other, reading it again and again and wondering where she was going to get the money to pay not only for the office call, but for the treatments that had to follow. She had just begun to cry softly when a man sat next to her, said, "You look like you could use this," and handed her an envelope. Thinking it was a religious tract, she shook her head and looked the other way. But when the man said, "It's money," she looked at the envelope again, then at the man's face.

"What I gotta do for it?" she asked suspiciously.

"Hold out your hand."

Her eyes flashed to the envelope, to the man's face, to his other hand, which she saw was empty. "I don't get it."

"I'm giving you this money, that's all. No strings attached."

She snorted a little laugh. "They's always strings attached, Mister. I don't think I want your money."

235

"Listen to me," the man said intently. "I know you can use it. You don't look like a junkie to me, and that's a medical bill you've got there. I'm giving this to you, if you want it."

"But . . . *why*?"

"No why. No reason. You need it, I've got it. Take it and never see me again."

"Are you . . . are you tryin' to buy my soul?"

The man raised his head a bit, as though the suggestion surprised him. Then he smiled. "Maybe I'm trying to buy back my own."

So Jesse gave away Bob Montcalm's money. He gave the majority of it to priests and nuns, since they were easy to identify. He gave much to people who were crippled or had deformities, and was once cursed soundly by a poorly dressed man on crutches who informed Jesse that he was not a charity case. Jesse took him at his word and apologized.

It took him seven hours to distribute the nearly fourteen thousand dollars.

Claudia saw Jesse Gordon sitting on the first bench of the downtown side of the 86th Street station, right where he had said he would be when he called her a half hour before. He was empty-handed and smiling.

"What's up?" she asked him as she sat down on the bench beside him. Although she was excited she tried to hide it. This was the first time that he had gotten in touch with her for an unscheduled meeting.

"There's something I want to tell you. Something I want you to write down. A piece of your story."

He told her about Montcalm, although he didn't mention him by name, about Rodriguez, whose name he *did* mention, and about breaking into the locker and giving the money to people on the trains.

When he finished, the first thing she said was, "This should be reported. This man should be turned in, prosecuted."

"There'd be no point. There's no real proof. Nothing in writing. No witnesses except maybe some skells. They know everything that goes on down here, but who'd put them on the stand? What jury would believe them? No, I've hurt this guy as badly as he can be hurt. He did it all for money, and now that money's gone." Jesse shook his head and looked away. "Besides, he's just a tool of someone else anyway."

"This Rodriguez?"

"Somebody a lot worse than Rodriguez."

"Who's that?"

He shook his head as if to clear it. "I can't tell you any more now. Maybe some day I will."

"What about the name of this policeman?"

"Some day. Not now. Besides, I know you. If you snoop around, you can find out the name on your own." He smiled at her. "You don't want me to make things *too* easy for you, do you?"

"You never have," she said petulantly, and his face immediately sobered.

"Don't pout. It won't work with me."

"Why did you tell me all this?"

"So someone would know, that's all. If anything happens to me."

"When are you coming up, Jesse?"

"I've got too many things to do down here first."

"First? Then you will come up? Eventually?"

"I don't know. I don't think so . . . I don't know." He stood up, and the strength of the move indicated to her that she had been dismissed.

"If this policeman . . . if something was to happen to him, would you be content then? Would you come up then?"

He looked at her and shook his head sadly. "It's not him," he said, then turned and walked away from her.

"Who, Jesse?" She called after him, but he did not look back. "Jesse . . ." she whispered, thinking how strange the name sounded to her.

CHAPTER

21

Bob Montcalm had just taken a cup of coffee from the machine and was returning to his desk when he heard several of the men talking loudly in the hall:

". . . but the dumb shit brought it *in*, Carlin told me. Can you fuckin' beat that? Some guy hands *me* a thousand bucks on the subway, I sure as shit'll *take* it, no questions asked."

"What are you talkin' about, Rocco?" Montcalm asked a short, squat uniformed cop around whom the others were circled.

"Aw, a report from downtown, Bob," Rocco Petrocelli answered in a voice made rough from smoking. "Some priest walks into a precinct house and tells them some guy in the subway gave him a thousand bucks for the church. Well, the good father smells something fishy here, and thinks maybe the money's been stolen, so he brings it in."

Montcalm's knees suddenly felt cold. He told himself there was no connection between this incident and Jesse Gordon, but something else told him there was. He forced himself to grin. "No shit. Who was this good Samaritan? Get a description?"

Petrocelli shrugged. "Not much of one. Guy had a beard, T-shirt and jeans. White guy, that's about it."

The description could have been of thousands of men other than Jesse Gordon, but Montcalm knew that it wasn't, that only a crazy man would give away a thousand dollars on the subway, and that Jesse Gordon was sure as hell crazy.

All of which meant that if it *was* Jesse Gordon, he was either giving away his own money . . .

Or somebody else's.

Either way, it was money in which Montcalm had a claim, and he felt sweat break out on his forehead as he told himself that it had to be Gordon's own money, that there was no way that Gordon could have found Montcalm's locker, and that if he did, there was no way he could have gotten inside it to take Montcalm's money, Jesus, no, there was *no* way . . .

But he didn't believe a word of it.

Trying not to run, he threw on his blazer over his service revolver and left the office. As the train took him closer and closer to Penn Station and his locker, the knowledge that Gordon had somehow taken his money beat at him so brutally that it was an anticlimax when he opened the locker. Still, even though he had run through the experience in his mind a dozen times, actually seeing the empty locker and the hole cut through from the other side maddened him. Enraged, he smashed both fists against the metal over and over again, and began to cry, thinking that it wasn't fair, that it wasn't for himself he wanted the money, it was for Gina, and how this son of a bitch

Lowland Rider

had just signed her death warrant by making it impossible for him to get her away from this vile, stinking city where people on every fucking corner were willing to sell you shit that killed you by inches or all at once.

After the initial fury had swept through him, he reached through the hole and pulled out the metal shears and the chisel. He thought about having them fingerprinted to see if they would match the prints that were taken from Gordon's apartment, but then decided that it would only affirm what he already knew. Besides, he couldn't tell anyone about the break-in, or what was in the locker. Christ, he couldn't even get back that lousy thousand dollars from the priest without spilling the whole thing.

No, this was a score he had to settle himself. He would get the bastard and whatever money the bastard had left. He had never killed before, but it occurred to him that now was the time to start.

At headquarters he told his captain that he was going to go below as a shoefly for a few days to check out his men, watch them unawares. The captain, though hesitant, agreed after Montcalm assured him that all his paperwork was caught up. Montcalm returned to his apartment and dressed in khaki slacks, a work shirt, and sunglasses. Over his shoulder holster he wore an old jeans jacket, and tugged a Yankees cap down over his forehead. He grabbed a handful of tokens from the always filled box by his apartment door, went down to the street, down to the tunnels, and began to ride.

CHAPTER 22

If you just keep your ears open, Butch Devlin thought, you can learn a lot of things. By keeping his own ears open for a few weeks, Devlin had learned who had the master keys to the storage lockers. However, in those few short weeks, Butch Devlin had also become more heavily addicted to crack. He no longer went to the base house with Mike. He didn't have to. Mike brought him his crack now, Devlin paid him for it, and he smoked it at home alone after work. Maybe it wasn't as social as going to the house uptown, but it was a hell of a lot more convenient. Besides, those uptown dudes were weird, and the place scared him. When that girl who couldn't have been more than fourteen had walked up to the corner of the room where he and Mike were smoking, and told them that she'd blow them both for ten bucks worth, well, that had really freaked Devlin out. It was a scene he didn't want to see again. But he realized that if he didn't either stop doing crack or win the goddam lottery, he might be offering to blow people himself before too long.

Lowland Rider

The crack was making a crack in his personal finances, and that crack was widening so that everything was falling into it. He'd sold his stereo and all of his records, and had been eyeing his TV lately, wondering how much Sam down the block would give him on it. But Jesus, with his TV gone, what the hell else would he do? He didn't have the money to go to the movies anymore, didn't have the money to do squat except eat and pay the rent and buy his crack. Butch Devlin netted $36 a day scrubbing tile, and $25 of that went to Mike. It didn't leave much, and he was falling further and further behind.

And lately he was thinking more and more about that dealer and his locker full of money. Yeah, thinking about it more than ever now that he knew who had the key. Dave Harnett was the guy's name. He worked for the locker company and came around three times a week to empty the coin compartments into a big cloth bank sack that he carried like a club. He carried a little zippered case with some papers in it, and that case was where he kept the key ring. There were about a dozen keys on it, all of them fat and squatty plastic things with the metal key part sticking out the one end. Devlin had hung around the room where the janitors ate their lunch and shot the shit with the guy the week before, asking enough questions to learn some things but not make Harnett too curious himself. But what he'd needed to learn most was something that Harnett had shown him rather than told him.

After gathering up the hundreds of quarters that filled his huge sack, Harnett then took them somewhere—bank, security office, Devlin didn't know or care. What he cared about was that Harnett left his little zippered case on top of the refrigerator for the twenty minutes it took him to get rid of his quarters.

Devlin thought twenty minutes would be enough—take the case, walk right to the alcove with locker number 4602, try the keys until he hit the right one, open the locker, take the gym bag, stash it in a nearby locker, and return Harnett's case. If he moved fast, it would take him ten, twelve minutes tops. And then, after work . . .

Of course there was the possibility that he might not be alone in the lounge when Harnett left, but in that case all he had to do was to grab the case and run out the door a minute after Harnett left, and say something like, "Holy shit, Harnett forgot his stuff—I'll see if I can catch him . . ." and hope to God that nobody else noticed that Harnett always left his case there. Odds were no one did. Then all he had to do was come back after he'd gotten the money, toss the case on the refrigerator, and say that he'd missed him. If a robbery from a locker was reported, maybe someone would remember that he'd taken the case, but drug dealers weren't too likely to report a robbery like that, were they? All in all, it looked to Butch Devlin like a foolproof plan.

CHAPTER
23

After two days of living on the subways, Bob Montcalm found Jesse Gordon. He spotted him at 6:30 in the morning in a car on the Lexington Avenue line between the 86th and 96th Street stations.

Montcalm had been walking through the cars, pausing before he entered each one, looking into it in order to see Gordon before Gordon saw him. The procedure had worked, for now he gazed through two panes of dusty glass at Jesse Gordon sitting with his eyes closed at the end of the next car.

Montcalm reached inside his jeans jacket and touched the rough checkered butt of the pistol, not because he intended to shoot Gordon immediately, but to make sure the gun was there, and had not magically vanished as had his money through that round hole in the steel. He almost looked on Gordon as a magician, and would not have been surprised to find that his pistol had become useless in the man's presence.

With an effort, he dismissed such foolish imaginings, and tried to think of Gordon as nothing more than a subject for surveillance, for he could do nothing to him until he found where Gordon kept his money.

At Grand Central, Gordon transferred to the crosstown, and from there to the Seventh Avenue–Broadway line, and got off at Penn Station. Montcalm had no difficulty in following him without being seen, for Gordon did not look around once. It seemed to Montcalm that Gordon walked as though he had a mission, a fancy undermined by the fact that the first place the man stopped was the hot dog stand in the main terminal. Montcalm waited impatiently while Gordon ate, thinking that he might have to do a lot more waiting before he went to where he kept his money stashed. But he would have to wait no more than twenty-four hours, for Gordon had to put quarters in the locker every day. And Montcalm would watch him, and follow him, and kill him, out of hatred and revenge and in the certainty that Gordon would never bother him or Gina again. Although he had never killed anyone before, this time he would. This time it was not a bluff. This time he would do it. And he prayed to God to let him, and then he prayed that Gordon would go to his money soon.

Bob Montcalm didn't believe in God, but something that he prayed to that day was kind. After Jesse Gordon finished his hot dog and coffee, he walked across the terminal and down a flight of stairs. Montcalm followed, and before long he saw Gordon enter an alcove which he knew had lockers in it. His heart began to race, and he looked down the short corridor in which he stood, looked and saw no one. He listened

Lowland Rider

as well, and heard nothing, no footsteps of anyone approaching. There would be time to kill Gordon, open the locker, and take whatever was inside. Montcalm took out the gun, held it at his side, and stepped into the doorway.

Jesse Gordon was standing at his locker, but the first thing Montcalm noticed was a uniformed policeman leaning against the wall, smoking a cigarette. The officer had his eyes on Gordon, so Montcalm had the time and the presence of mind to put the gun behind his back. When the officer turned and looked at him, Montcalm saw that it was a man he did not recognize. He glanced at Gordon, who was standing at the open locker with his back to him, then turned, keeping his gun hand away from the policeman, and walked out of the alcove and down the corridor.

He rounded a corner, pushed the pistol into its holster, and waited, remembering where Gordon had been standing, remembering the position of the locker —second one in the top row. That was good, that was fine. When Gordon came out he would follow him, and when they were alone he would kill him and take the key, then go back to the locker and take his own sweet time opening it and cleaning it out.

Montcalm looked around the corner and saw no one. He waited five minutes before he began to suspect that he missed Gordon, that the man might have come out of the alcove right behind him, or in the time it had taken for him to round the corner, think for a second, and look back. Sweat sprang out on Montcalm's forehead, and his face felt hot as he trotted down the corridor the way he had come.

Chet Williamson

This time, there was no one in the alcove. Both Jesse Gordon and the policeman were gone. The locker at which Gordon had been standing was closed and locked. Montcalm clenched his fists until the nails dug tracks in his palms. He had lost him. He had had him with the money and had lost him, and might never find him again. But then he made himself relax and start to reason calmly. The locker, which he saw now was number 4602, was still locked. That meant that Gordon had locked it, and he had locked it because something was in it, something that he would be coming back for sooner or later. And when he did, Montcalm would be ready for him . . .

Or would he?

Then the plan all fell into place for Bob Montcalm, full-blown and beautiful. He would not have to kill Gordon after all.

Duke Sinclair would do it for him.

"The sweetest part is that this guy is wanted for questioning in a murder—killed a kid or something—so whoever nails him might just nail a citation as well."

Montcalm grinned over his beer, but Duke Sinclair didn't grin back. "But I gotta *kill* him," Sinclair said softly.

"Only way," Montcalm answered. "You do him, right away put the stuff in his locker into the one next to it, lock it up, and then go get assistance. For all anybody knows, you surprised this guy, he thought you recognized him, pulled out a piece, and you had no choice, you hadda shoot him."

Lowland Rider

Sinclair took a sip of beer and a drag on his cigarette before he spoke again. "The money be worth it?"

'It should be. Three, four thousand apiece."

"That ain't much." Sinclair's mouth twisted. "Not for a hit."

"This isn't any goddam hit."

"Hell it ain't. What is this shit, Bob? We into killing people now? It come to that? I've never killed anybody for you, man."

Montcalm's smile was long gone. His mouth was nothing but a thin, straight line that opened only a fraction of an inch when he spoke. "It has to be a stakeout, Duke. The guy would recognize me if he saw me. He won't recognize you. It has to be done. You can do it, I can't."

"This guy *knows* you? What the fuck is this, some personal stuff you got going?"

"Look, the guy has no connections, none at all. In fact, Rodriguez would be very happy to see him disappear, and I think he'd be deeply grateful, if you get my meaning."

"This guy's not working for anybody else?" Sinclair said, terrified of killing someone he shouldn't, terrified of killing someone, period.

"He's a maverick, a nut case. He's a fucking *skell*, Duke, who put his nose where it shouldn't be, and that's all he is. I don't know why the hell you're so dainty about this. Odds are you can just do the thing, take the money, and walk away. If a cop's around, you got the perfect excuse for killing the guy. He'll have a gun in his hand, for crissake."

"And you got a clean gun."

"That's right. I do."

Sinclair shook his head. "I don't like this."

"Duke, I don't give a fat fuck whether you like this or *not*!" Montcalm spoke softly, but so forcefully that his spittle cast droplets onto Sinclair's beer glass. Sinclair was afraid to make a move to wipe it off. "Now you listen to me. You've been on the tit for a helluva long time with me, doing little crappy things that have made you a helluva lot of money. Now, when I ask you to do one goddam job that's a little more complicated than rousting winos on trains, all of a sudden you're Mister Clean, you're a fucking prom queen, and that doesn't sit too well with me, pal. Three thousand dollars you get, and—"

"Three? I thought you said four."

"Three, asshole. You just pussied yourself out of an extra grand."

Sinclair swallowed hard. "Yeah? Well, maybe I'll pussy myself out of this whole damn deal."

Montcalm looked at him so hard that Sinclair thought he was going to come across the table at him right there, in front of the whole damn cocktail lounge. "Yeah, well, you might just pussy yourself into the cemetery, and I'll tell you one thing that's for damn sure—you don't do this for me, at the least, at the very, luckiest *least*, you're off the tit. No more good times, Duke. You pull your weight or you don't play, that simple."

"But you're asking me to *kill* a guy."

"That's right. And it's just like anything else. Just easy money and no risk."

"No risk?"

Lowland Rider

"All right, a little risk, there's a little fucking risk in anything." Montcalm sighed, sat back, and looked at the two empty glasses, the dried, white foam webs inside. "You want another beer?"

Sinclair shook his head. "I don't like being threatened, Bob. I really don't like that."

"Okay. Okay." Montcalm suddenly seemed very tired, as if all the anger had gone out of him. "Sure, hell, nobody likes that. Fuck. Fuck it. If you're scared, you're scared, I can't blame you . . ."

"I didn't say I was scared, I just don't like it, that's all."

"Look, don't tell me you're not scared."

"I'm not scared."

"Then do it. No reason *not* to do it, good reasons *to* do it. I meant what I said about being off the tit, Duke. I did mean that. And I need this done now. Right away. Otherwise I might lose this guy forever. Now. Can I count on you?"

"Why do we gotta hit him at this locker? I mean, why not wait till he comes back to it, then follow him, hit him somewhere safer, and take the key?"

"There *isn't* anywhere safer. He's a *skell*, Duke. He's on trains, in stations, hell, there's always the chance of people around. But this place with the lockers has got a long hall running off in both directions, you can hear anyone coming, and you can leave either way. It's not perfect, but you're not gonna find a better place. Besides, even if the fucking *mayor* walks in on you, you got your story all set up."

Sinclair pondered. There was no reason for Montcalm to be setting him up in something that wasn't safe. If he got caught doing something shitful, then Montcalm got caught too. And if this thing came through all right, he was a couple grand richer and further in with Rodriguez. Besides, he'd heard rumors of a white dude who'd been messing up deals with both Rodriguez's people and with the people he had, unknown to Montcalm, been watching out for. Maybe, if this was the same guy, he could ingratiate himself with two factions by killing this one bird. And if the guy was wanted for murder . . .

"All right," Sinclair said. "I'll do it. Tell me where."

CHAPTER 24

She could not return to him empty-handed. But she *had* to return. Enoch had worked on Gladys H. Mitchell like alcohol had worked on her years before. He was in her blood, *was* her blood, that part of her without which life was colorless, devoid of feeling, warmth, sensation itself. She remembered the first line of an old hymn that she had sung with her mother when she was a little girl—*Jesus is all the world to me*—only it wasn't Jesus anymore, was it? It was Enoch now, not that coward Jesus.

What had Jesus ever done for her in all the years she had prayed to him, prayed even while the strangers were lying between her legs, filling her up with their seed, trying to make a breeder out of her? Where was Jesus those times she was ripped open, when she called out his name, called for him to come and help her? She never even saw his face. He never even *tried* to come and help her, to pull those bastards off, nail *them* to some wooden crosses for a change, drive those big spikes up their *ass*, make *them* feel what they did to her. God of justice? Jesus fair? Bullshit.

But Enoch would have done that. He would have spiked them out, hung them up by their balls the way they did that young boy, that damned little dago breeder who was stupid enough to try and lie to Him. Imagine lying to Enoch! Imagine trying to get away with that with a man who looks into your head and heart as easily as reading a station sign.

Baggie sat on her bench and chuckled at the foolishness of it, then sighed deeply and wiped a ball of mucus from her upper lip. If she could have gotten to that dago boy quickly enough, before he was dead, she might have taken something from him, a sacrifice to give to Enoch. But the others who had worshipped before were too fast for her. They knew what was happening, she did not, and she could only stand there stunned into immobility by the glorious power of her savior, those eyes that blazed at that stupid liar.

Oh, she would have loved to have gotten one of that liar's eyes, those bright and shining and still living eyes that the faster ones had plucked from the sockets and held out to Enoch. The way He had *smiled* at them! The way He had laughed when they tore that fool apart, her own rollicking God, His hands crossed upon his chest once again, oh God, how she loved Him, how she wanted to bring Him something, not just an eye or a tongue or an ear or a hand, but a whole body, a full carcass to show that she would slay for Him willingly and lovingly . . .

But the time was never right. No matter how she hunted and waited and stalked, the time had never been right, and she felt like those in the purgatory in which she no longer believed, in torment from no

Lowland Rider

induced pain, but at their absence from their God. She felt as though she could stand it no longer, felt like rushing into a crowd, slashing as she went, killing for Enoch, and at last, when they were about to take her, turning the knife on herself, making herself the last sacrifice to her white and red Lord, giving all for Him.

But she could not. She was still afraid to die.

She would go above then. She would go above and look for a victim, and kill it, and bring it back down to Enoch. This time she would not fail Him.

When Baggie pushed herself to her feet, her muscles felt unaccustomedly strong and vital, and it occurred to her that perhaps this sense of refreshment was a sign, an indication that today—this night—she would find her prey, reap her harvest. She walked up the stairs of the 86th Street station, and found herself on Central Park West. Across the street, one of the streetlights was out, another sign, and she chose that spot to sit and wait. It didn't take long for the cattle to begin to pass by. It was early in the morning, Baggie thought perhaps three o'clock, but people still walked the street, breeders, all of them, on their way to fuck and breed and spread their seed and make more of themselves, over and over and forever. Most, at this hour, walked together, as if they knew what they were and were afraid to be alone, afraid of Enoch's justice. And there were men together with their arms around each other, or their hands on each other's asses, and that was bad too, but at least they didn't breed, at least there was that comfort, and Baggie watched them approach, and glance at her, and chuckle, and move away again.

Two boys in leather jackets came near to her bench and one said, "Hey, grammaw, what you got in your pockets?"

She reached in and took out the knife, its blade open and long and gleaming, and held it up so they could see it. "Go away," she told them. "You little fuckers."

The boy who had spoken laughed. "Right on, grammaw. You're not worth the hassle." As the two walked away, she heard the other one say, "Old ladies with blades, shit, what's this town coming to?"

Coming to Enoch, you little fucker, that's what it's coming to. It's all coming to Enoch.

The man came walking alone down the street, a half hour before dawn. He was short and seemed frail, and carried a bundle in his right arm. He never looked up, never saw her as he got closer, never even raised his head as she stepped behind him and drove the knife into his back. He made a gargling cry and fell to his knees, still clinging to his bundle. She wrenched out the knife, feeling the *tick tick* as it ratcheted along the man's ribs like a stick on a picket fence, and drove it in again, this time into the flesh at the back of his neck. Another gargle of blood and spit escaped him, yet he remained on his knees, continued to clutch his parcel. She yanked the knife sideways, ripping through the muscles of the neck, then came back again into the side of his body beneath his right arm. The blow drove him over onto his left side, and what he was holding at last left his arms, flopping onto the pavement with a soft crack and a muffled cry that lasted only a moment.

Lowland Rider

Baggie was aware of the peculiar sound the package had made, but she could not investigate it immediately. She was solely possessed by the violence of her attack, by the fact that yes, she was *doing* this now, that she was no longer afraid, and the swing of her arm up and down and in and out were like great gestures of praise to Enoch, the blood spraying up and over her head like palm branches, and blessed is she who killeth in the name of the Lord . . .

And she laughed and swung the knife until what she sank it into felt like a sack of pus, with no resistance except when the blade slipped on bone and felt like fingernails on an old chalkboard. Only at the end, only when she was totally exhausted, did she remember the parcel and the quick whimper that had come from it.

Glancing up and down the street, she roughly pushed aside the wrappings and saw a baby, its eyes closed, a bruise discoloring its forehead, but breathing, still breathing. Her breath caught, and she pushed the wrappings back further, exposing a paper diaper, which she frenziedly tore apart.

A boy. It was a breeder.

One of those goddamed, fucking breeders.

And this would be her sacrifice. The whole carcass, as she had wished for, dreamed of. Her gift to Enoch. She needed no eye now, no balls, no cock from the man who had died so easily for Enoch's glory. She had all those and more.

Now, if she could only find a bag . . .

CHAPTER

25

While Gladys H. Mitchell, carrying her sacrifice, was looking for a shopping bag, Duke Sinclair was standing in the hall outside the alcove that housed locker number 4602. Tucked behind his back was his .38 police special, and in the pocket of his lightweight jacket was a .32 caliber Saturday night special Montcalm had given him to put in the dead man's hand. His orders were simple: When a tall man about thirty-five years old went into the alcove, Sinclair was supposed to follow. If the man opened locker number 4602, Sinclair was supposed to say something to him and, when the man turned around, shoot him, then put the .32 in his hand and move the money from locker 4602 to locker 4614 next to it, and lock it. If anyone came in after the shooting, Sinclair was to declare himself a police officer and go for assistance. Otherwise, he could simply walk away. Montcalm could come back later to get the money.

Sinclair waited, one hand in his pocket clutching the key to locker number 4614 so tightly it hurt. His bowels were full, and he wished he could go to the

Lowland Rider

lavatory, but he was afraid that he would miss the man he was looking for. He had never killed anyone in the line of duty, though he had killed, he supposed, in Vietnam, even if he had never seen what the shells from his mortars actually did to those human targets. Still, that was different, that was war. This was shooting a guy face-to-face, a guy who would probably be unarmed, who Duke Sinclair didn't even know and didn't give a shit about, and *goddam*, he wondered, *why the hell am I even doing this*?

Because of Montcalm, he decided quickly. To show Montcalm he wasn't afraid, to stay on Montcalm's tit, to maybe make an impression on Rodriguez and the others. Hell, if they knew he could pull off something like this, maybe they'd be willing to expand his opportunities. There was little enough on the transit police, that was for damn sure. Thankless fucking job. He didn't understand how ninety-nine-plus percent of his colleagues went from day-to-day without messing in the kind of stuff he was messing with. Jesus, they even had families to support, and Sinclair couldn't figure out how they did it. No, he sure as shit wasn't going to be a transit cop all his life. Get into the drug business, that was the ticket. Buy in bulk, sell to the dealers, that was where the money was. Middleman. Never touch another gun, never hustle butt down in a tunnel again.

Montcalm would never be able to do that. Montcalm was nothing but a fucking toady. And although Sinclair was *Montcalm's* toady, Sinclair knew he had something Montcalm didn't—he had ambition. No, Montcalm was too old for that. He'd die in the tunnels if he didn't get his ass caught first and go to prison. Sinclair smiled in spite of the pressure in his gut. Montcalm wouldn't last two days in jail. There were too many people he'd sent there. No, Montcalm would probably take the crooked cop's hara-kiri if things came to that. A bullet in the head. Sayonara.

Sinclair tensed as he heard footsteps coming down the hall, but it was only a businessman in his fifties who poked his head in the alcove, then asked Sinclair if he knew where the rest rooms were. Sinclair told him, wished he could go there, and allowed himself to relax a bit as the man walked away. Christ, he couldn't let himself get this tense. If the guy did come down the hall and saw Sinclair poised there like a coiled spring, he'd know right off something was fishy. Relax, that was the key. Look like some dude waiting for a deal or something. Look cool but not threatening. Just look cool.

Duke Sinclair waited for another five hours before he decided that he either had to go to the lavatory or do it in his pants. He chose the former, and scurried down the early morning halls into the men's room and the nearest booth, unbuckling his belt as he went, so as to waste no time. If the sonovabitch came and went while he was taking a crap, he'd never even know it. Shit, he might have to hang around for days before he got another crack at the guy.

He defecated as quickly and forcefully as possible, cleaned himself up, and started out, but paused when he realized he hadn't washed his hands. Wash my fucking hands, he thought with wry humor. Mama, I

Lowland Rider

learned my lessons well. He chuckled and went back out into the hall.

A few feet from the alcove, he heard the rattle of keys and froze. A quick glance up and down the hall told him there was no one else around, and he moved quietly to the door of the alcove. He looked around the corner and saw a man standing at the row of lockers, fitting a key into number 4602.

Jesus, he thought, taking out his pistol. This is it, so damn fast. Shoot him in the head, shoot him in the goddam head. Kill him quick so he'll never talk.

The key turned, the locker opened. Inside he saw a leather bag, which the man grasped and started to remove. It was halfway out when Sinclair said, "*Hey*," softly but sharply.

The man turned, and there was fear in his face. Sinclair shot him, the explosion surprisingly loud. They were so close that he saw the bullet go in, right above the man's left eye. The head snapped back, and the man collapsed, Sinclair thought, just like a gray, burst balloon. It was almost funny, the way all the air went out of him at once. Whoosh—and gone.

Sinclair stood for a second, looking at what he'd done. He had no doubt that the man was dead. A foot was twitching, but nothing else moved, and blood trickled freely from the hole in the forehead. The eyes were wide open.

Footsteps pattered down the hall, or so Sinclair imagined. The noise of the gunshot had deafened him for a moment, but now he shook his head and took the smaller pistol from his pocket, wiped it on his jacket, and pressed it into the dead right hand. Then he grabbed the leather bag, zipped it open, and looked inside.

Clothes. Nothing but clothes. There was no money at all. Just a T-shirt, a pair of jeans, some underwear and socks.

Sinclair rummaged frantically through the items, his fingers crooked into claws, scrabbling for a wad of bills, but there was nothing to find, nothing to jam into locker 4614, hell, goddam, *shit*, no money at all! He stood up, shoved his pistol into his holster, and ran out of the alcove, right into two uniformed policemen.

There was a brief scuffle, and the officers grabbed Sinclair by the arms, roughly frisked him, and took away his .38.

"Police officer, goddam it!" Sinclair wailed. "*Police officer!*"

"Yeah, we'll see . . ." growled the larger of the two officers, as they manhandled Sinclair back into the alcove where the body lay.

"Holy shit," said the other officer, a thin but wiry black man whose grip Sinclair was not able to break. The pair shoved Sinclair facedown on the floor, his arm pressed behind his back. The black officer pulled out his service revolver and jammed it behind Sinclair's neck. "You just ease off now, just relax."

"I'm a fucking *police officer*," Sinclair said again.

"Yeah, okay. He dead, Sam?"

"Dead as hell," said the big officer. "Better pat him down again."

Together, they emptied Sinclair's pockets, and the

black cop looked in the wallet. "He *is* a cop, Sam. Transit."

"That's what I *said*, man! Now will you let me the fuck up?"

The cop holstered his revolver and released Sinclair, who pushed himself painfully to his feet. "What the hell happened?" asked the white cop the other had called Sam.

"I saw this guy out in the hall . . . thought he was acting suspicious, looking around and all," Sinclair babbled. "So I followed him in here and he's standing at the locker. He turns around and sees me and all of a sudden he takes out this pistol, see, there, he still has it, and starts to point it at me. Well, shit, I mean, the guy's gonna *shoot* me, so I got out my gun and shot first."

The big white cop made a sour face. "You always shoot in the head?"

"I . . . I didn't have time to aim, for crissake . . . I mean, the guy could've killed me . . ."

The big cop shook his head. "I don't think. Not this guy."

"What . . . what do you mean?"

"Why were you *running* out of here?"

"I . . . I was going for assistance, what the hell else?"

"Uh-huh." Sam showed the locker key he had taken from Sinclair to his partner. "4614," he said. "Quite a coincidence."

"I . . ."

"Read him his rights, Tony. We'll take him downtown and see if he can explain what this is all about."

"I just *told* you!"

"Yeah, you wanta tell us about that key? About why your locker and his locker are side by side? You wanta tell us why you shoot station janitors in the head?"

"Station . . . station *janitors*?"

"You maybe got mixed up and thought the gray uniform meant he escaped from prison?"

CHAPTER 26

It was ten o'clock in the morning when Jesse Gordon put two more quarters into the locker at Grand Central Station that held his nearly fifty thousand dollars in cash. He smiled as he pocketed the key, and wondered if Montcalm had figured a way to get into his old locker. He hoped that his jeans would fit the man all right.

Jesse had seen Montcalm following him, had figured that he had somehow learned that it was Jesse who had taken his money and given it away. He was surprised, though, that he had been found so easily in the labyrinth of tunnels that honeycombed the city. It seemed like more than luck. It seemed like a miracle. But it would surely be a miracle to Montcalm when he found that Jesse's money was no longer there. He had taken the rolls of bills out of the locker right in front of the lounging policeman who had apparently scared off Montcalm long enough for Jesse to lose him. He knew, though, that Montcalm had seen what locker he'd been in, and that would be enough to keep him busy and off his trail, at least for a while.

At least until he found Enoch.

In the past few weeks, the rumors had been increasing among the skells, and most of them were scared. There was something that was down there in the tunnels, they said, something that had always been there, but which was now growing in power and influence until it threatened all of them, anyone who lived beneath the city.

Anyone who was not already part of it.

Part of what? Jesse had asked the skells who were willing to talk to him. Part of Enoch, they would answer, telling him what he already knew. Part of Enoch.

Enoch was the power and the evil. Enoch, Jesse thought over and over again, was the reason he had been drawn below. Enoch and his white, glowing angel's face, a mask behind which lay the horror of the city. It was all in him, all in Enoch.

Jesse's destiny. Enoch.

It was because of Enoch that Jesse could not take the menace of Montcalm seriously. Montcalm, despite his own corruption and the extent to which it corrupted others, was unimportant compared to the absolute horror that was Enoch's domain. At the thought of Montcalm, Jesse shook his head in pitiful disgust. Small change. But Enoch . . .

The day before, after Jesse had lost Montcalm, he had ridden the Jamaica Avenue line back and forth until midnight, when he disembarked from the train at the Woodhaven Boulevard station. He sat on the benches for a while, dozing occasionally, and some time after one in the morning went into the men's

Lowland Rider

room to wash himself and clean his teeth. When he came out he saw, in the dim light at the end of the platform, a man in his sixties bent over the body of a teenage boy. Months before, when he had first descended, he might have thought the boy had fainted and the man was trying to help him. But his innocence had long since fled, and he saw the act for what it was, and walked slowly and silently down the platform.

The man was working something in his hands with a sawing motion, like a diner bent over a particularly tough steak, and Jesse finally saw that he was attempting to sever the boy's hand at the wrist. The boy was beyond help. A gash showed wetly across one side of his neck, and his eyes were already glazed over. The man did not hear Jesse until he was three yards away, then turned and looked up at the tall form standing over him. His eyes widened, and he tensed like a gray cat too old to spring. Still, he made an effort at it, and leaped feebly, the knife scratching on concrete as Jesse easily sidestepped and kicked the man's knee so that he fell heavily, the knife skittering across the platform.

Jesse snatched it up, pushed the man over, placed his left elbow on the man's chest, and held the knife across his throat. The man's body shook beneath him like a mass of congealed rage, but he made no attempt to push Jesse off, his energy depleted by his stalking and killing the boy.

"What?" Jesse asked him. "What is this for?"

The man's head shivered, the jaw jutted upward, as though he were possessed, and he tried to spit into

Jesse's face, but the gobbet fell back weakly on his own.

"The hand," Jesse went on. "Who the hell is the hand for? Answer me, you bastard." He pressed the edge of the knife against the white stubble that covered the wattled neck, and a thin line of blood appeared, though the man made no outcry. "Who is it *for*?"

Suddenly there was recognition in the man's face, and he smiled so that Jesse could see the yellowed teeth, a brown stain capping each one like a wig on a skull. "For *you*," the man whispered wetly. "For *you*, Lord!"

Jesse shuddered, then slashed the knife across the man's throat. After he rolled the body off the tracks, he could still see the man's smile.

He saw it even now. The man had been insane, that was certain. He had to be insane to do what he'd done in the first place, and he had to be insane to mistake Jesse for Enoch, for surely that was what he had done.

The hand was for Enoch, the murder was for Enoch. Somehow all of it, every death down here, every beating, every crime of man against man was for Enoch. How far did his influence reach, Jesse wondered. How long were the fingers of that bloody hand? Did they reach to the surface of the city? And if so, how far beyond the city's edges? Where did they stop?

Did they stop?

And what, he wondered most of all, would he be killing when he killed Enoch?

PART
4

CHAPTER

27

It was beginning to grow quiet on the trains. Rags figured it must be about 11:30. The theater crowds were all home, the middle-shift workers were at their neighborhood bars. Nobody riding the trains now except for the people who really had to get somewhere and couldn't afford a cab.

The car Rags was on was empty, a Lexington Avenue local going downtown from 241st Street. It was a nice long ride, safe and secure, a good train to sleep on. Not many transit cops this time of night, and the ones you did see didn't bother you unless you were making a nuisance of yourself or smelled like shit or something. Rags took a deep whiff of himself and decided that he didn't smell too bad for a summer night. He had been washing more frequently in the months since he met Jesse. It just seemed like something he wanted to do.

Get himself clean again.

He had been having weird thoughts ever since he told Jesse about why he came down into the tunnels. He had never told anyone before, and he wondered

Chet Williamson

why he'd gone and told Jesse something so secret, so personal, so terrible about himself. Still, he was glad he had. Jesse hadn't said or done anything that led Rags to believe he thought Rags's sin was unforgivable. Instead, he'd said some things about being forgiven, about good works saving his soul. And he'd said that when Rags died he wouldn't go to hell. Now how did Jesse know that?

Then Rags remembered the poem that had affected Jesse so much when he'd read it, that Lowland Rider poem. He fumbled in the layers of cloth and brought out the book of ballads. As if by chance, it fell open to *Jamie Gordon, The Lowland Rider*, and Rags read:

"So take thy saddle and thy sword,
Avaunt into the night,
Nae seek for rest, nor walk again
Beneath the bright daylight."

Well, *that* was on it, sure enough. Jesse hadn't seen sunlight since he'd come below. Rags read on:

"But be my faithful harvester,
And ride the lowland dark,
And gather in the men of sin
On whom I place my mark.

"For when their time is come to die,
Then shall they see thee ride
Upon the path that they must cross
Til you be by their side.

"Then hold thy sword in front of them,
That sword that brought thee woe,
Command them, in sweet Jesu's name,
Away with thee to go.

"Then bring them to the Judgement seat
Where God alone may tell
Them whether to fly Heavenward
Or sink, condemned, to Hell."

Rags hadn't read the ballad for a long time, and the words made him feel funny, as if something really strange was happening down here with Jesse. "Gather in the men of sin . . ." Wasn't that just what Jesse had been doing? Messing with all these people he had no business to be messing with? Still, all the same, Rags respected him for it. He didn't remember ever respecting anybody as much, unless maybe it was his Daddy, who'd died when he was just a little boy.

But if Jesse was making the ballad come true, and it surely looked like he was, then he wouldn't be the final judge, would he? It was God alone that would tell Rags whether he went to Heaven or Hell, not Jesse. Still, if Jesse had some inside information . . .

Stop it, Rags told himself. It was stupid—worse than that, it was blasphemy—to think that Jesse was some kind of messenger of God or something. Hell, no. He was just some poor soul like Rags, down here for much the same reason. Trying to pay. Just trying to pay for what he'd done. But Rags wondered if maybe Jesse wasn't getting more sins to his account than he had when he started.

Rags closed the book of ballads and tucked it away into one of his soft crevices, then sat back with his head against the glass. No matter what Jesse's sins were, he thought, he'd profited by knowing him. Even though Rags thought he was going to die, knew the cancer on his neck was going to kill him, he wasn't as afraid anymore, and that was good.

Rags was dozing, and only dimly aware that the train had stopped at the 86th Street station. The doors were open for only a short time, and he heard a pattering of feet, the unequivocal crash of the doors closing, a choked exclamation that was definitely out of the ordinary. Rags's eyes opened.

Standing five feet away from him was Baggie, a snarl smeared across her face like blood. Her elbows jutted outward, and she held to her chest by twine handles a shopping bag, the contents of which rounded the bottom. Her shoulders hunched over the bag like a bat's wings.

Rags's mind was still dulled by sleep, but he was awake enough to realize that this was not the Baggie of old. That woman had been insane, not dangerous. But now there was something about her that terrified Rags, a look in her eyes that went far beyond the aggressive madness she had previously displayed. There was violence, murder, blood, and although the bag she carried bore no red stains, he knew that inside there was something alive, possibly dying. Possibly human.

"What you got?" he asked roughly, ready for her to leap at him with those clawlike fingers. The train lurched as it pulled out of the station, and Baggie

Lowland Rider

smoothly moved with it, years of long tenure underground giving her the motion of the train itself.

"Not for *you*, nigger!" she spat at him. "Not for *you*!"

Rags got to his feet. "You show me what's in that bag."

Baggie looped the handles over her left arm, and dipped her right hand into a pocket, from which she drew something hard and shiny. Rags heard a clicking sound, and found himself looking at a long-bladed knife, its blade dulled by something that looked like, but that Rags knew wasn't, rust. "You get back, nigger. Nigger breeder. All want to fuck me, don't you? Fuck me and take what's mine, take what I done for *Him*. Oh no you won't. I'll cut off your black balls first, cut 'em off and take 'em to Enoch."

Rags felt suddenly, horribly cold. "What you got?"

"For *Him*, not for you. You get back now. I don't need no more, but I will, you try and take it . . ." She started to back toward the door to the next car.

They were at a standstill. Baggie did not want to have to fight while she carried the bag in her arms, and Rags didn't want to go up against the knife. It was long and sharp, and he knew she had used it recently and would be willing to use it again. When she bumped against the door, she reached back with the arm that bore the shopping bag and pulled the handle, then pushed her way through, closing it firmly behind her.

Rags waited for several seconds, then went up to the door and looked through the window. Baggie was walking down the aisle of the next car, which was empty except for a young Hispanic boy, his head buried in a comic book. He glanced up when Baggie passed him and watched her until she went by and looked through the window into the car ahead. Rags figured she saw more people, for she sat at the end of the car, her eyes fixed suspiciously on the boy, who now ignored her and read his comic book.

At 14th Street she got off the train and transferred to the BMT west, then, shortly afterward, to the IND train that, when it went beneath the East River, became the Beast. Rags followed her every step of the way, slipping behind posts the few times she looked behind her. Her monomania concerning the contents of the bag seemed to free her mind of a minor disturbance like Rags, and he could see that she now had a smile on her face, and her shoulders shook with what Rags, at a distance, could only imagine to be laughter.

He positioned himself in the car behind hers and continued to watch her through the window. At one point he could have sworn the bag moved, and Baggie's head jerked down and looked inside it. Her long fingers joined to make a fist, and he saw her punch into the bag once, twice, then smile and nod calmly. Though the noise of the train was loud, just before she had struck the thing within, Rags imagined that he could hear a high-pitched wail like a cat's. He wondered if it was, after all, just a cat, and if he was on a fool's errand. But then he remembered what she had said, and what her eyes had said, and he leaned back against the metal, following without motion.

Baggie got off the train at Van Siclen Avenue

Lowland Rider

station, the next to last stop on the line. Rags got off as well, and lurked behind a stanchion, peering out with one eye. They were the only ones who had left the train at the stop, and the hard surfaces of the station amplified every sound. Rags scarcely dared breathe.

Finally he heard Baggie's footsteps move off in the direction of the tunnel out of which the train had come, and he moved slowly around the stanchion so that it would remain between them as she passed by. She walked to the end of the platform without turning around, then set down her bag and lowered herself heavily to the track bed. She reached up, took the bag, and walked off over the loose stones into the darkness. Rags waited until he could barely hear her footsteps, then dropped over the edge of the platform and followed her. He hugged the wall from fear of trains, and so that if Baggie turned she would not see his silhouette against the light of the station.

Walking through the tunnel was a nightmare. The stone walls seeped water which collected in puddles, and often Rags heard things nearby splashing their way through them. They sounded big enough to be dogs, but Rags suspected they were rats. In a way he was glad there was no more light than the small blue bulbs spaced every fifty feet or so. He didn't want to see what was down here, skittering along near him. When he began, he stopped frequently to listen for Baggie's footsteps, but was so appalled by what else he heard that after a while he stopped listening and simply walked, as quietly as possible.

They had traveled what Rags estimated to be three or four blocks, when a light brighter than the dim blue globes began to shine somewhere up ahead and to the side. A spur, Rags thought, remembering the term his grandfather, who had been a porter on the Southern Central, had used. A spur, probably unused for years and years. And suddenly he thought, what am I *doing* down here? It had begun as curiosity, to assure himself that the worst he suspected about Baggie was true. And now that that curiosity had brought him into a situation he didn't want to be in, he found it impossible to turn around and walk back to the station. What was the matter with him? Why was he here? And what if she was taking that thing in the bag to Enoch? Sweet Jesus, what then?

Nevertheless, he followed.

And at last he peered around an archway of stone, and saw Baggie on her knees before a man dressed all in white whom Rags knew could only be Enoch. Rags didn't know, however, where the light inside the spur was coming from, that light that shone on Enoch's smiling face, illuminated Baggie's wiry talons that plucked from the bag, as a falcon snares a mouse, a small and mewling form that was neither dog nor cat nor rat, but which bled as profusely as any other animal when the woman's long and filthy nails raked across the gleaming whiteness of its extended throat.

And to try and drive the sight away, Rags wondered over and over again, where is that light coming from?

And as he turned and ran away into that safe, sweet darkness, he tried to keep thinking, where is that light coming from?

Where is that Light coming from?

CHAPTER 28

"Virgil, you don't want to be an asshole, do you?"

Duke Sinclair hated to be called Virgil. He'd hated it ever since he found out it was his name.

"I mean, I think we'd be a whole lot better off if you'd just tell us what the hell this shit is all about . . ."

The voice went droning off again as Sinclair tried to concentrate on his surroundings, tried to keep from answering anything stupid or incriminating. He looked around the room, and saw that nothing had changed in all the hours since they'd kept him here. The walls were still institutional green, the chairs were still heavy metal with padded, dark green backs, the table over which Detective Barton now leaned toward him for the hundredth time was surfaced with that dark gray, claylike crap that you could leave marks in with your fingernails.

"Virgil!" The voice made him raise his head. "It's four in the fucking morning, Virgil. I've been talking to you, and I'm getting tired of talking to you."

"Well, I'm getting tired of *having* you talk to me."

Sinclair was pissed. It had all come off wrong. Fucking Montcalm. First of all they'd brought him to the Midtown South precinct station, where he didn't know a goddam soul, they'd kept him in a holding cell for hours, said they'd let him call an attorney "if he really thought he needed one," by which they meant *if you do, asshole, we'll know you're in it deep*. So he didn't. He thought he could dumb it out, stick to his original story. He wasn't so sure anymore. He was sleepy as hell, and when he got sleepy he was afraid he might say something he shouldn't.

There was still the gun he had put in the guy's hand. There was still that.

Detective Barton leaned back against the wall and sighed. "Okay, Virgil—"

"And stop calling me Virgil. Call me Duke, or Officer Sinclair."

"I don't think you'll be an officer for long. And your mama named you Virgil."

"Fuck . . ."

"Fuck your mama?"

Sinclair sat up straighter in his straight-backed chair. "Listen, whitey, don't try and pull that brother shit with me. You white guys try and sound like us, you sound like dickheads."

Barton nodded his round, huge head. "Okay, Virgil. *Officer* Sinclair. I tried. I tried to be nice, and it didn't work. You want to talk to a brother, you can talk to Tyrone."

Sinclair snorted a laugh. "*Ty*-rone. Shit."

"Tyrone—or Detective Jackson—does not like

Lowland Rider

crooked cops. Tyrone especially does not like crooked TA cops, since he doesn't like TA cops to begin with."

"Fuck, man, I know what this is. This is the good cop–bad cop routine. I know this, hell, I *done* it. Big nigger comes in, tries to scare me, rough me up, and you say hold it, *Ty*-rone, and then you tell me you can keep *Ty*-rone from killing me, all I have to do's tell you the whole truth, which I already told you, so it's not gonna do you a little white dick's worth of good, okay?"

"Tsk tsk tsk. You have got one hell of an unquenchable spirit there, Virgil. I just hope it doesn't get you into any trouble. With *Ty*-rone." Barton sidled to the door and opened it. "Detective Jackson?" He stepped out of the way. He had to. Tyrone Jackson looked like a walking mountain. His skin was as shiny and black as coal, he stood well over six feet tall, and had the build of a power lifter. The wire-rimmed glasses he wore should have softened his appearance, but instead they enlarged his eyes, making them look more yellow and more menacing.

Sinclair chuckled, but it trembled more than he wanted it to. "Oh man . . ." he sighed. "You lost out not calling this one Bubba."

Jackson looked at Barton. "What has he told you?" There was not a trace of street dialect in the voice, which was soft and fat-sounding.

"Nothing," Barton replied. "Virgin territory. You want me to stay?"

Jackson shook his head, and Barton walked out of

the room, closing the door behind him.

"So what's it gonna be?" Sinclair asked. "You gonna use a cattle prod, or wire my testicles now or what?"

"Later." Jackson didn't smile. "You can just tell me everything now and save us a lot of trouble."

"You don't sound black."

Jackson passed a hand across his cheek and held his fingers up to Sinclair. "It doesn't come off." Sinclair smiled, and tried to look cocky. Jackson didn't smile at all. "I've been sniffing around about you. Word on the street is that you're not exactly an upstanding officer. Word is that probably you're on the take. Maybe on the take from more than one customer. Now when I hear that a cop is on the take from one person, or group of people, I'm not too concerned. You make enemies out there . . . *down* there, in your case . . . and people are likely to bad-mouth you. But when I hear it consistently, such word of mouth is enough to convince me that I have a crooked cop on my hands."

Jackson walked behind Sinclair and rested his hands on Sinclair's shoulders. Sinclair shuddered. The fingers felt like baling wire.

"I don't like crooked cops. They stink. They stink bad. I don't often get to talk to crooked transit cops because they deal with their own. But because you shot Lawrence Devlin where you did . . . well, that means that you're ours. Now. I know you say that Devlin had a gun, but I don't believe that. I believe that you put that gun in his hand after you shot him. But I don't know *why* you shot him."

Lowland Rider

"Hey, man, it's the truth. He pulled that fucking gun on me."

"He pulled the gun on you. And why were you there?"

"I . . . I had a locker there."

"That's not what you told the officers. You told them that Devlin looked suspicious."

"I was confused. Shit, they had me on the floor, the guy had just pulled a gun on me—"

"You had just shot him—yes, I guess that would tend to make you confused."

Sinclair pressed his lips together, determined to say nothing stupid.

"Why did you have a locker there?"

"I just . . . wanted a locker, that's all."

"But there wasn't anything in it. You weren't carrying anything to put in it either. Were you just going to open it to make sure the air was still there?"

Sinclair didn't answer.

"Devlin was suspicious, though. At least you had that right. He was carrying some stolen keys. Master keys to the lockers. Which leads me to think that he wanted to get in one of those lockers very badly, what do you think?"

"I . . . yeah, I guess maybe."

"You guess maybe. You sure you didn't find out about Devlin stealing those keys and then maybe you followed him because you wanted what was in there as much as he did? You guess maybe that?"

"I . . ."

Jackson's next words came with machine-gun rapidity. "And then you guess maybe you shot him because you wanted what was in there for yourself and you were going to put it in the locker that you had the key for? But then you guess maybe that you got caught? And you guess maybe that your story might have held water if you hadn't been caught with that key? You guess maybe you're a fucking son of a bitch liar and killer and thief?"

Before Sinclair could respond, Jackson had snapped a cuff on his right wrist, yanked his arms behind his chair, and snapped the other on his left. Then Jackson pulled out Sinclair's chair, turned it toward him, and sat in another chair so that he faced Sinclair.

"What the fuck you doing?" Sinclair yelped.

"Interrogating." Jackson held up his big right hand for Sinclair to see, as though he were displaying a weapon. Then he pushed Sinclair's legs apart and shoved his fingers under Sinclair's crotch, keeping his thumb on top, against Sinclair's penis.

"Whoa! *Whoa!*" Sinclair husked out, his breath coming faster and faster. He could feel the sweat forming on his forehead and upper lip. "You can't do that, man," he half-laughed, half-moaned. "This is so fucking illegal they'll rip *your* balls off."

"But I'll have yours first. And I'm not going to rip anything. There'll be no permanent damage. Not a bruise, not a mark. Just a great deal of pain, unless you tell me the truth. And you will. It's just a question of how much you want to suffer first. And how tired my hand gets. But even if it does, I've got two of them."

Jackson held the left hand up and made a fist. When he did, Sinclair felt as though the hand holding his

Lowland Rider

genitals had made the move, and sobbed in anticipated pain. "Now wait, now wait . . . nobody *does* this, brother!"

"I do. And I do it well. I could say I don't really enjoy this. But I do. All I have to do is keep in mind what you are. A crooked cop. And then I enjoy it." He gave a slight squeeze that would have toppled Sinclair out of his chair if Jackson hadn't held him with his free hand.

Within ten minutes, Sinclair was telling as much truth as he knew into a tape recorder in the presence of Detectives Jackson and Barton. He told how Montcalm had set the whole thing up, had given him the gun to put into the dead man's hand. He said that he thought there had been a mistake, that Montcalm had not intended for him to shoot Lawrence Devlin, and that he thought maybe Devlin had found out about the money that Montcalm had said was in the locker.

After Sinclair had finished, he was formally charged, and waived his right to call an attorney. He could do that, he decided, after he'd gotten some sleep. When he left the interrogation room, Jackson spoke to him. "You tell anybody about any coercion, they won't believe you. People don't do things like that. Besides, Detective Barton was with us all the time, and he saw nothing of the sort occur."

When Sinclair left the room, Barton turned to Jackson. "You know this Montcalm?"

Jackson shook his head. "Heard about him when I was sniffing around about Sinclair. Word is he's as crooked as the other, if not worse."

"So who the fuck did he set Sinclair out to kill?"

"I think we'd better get Sergeant Montcalm to give us that information."

"You think he will?"

Jackson smiled for the first time that morning. "I think he will."

CHAPTER 29

The phone call woke Bob Montcalm from a restless sleep. The previous day at headquarters had been nothing but a waste of time. He hadn't been able to concentrate on any of his desk work, and he couldn't make himself go down to Penn Station to see if Sinclair was where he was supposed to be. He could only assume that he was, trust him. Sinclair was a good guy after all. Sure, he'd been pissed when Montcalm had put the screws to him, but who wouldn't have been? Duke could be a pain in the ass at times, but Montcalm believed he'd always been straight with him. And after this killing, Duke Sinclair would have to be straighter than ever with Bob Montcalm.

He had thought about going down to 34th Street, but what if Gordon was there and spotted him just as he was checking out Duke? No, better to let things go. Hell, in all likelihood Duke would get tired or hungry and eventually have to give up. And if he did, he did. Montcalm would get Gordon sooner or later, damned if he wouldn't.

Still, he slept poorly, thinking about it all. He had hoped that Sinclair would call before he went to bed, would say, *Yeah, I got him, no problem. Put the money in the locker and walked away. Nobody saw me.*

But Sinclair didn't call. Montcalm stayed awake in the dark until long after midnight, waiting for the phone to ring, and finally slept. But now, as the sound of the telephone threw him into wakefulness, he felt as though he had just closed his eyes for a moment. He glanced at the digital alarm clock as he reached for the phone. Five-thirty. It had to be Sinclair then, had to be.

"Yeah," Montcalm said sleepily into the mouthpiece.

"Bob?" It was a voice Montcalm knew, not Sinclair's, and in his groggy condition he could not put a face to it.

"Yeah, who's this?"

"Listen, Bob. They got Sinclair."

A gobbet of phlegm lodged in Montcalm's throat, and he coughed it away. He felt cold inside. "They . . .? Who's . . ."

"Got him for shooting a guy, janitor at Penn Station."

A janitor? Jesus! "Who is this?"

"Bob, I . . . you're maybe tapped." Rooney. Now he had it. It was Rooney. Rooney was always a friend. "But he spilled his guts. Told them you wanted it done. I don't know if they'll be coming for you, or if they'll just wait till you get in today. But I . . . thought you ought to know."

The man he thought was Rooney said no more.

Lowland Rider

Good old Rooney. He could always count on Rooney. Rooney knew what Montcalm would want to do.

"Okay. Thanks." Montcalm hung up the phone and sat on the edge of the bed for a minute, thinking. Things had ripped. The whole fucking thing had fallen apart on him, the stuffing coming out all over the streets, all over the goddam corruption task force or whoever the hell it was that had gotten Sinclair to shit his pants. It had ripped wide open.

It was all over.

If he had said to hell with the money, if he had just followed that goddam Jesse Gordon to some lonely station somewhere and blown out his goddam brains —*forget* the money—then it would have been all right. His money would have been gone, but so would Gordon.

But he couldn't have done it. He couldn't have killed anyone, not even Gordon, who he hated more than death, more than hell, more than that chickenshit Duke Sinclair who he hoped would be sliced open with a homemade knife the first prison he walked into. No, he couldn't have killed him. Even now, if he'd had Gordon in front of him and a gun in his hands, he couldn't have done it. He'd gotten Sinclair to do it because he couldn't, wasn't man enough, and Sinclair had fucked up, fucked up everything.

Montcalm stood up, pulled on a pair of slacks over the underwear he slept in, and walked into the kitchen. He opened the refrigerator and looked into it, then closed it. He went into the bathroom, brushed his teeth, combed his hair, shaved with an electric razor, and splashed on after-shave lotion when he was done. Back in his bedroom, he finished dressing, loaded a .38 caliber police special with six cartridges, cocked the hammer, and very carefully wedged it into the small of his back, making as certain as possible that nothing would bump the trigger. Then he put on a light jacket and walked out of his apartment, leaving his keys behind.

A soft summer drizzle was falling on the early morning streets, and Montcalm stood in it as he waited for a cab to drive past. He put his hand up to his head, touched the mist that had settled on his hair, and looked at his damp palm as though it were a mirror in which he could see his face. A cab came, and he gave the driver the address of Gina's apartment house. As it pulled away from the curb, Montcalm saw a police car round the corner and come to a stop, double-parked, in front of his building. They wouldn't even give him the grace to come in on his own. Or to go out.

When the cabby let Montcalm off in front of Gina's building ten minutes later, Montcalm gave him seventy dollars, the total amount that was in his wallet. "You serious?" the cabby asked. Montcalm only nodded and walked away, barely hearing the driver's thanks, or the cab as it pulled back into the light traffic.

Without hesitating, he walked into the lobby and pushed the button next to Gina's name. *Gina Montcalm*, he read. There was the heart of it: Gina Montcalm, and the events that had created Gina Montcalm. How did he think he could change her?

Lowland Rider

Could even the house in Pennsylvania have done it? His love hadn't changed her, never could.

Finally he heard her voice, distorted in the tinny speaker. "Who's that?"

"It's me. Bob."

"Bob?"

"Let me in, Gina." There was a brief pause, and then the buzzer sounded at the lock. He pushed the door open and walked in. The Out of Order sign was no longer on the elevator, but he took the stairs, trudging up them slowly, as if he wore heavy weights on his feet. She had the door of her apartment open when he reached the fifth floor, and he smiled when he saw her. Her hair was tousled with sleep, but her eyes were clear. She looked young and innocent, and he loved her.

"What is it, Bob?"

"I had to see you, Gina, that's all. I just had to see you."

"Well . . . come in. You want some coffee?"

"No," he told her, following her in and walking to the couch. The room was a mess, as usual, but it didn't matter to him, and he picked up the magazines on the couch and set them on the coffee table, then fell back onto the cushions with a sigh. It was a nice apartment, he thought.

"Can I . . . can I get you anything?"

He shook his head. "Have you been all right?"

"Yeah. Yeah. The stuff you brought me last time was good, so I cut it a lot. I've still got some left."

"Good. That's good. Come here. Sit down with me." She moved to the couch and sat beside him. He put an arm around her. "You won't need any more."

"Any more . . . heroin?"

"No. We're going away. Finally. You're going to get clean."

"Bob, I . . . I don't think I can."

"Yes, you can. Where we're going. It's a beautiful place, Gina. A little house back in the woods. Not a city for miles and miles. Just clean air and trees and animals. And you and me together."

"Bob . . ."

He hugged her more tightly, and she put her head on his shoulder. "Do you know, Gina, that you're my first?"

It was early, and she was still sleepy. She closed her eyes and listened to his voice, soft and comforting. "Your first?" she whispered.

"Mmm-hmm. It's love that lets you do it, you know. I can do it now, for you. I love you, Gina."

"I know, Bob. I love you."

He shifted slightly, pushing his hips forward so that he could reach the pistol behind his back with his left hand. He removed it quietly and brought it around, holding it down over the side of the couch so that she would not see it. He did not want her to see it, did not want her to know.

"Turn around," he said. "Turn around and put your head in my lap." She sat up, turned, put her legs over the right arm of the couch, and he aimed at the nape of her neck, at the place where the round hardness of the skull ends, and pulled the trigger.

The bullet snapped her head forward for a second,

and he saw the hole it made in the wispy tendrils that covered her neck. An instant later, she fell back with her head on his lap, and he felt the warm blood run from her body, dampening his groin. Her eyes were still open, but he knew they saw nothing.

"You are my first," he told her, in case she could still hear him. "You were always the first, the only thing with me. This is the only way I can get you loose from it now, the only way we can be together."

He thought for a moment that he saw her eyes move, that somehow, somewhere in death she heard him, and was even now waiting for him. A sound came from out in the hall. It might have been a door slamming, but he wasn't sure. He only knew that he didn't have much time left. The sound of shots kept people away in this city, but not forever. Sooner or later someone would come, and he had to leave before then, or the fate he had wished on Sinclair would be his as well—there were too many people in the jails of the state who hated him for him to live longer than a few days, even if he had wanted to. He didn't.

Finally, he thought, he had killed someone. And it made so much sense. She was the only person other than himself that he *could* kill. You had to love someone to kill them, he didn't know why he'd never realized that before. He hoped he could love himself, poor, foolish man that he was, enough to pull the trigger again.

He looked into Gina's wet eyes, and put the barrel of the pistol into his mouth.

Love. It's all because of love.

He pulled the trigger and entered darkness.

And in the darkness, a hundred feet directly beneath where Bob and Gina Montcalm lay, Enoch stood within a tunnel, gazing upward, the only light around him the pale glow which radiated from his perfect face, a face suffused with love.

CHAPTER 30

Rags had been looking for Jesse for hours, ever since he had run from the spur where he had seen Baggie and Enoch together. As he ran, he expected to hear footsteps behind him, growing ever nearer until he was dragged to the stones and . . .

And what? Torn? Devoured? Or something worse? But nothing had happened. He had heard no sound behind him, no laughter, no shrieks of fury. It was as though Enoch had wanted him to see, had wanted him to run and tell someone, to spread the gospel . . .

Now what had brought that idea into his mind, he wondered uncomfortably. Connecting the gospel to the hideous thing he had seen done was the worst kind of blasphemy, and he struggled to get the word out of his mind.

He finally found Jesse at the Times Square station, standing beneath a clock, looking up at it as if he expected it to tell him something more than the time, for of what use was time to skells? "Jesse," Rags panted as he scuttled up to the man, then stopped.

Jesse's eyes were more intense than Rags had ever seen them. There was something else too. If he could have put this Jesse Gordon beside the Jesse Gordon he first met down here months ago, he doubted if he could have told that they were the same man. It was not so much a matter of physical appearance as it was of attitude. The man who stood before him now was a creature of the tunnels, but not a skell. There was none of the secretiveness, the shabbiness, the sense of subservience, of being something less than human, about Jesse Gordon. Rather there was a sense of place, there was purpose, there was mission in the lines of his face, in the set of his shoulders. This was a man who was home, who was where he was always meant to be.

Jesse was no longer wearing a white T-shirt. Instead he had on his black turtleneck. But despite the heat of the station, there were no signs of perspiration on his face. He looked cool and ready and unafraid. He looked, thought Rags, like a Deliverer.

"Jesse," Rags said again.

"What is it, Rags? Is it Enoch?"

How did he know? "Yeah, oh sweet Jesus, it sure is. I seen Baggie, that old woman, she had a baby, Jesse. She took somebody's *baby*, and she *killed* it, she killed it right in front of Enoch, like they done for Baal in the Bible."

"What did you do, Rags?" Jesse's voice was quiet and still.

"What did I *do*?"

"Did you try and stop her?"

"I . . . I didn't know for sure till it was too late. I

seen her on the train and she . . . she had a knife, Jesse."

"Find her, Rags. Take her knife. Stop her."

"Stop her? I can't . . . she got a knife, Jesse."

"This is your chance, Rags. The chance to make up for what you did, why you came down here. Children, Rags. To *save* children."

"Jesse, I . . ."

"You think she'll stop now? You think Enoch will stop, will say that's enough, that's fine, go and kill no more?"

"Jesse . . ."

"Find her, Rags. Stop her."

"You're telling me to kill her."

"Yes."

"But . . . but even if I do, that won't stop Enoch. Somebody else'll do for him, bring him babies."

"I'll stop Enoch."

"You?"

"I'll stop Enoch," Jesse said again.

Rags looked into Jesse's face for a long time before he spoke again. "You been sent, Jesse? That it? You been sent?"

For the first time, Jesse looked down, and a touch of humanity in the form of confusion and uncertainty crossed his face. "Something sent me. Something . . ." He paused, then said, "Walk with me."

It seemed to Rags that they walked hundreds of yards through a honeycomb of tunnels before Jesse spoke again. When he did, his words were slow and measured, as if he had never before dared to think the words, let alone speak them.

"I think I *was* sent, Rags. By what I don't know. Maybe it was by God." He smiled bitterly. "After it happened, I thought there was no God, that there could be no purpose in it, that a god wouldn't let such things happen. But I think I was wrong. There was a purpose. Sit with me."

They sat together on a bench at the end of an uptown platform. Jesse leaned forward, resting his arms on his thighs. His eyes looked at the edge of the platform, but Rags knew he was seeing far more. "Random violence. That's what I couldn't accept, what nobody can really accept. It means an unstructured universe, Rags. It means that there's no reason for anything. Why go on living and struggling when a random act can kill us in an instant? What's the point? But the longer I've been down here, the more I've seen. And the more I've thought about it, the more I see patterns. Reasons. Reasons for everything. And there are reasons we *can't* see, and those are the ones that drive us mad, that make us think the world is a madhouse."

Rags shook his head wearily. "I see what you mean, Jesse, but I don't know what difference it makes. It's just a way of looking at things."

Jesse put a hand on Rags's shoulder. "All life is a way of looking at things. And how we look at things makes us who we are, makes us do what we do."

"But what's the reason for your wife? And for your little girl? For the boy you killed?"

"To bring me down here. Nothing less would have brought me here. But that chain of events—their deaths leading to my killing the boy who tried to help me—that was enough. They were sacrifices, Rags. As horrible as that seems, they were necessary sacrifices to the final purpose."

His eyes were alive now. Rags did not want to ask the question, but he had no choice. "What . . . what's that purpose then?"

"To kill Enoch."

"Jesse . . ."

"The evil that comes from him is unbelievable, Rags. I don't know what hold he has over people, but I do know it's incredibly strong. You've just seen it with Baggie, and I've seen it several times. These tunnels stink with his power."

"It ain't no earthly power, Jesse," Rags said.

"I don't know about that, Rags, but if it isn't, then no earthly power sent me down here to deal with him."

"How you gonna find him, Jesse?"

"I can find him. I can do whatever it is that I have to do. And so can you, Rags. Find Baggie. Stop her. With whatever it takes. Bring me the knife."

"Jesse . . ."

"Rags," Jesse said, laying a hand on his friend's shoulder, "You're going to die soon. Nothing is going to stop that from happening. That growth is going to kill you. If you stop Baggie, that will mean something. It's good you're doing, Rags. Good."

Rags began to raise a hand to his neck, but stopped before he touched the hard swelling beneath the cloths. The hand closed into a fist. "I'd be doing . . good?"

"Yes, Rags. Good. Go. Stop her. I'll find Enoch." Jesse walked away.

Rags looked down at his feet. Jesse's words had hurt him, but in a strange way they had also given him hope. Maybe, he thought, Jesse was right. Maybe the way for Rags to redeem himself was to kill Baggie, just as Jesse wanted to redeem himself by killing Enoch.

All right then. All right. If he was going to die, he had nothing to lose. He'd find her then. He'd find Baggie. One thing was sure—it would be a damn sight easier dealing with her than dealing with Enoch. Baggie could take your life, but Rags was all too certain that Enoch could take your soul.

CHAPTER 31

Enoch. She heard the name echo over and over in her mind. She saw His face before her, filled with love and peace and satisfaction, and she knew that she loved Him too, and that what had passed between them would last her the rest of her life, even if she was never to see Him again.

But she would see Him again. She had brought Him her sacrifice, and He had loved her for it, and she had told Him that there would be more, she would not make Him *ask* for more, oh no, never make Enoch ask again. Now she knew all, now she was one of the blessed, and she looked around her at the teeming thousands who scurried through the tunnels, and knew that they were there whenever she needed them. They were ready for the harvest, ready for Enoch. All she had to do was pick them.

She carried no bags now, nothing but the clothes on her back and the knife buried deep in her pocket, and the ruby that He had given her, that stone as large as the baby's fist, red as the baby's blood. He told her to do what she would with it—sell it and use the money to live on if she liked. But she would never do that. Sell a gift from Enoch? It was unthinkable. She would keep it always, and take it from her pockets when no one was looking, stare into its red depths, and see Enoch's face. That was all she wanted from life now.

To see Enoch's face.

CHAPTER 32

"Son of a *bitch*!" Tony Rodriguez said in English. He had just woken up and flicked on the color TV at the foot of the bed to see a black and white photo of Bob Montcalm on the noon news. Angelina, his most recent lady, was singing a salsa song at the dressing table. "Shut up," he told her in Spanish, and she did, allowing him to hear the rest of the story. When it was over, Rodriguez hit the remote and turned the set off. "Son of a bitch," he said again, more quietly.

"What's wrong?" Angelina asked in Spanish. Her English was poor.

"Guy I know. Transit cop I paid to let me do business on his line. He killed himself this morning. Something about the murder of a janitor. Now what the fuck . . ." he added in English, shaking his head.

"I bet there was a woman," Angelina said, straightening the straps of her filmy nightgown and cupping her breasts.

"What?"

"A woman. Men always kill themselves over a woman."

Rodriguez frowned, feeling himself grow semierect and wondering if maybe they had time to do it again before he hit the street. "Yeah, there was a woman all right. His wife. He shot her too."

"Ah," Angelina said, crossing to the bed and smiling at the bump Rodriguez's spiky penis made under the sheet. "You see? She was cheating on him. Was she beautiful, I wonder?"

"All I know about her was that she was a junkie. I used to give him heroin for her." He reached up and touched a breast. Angelina slid onto the bed and licked his neck.

"And he killed her for love," she said, grasping his penis through the sheet.

"He didn't kill her," Rodriguez said, unmoving. "He . . . paralyzed her."

"What?"

"She can't move, can't speak."

"Poor woman," Angelina said, pulling her nightgown over her head and slipping between the sheets. After a minute of working on him, she looked up, a child's petulant frown on her sixteen-year-old face. "What's wrong?" she asked him.

"I was just thinking," Rodriguez said, looking at the ceiling, "about what she will feel when that first craving hits her. Mother of God, what will she feel?"

His lust was gone. He got dressed and went out onto the street, hoping that the dead man had not mentioned him in any notes, looking for new territories, thinking of tortured Gina Montcalm, hearing her silent screams.

CHAPTER 33

It was rush hour when Rags found Baggie in the 66th Street IRT station. She was standing against a wall, watching the people pass. There was none of the misanthropy that had previously sat on her face like a cloud. She seemed, Rags thought, to be enjoying herself, like a patron of an outdoor cafe, sipping a drink and watching the people pass, in love with life and the city. If her appearance had not been unmistakable, he might have thought she was a different woman.

Everyone was changing—first Jesse, now Baggie, and even himself. Was he really going to kill this woman in cold blood? Even as he asked himself the question, he knew that he was. And why? Because Jesse had told him to do so. And didn't that make him the same as Baggie, with her blind obedience to Enoch?

No. He didn't think so. There was a difference. He was killing something evil to stop the evil from killing more good. That had been done before, in the Bible. God's people had destroyed the people who were evil.

But Rags, said a voice within him, who made you one of God's people?

Jesse did, he answered. Jesse did, and he's enough.

He didn't know how he was going to kill her. He had no weapon, and, though he was big and strong enough to kill her with his hands, he did not know how he could do that with all these people around. Then the thought occurred to him that it worked both ways. How could she do anything to him?

He moved toward her through the crowd, and was soon close enough to reach out and touch her. "Hey," he said, and she turned and looked at him. Her eyes narrowed, but there was none of the hatred that she had shown whenever she had seen him before. There was rather a bland curiosity, and she cocked her head and looked at him as though she recognized him as an old acquaintance, but couldn't be sure, and was afraid of getting his name wrong.

"I wanta see you," Rags said, and she cocked her head to the other side. What the hell, Rags wondered. Had she gone simple? Like a kid? "You hear me? I wanta see you."

She turned away from him then and walked off. He followed her through the milling mob, pushing aside the owners of the thigh-high forest of briefcases and handbags that struck at him. Baggie didn't look back to see if he was coming, but plowed ahead, her arms hidden by her body and the throng.

At last, near the turnstiles, the crowd began to thin, and he was able to get close to her again. But she walked faster, toward a short passage he had never been down before, with gray, unmarked, closed doors

Lowland Rider

on either side. "You wait a minute," he said, and put out his hand, grabbed her shoulder.

She whirled on him, and he saw that the fury had returned to her face. It was alight with hate as she swung her knife in a savage backhand across his throat.

The rags saved him. He felt a coldness beneath his chin, a sudden shock, but no pain, and he realized that although the knife had cut him, it was now tangled in the layers of cloth that wrapped his neck, and Baggie was tugging at it frantically, the exertion spraying a fine mist of spittle into Rags's face.

He brought up his arm and shoved her backward so that she stumbled, losing the grip on the knife. Rags wrenched it from the cloths with his right hand and pressed his throat with the other. He felt wetness, but did not look at his hand. His eyes were on Baggie.

She started to growl, a low, bubbling roar that sounded more to Rags like the approach of a faraway train than anything from a human throat. And, like a train, she came at him, hands in front of her, her white, twiglike fingers crooked into claws to tear his eyes. He thrust out the knife and caught her on it.

The breath left her in a cloud of blood as Rags's hands, pushed by rock-hard arms, sank into the wound the knife had made and pressed through the woman's ripped flesh, which bathed his forearms in red warmth. Her arms fell to her side, her head rocked back, and the two of them stood there, the man holding the woman in a dance of death. At last he drew a shuddering breath and stepped back, but she fell against him, as if reluctant to break their embrace.

He yanked his arms away, leaving the knife deep within the cavern of her torso, and the body fell to the floor with a soft, wet sound. He looked at it for a long time, unable to believe that anything that alive with hatred could die so easily.

But there was no motion, not even the twitch of a finger. Rags raised a hand to his neck and felt where the knife had scored his skin, cutting into the edge of the tumor. He looked at his fingers and saw a darkness deeper than blood.

He was just about to make himself turn, walk away, and seek some help when he remembered Jesse's admonition to bring him the knife. At first he intended to ignore it. Jesse didn't need it, it would prove nothing. But the more he thought, the more he felt that he should do what Jesse asked. So he knelt by the side of the body, and was trying to work up enough nerve to roll it over and look at the ruin he had made, when he heard the gray door behind him open.

He did not turn immediately, for he knew who was standing there, but he realized he could not outwait Enoch, and turned slowly, still on his knees, feeling weak and vulnerable despite the killing he had just done.

Enoch stood framed by the doorway, a blaze of white light against the utter blackness of the room out of which he had come. It did not occur to Rags to wonder why he was here, how he had come to step out of this particular room in this particular station hall. As Rags gazed into those clear eyes, it seemed the most natural thing in the world for Enoch to be here.

"What is it you want?" Enoch asked, and Rags did

Lowland Rider

wonder why he didn't see Enoch's mouth moving, although he heard clearly enough.

"I . . . I wanted the knife." His words sounded small to him, like a child's.

Enoch smiled at him as if he were indeed a child, and knelt next to Rags so that his warm and fragrant breath coursed in a gentle zephyr over Rags's face. "There is no knife," he said, and with surprisingly little effort pushed the body over so that Rags could see the seamless dress, the whole body, free of blood, still, but untouched by any tearing knife. "She died for love."

Enoch leaned over and kissed the woman's face, then straightened up and slowly extended a long-fingered hand toward Rags. The hand touched the cloths around his neck, paused there, then withdrew, the fingers spotless, unstained.

"*Live* for love," Enoch told him, and Rags knew without touching the spot that the bleeding had stopped, and his wound was healed.

Rags began to cry as he had not cried since he was a child. When the tears went away enough to allow him to see again, Enoch was gone. There was only him and Baggie, both of them whole, unmarked by knives, at the end of a short hall with many closed doors.

CHAPTER 34

Claudia looked at her watch. It read nine o'clock, and she wondered where Jesse was. Every other time she had met him he had been there before she arrived, waiting for her. But he was nowhere to be seen now, and it puzzled her. When she had asked him why he always got to their appointments first, he had told her it was because he didn't like her standing around alone in the tunnels, and then had smiled and added, "Besides, what else do I have to do with my time?" If what she thought about him was true, he had a great many other things to do.

She was doubly impatient for him to arrive, because she had news for him. She had heard all about Robert Montcalm's suicide on the evening news, and when the announcer said that Virgil Sinclair, Montcalm's alleged accomplice in whatever the hell they'd been doing, had also accused one Antonio Rodriguez, now in custody, of being involved in drug trafficking, Claudia fit the pieces together instantly. It had been this Montcalm who Jesse had stolen the money from. But now he was dead, and proven to be crooked

Lowland Rider

besides. So there was no reason that Jesse should not be able to come above to tell his story, to rejoin the human race, and she continued to look around for him anxiously. After all, there was no telling what else might happen once Jesse returned to a state of normality.

There were few people in the 86th Street station. It seemed to her that, except for rush hour, the trains were less populated than they used to be. Fear, she thought, although she realized with some surprise that she felt none. She supposed it was because of Jesse, and the fact that he was always around when she descended into the system, so that now, even when she was alone, she still felt safe, as though part of him were still with her, as though his courage and determination had rubbed off on her.

It was an apt description, Claudia thought. A great deal of Jesse had rubbed off on her. She found herself thinking of him constantly, and since she could not be with him as often as she wanted, she sublimated her desire for his company by writing about him. Her piece on him had grown over the past few weeks to eighty pages, and she toyed with the idea of expanding it to book length. It would be far too long for an article in *Manhattan*, unless Julia serialized it. It could be a book. An honest-to-God original *book*.

If Jesse agreed. Only if Jesse agreed.

She never wanted to do him any harm, or cause him any more pain. She respected him more than she had ever respected any man because of the way he had come back from his loss to do what he had done, no matter how bizarre his reasons. Their affair of years before was repeatedly on her mind, and she tried over and over to remember why it had ended. He had been an ardent and skillful lover, and they had been happy together. The only thing she could recall about the breakup was that outside the bedroom she had found him too unexciting.

Too unexciting. Jesus. He sure as hell was exciting enough for her now, even frightening, when she thought about it.

Yes, although the tunnels no longer scared her, she *was* frightened of him, just a little. There was something alien about him, something that she knew she would never understand, no matter how long she knew him, or how much he told her, or how close they might become.

She looked at her watch again, and hoped he would not keep her waiting too long.

CHAPTER
35

"Jesse," Rags panted. "Stop. Stop a minute."

Jesse turned and saw Rags limping toward him, his face the color of wet ashes. "Rags."

"It's done. She's dead."

"Baggie."

"Yeah. I killed her. But I didn't somehow, I don't understand it at all . . ."

"The knife."

"Wasn't no knife. I don't know what happened to it, maybe Enoch took it, I—"

"Enoch? He was there?"

"Oh Jesus God, yes, he was there. And I stabbed her, and she cut me, but my neck . . ." He fumbled at the rags, pulling them away from his skin, showing Jesse the intact tumor. ". . . there's no cut now. I was bleeding bad, but he touched me, and there's no *cut*."

Jesse's eyes narrowed, and he looked at Rags as though he were something even more unclean than he was. "Where is he? Enoch?"

"Up 66th Street. IRT. But it don't matter where, Jesse. I think he's anywhere, anywhere he wants to be.

He want you to find him, you find him—he not want you to, you won't."

Jesse whirled around and started toward the tracks. "Where you going?" Rags called, hurrying after him.

"I have to meet Claudia. I'm late," he said. "Then I'll see Enoch. For the last time."

Rags stopped and watched Jesse walk away. He almost called out for him to stop, to come back, to let Enoch alone, but it was as though something locked in his throat and stopped him from saying it. Instead he put a hand to his throat and felt the whiskery and wrinkled flesh, the hard egg of the tumor, searched again for a scar, a scab, a slash that he knew had to be there, but which he could not find.

CHAPTER 36

"Hey hey hey, pretty lady. You waiting for something?"

"Waitin' for us."

"Well, man, she's found us, haven't you, darlin'?"

They were not young. They were no possessors of that fresh, boyish bravado that could be humored, then intimidated, and eventually dismissed, leaving only filthy words and a few obscene gestures in their wake. These two men frightened Claudia, as they would have frightened anyone standing alone at night on an empty subway platform. They were big and brawny and ugly, their arms slathered with obscene tattoos. The larger of the men, the more outspoken one, wore a stained cowboy hat with a multicolored arrangement of feathers that would have looked more at home on a trout fly. They both wore tank tops that showed off their backs and shoulders, which were matted with dark hair. White men of no apparent ethnic origin, they constituted their own distasteful minority.

"I'm waiting for someone else," Claudia told them coldly, wishing she could turn away from them and yet hesitant to do so, afraid that they would touch her from behind.

"No, you ain't," said the first man. "You're waiting for us. This is Al, and I'm Roy. And what's your name."

She turned her back and looked toward the tracks, but Roy slowly moved around with her, like a storm cloud that refuses to blow away. "I don't mean to be rude," she said, afraid to offend him, "but I really am meeting a friend here."

"Lady friend?"

"A man friend. He'll be here any minute."

"So will Christmas. But I ain't shopping for presents yet, y'know?" Al chuckled behind her. "You want a present?"

"No. Thank you."

"You like to watch movies?"

She shook her head and looked down at the ground, praying for Jesse to get there.

"Aw, that's too bad. Al and I got lots of movies. We make 'em. Video movies. We sell 'em too. Get good money. See here?" He held out a fist and Claudia recoiled, but then saw that he was showing her a ring on his index finger. She didn't know if the diamond was real, but it looked as though it might be. It was large, and sparkled nearly green in the station light. "Bought that with what we made. Don't make many copies either. Be surprised what people pay for certain kinds of things. Things they can't see anywhere else, or if they do, they're fake. We don't fake 'em. They're real."

Claudia felt like throwing up and crying at the same time. She didn't know if they were liars or if they were telling the truth. She knew such people existed, but never expected to meet them, to be here now talking with them, alone. Except for the three of them, the station was as empty as the moon.

The only thing she could do was walk away and hope they didn't follow her or try to stop her. So she started to move between the pair of them toward the exit, but the one called Al grabbed her left arm. "Uh-uh," he said. "Goin' with us."

She gave a scornful laugh that she did not feel. "I'm not going *anywhere* with you."

Roy grasped her other arm, and she winced from the pain. His fingers felt like hooks, and she smelled garlic on his breath, stale and sour. "That's just because you weren't invited yet. They like to be invited, Al, you know that. Now listen. Darlin', wouldn't you like to come along with us and make a movie? Be a movie star?"

"Let me go," she told them through gritted teeth.

"Darlin'," Roy went on, "didn't you hear me right?" He reached inside his belt and drew a knife from a hidden sheath. The blade was five inches long and looked like a machete to Claudia. The handle was made from a deer's hoof. "You been invited."

"What . . . do you mean you're going to take me somewhere?"

"Uptown. Way uptown to Tremont Avenue. Where

we have our studio. Where we'll make you a star, darlin'."

"And how the fuck do you expect to get me there?"

"Whoo, nice mouth on you. We can *do* some things with that mouth. Why, we're goin' up on the train, darlin'. Trains aren't too busy this time of night."

"All it takes is one person," she told him. "All I have to do is yell."

"And all I have to do is stick this in you. I'd enjoy that just as much here as stickin' something else in you uptown."

She couldn't believe what he was saying. It seemed impossible. Everything seemed wrong, a dream, a nightmare. She tried to reason logically. "If I go with you, you'll kill me up there anyway, won't you? You'll kill me, and tape it. *Won't* you?"

"You can't be sure of that, darlin'. Hell, *we're* never sure what we're gonna do till we start to, you know, *improvise*. But you can be sure of one thing, and that's that if you *don't* come along, or you try to make a fuss, then you're dead for sure."

She choked back a sob. "Why?" she asked everything.

"We just like your looks," Roy said. "I mean, honey, you are just *right*. And you happen to be in the right place at the right time. Just like Lana Turner in that soda shop."

A train came, but it was a local. "Next one," said Roy. "We're waiting for the express, sugar. The Sugarland Express. That was a movie too. And we'll get on it real quiet and go uptown to Sugarland."

Claudia kept waiting for Jesse, kept praying that the

Lowland Rider

express would never come, but it pulled into the station only several minutes after the local. Roy and Al marched her down the platform until they saw that the last car was empty, hurried her into it and forced her down on a seat between them. Al started to rub her breasts, but Roy pushed his hand away. "Keep it in your pants, boy. We don't wanta mark the merchandise before we shoot it, do we? Plenty of time for squeezin' later. You can pretend her tits're lemons and you're makin' juice if you want, but wait till the fucking camera's rolling, boy."

When the doors slammed shut, Claudia felt as though they were slamming shut on her life. The only thing that could save her now was a policeman, and even that was not certain. If she cried for help, these men might be crazy enough to kill her anyway, or keep her alive and kill whoever she tried to get to help her. They might have guns, for all she knew. And she was sure that they were insane.

The train seemed to boil along forever before it made its next stop at 125th Street, where two rangy, black teenagers got on their car. They sat across from Claudia and the two men, but near the front, so that twenty feet separated them. The train pulled out again, and Claudia decided that this was her only chance, that she had to do something, anything, to avoid being led like a sheep to these madmen's slaughter. She looked at the boys and said, "Excuse me."

Roy and Al jerked their heads toward her in warning, and Roy hissed, "Shut *up*, bitch . . ." The boys had turned and were looking at her curiously, though they said nothing. Roy snapped his glare back toward them.

"What?" one of the boys asked with barely disguised hostility.

"Nothing," Roy snarled.

"I wasn't askin' you," the boy said.

"I'm telling you. Mind your own business."

Claudia's mind raced. This was her chance to start something, something to take their attention away from her for a moment, long enough for her to try to run. She didn't know where, but anywhere was better than this car, between these two men. So she said, as viciously as she could, "Stupid niggers!"

The boys bristled, and one of them got to his feet. Roy and Al were both looking at her, surprised by what she'd said, and too obtuse to realize what she was doing.

"Mind your own business, you black bastards," Claudia added venomously. "You mess with my friends here, they'll cut you up!"

Slowly awareness grew on Roy's face. "You little cu—"

He never finished the word, for the boys were on them, fists swinging. Claudia screamed, and threw herself on the floor and under a seat as one of the boys lashed a vicious fist at her, but Roy got between them and stuck the knife in the boy's belly. Claudia heard the crash of metal against metal, as the boy gave a choking cry and fell away. Al had tackled the second boy, and was on the floor with him, smashing his head against the green and yellow tile. She looked up at Roy, expecting to see him coming toward her with the bloody knife, to finish her before she had time to jump up and run into the next car.

But Roy was staring at something, staring with wide eyes toward the end of the car where no one had been, and suddenly she heard a loud explosion and saw a flower of blood bloom on Roy's face, directly under his right eye. Roy's knife fell from his hand. He sat down, then slumped over onto the seat and didn't move again, except for some spasmodic shaking that might have been caused by the motion of the train.

Al was still pounding the boy's head against the floor, but Claudia noticed that the sound it made had gone from hard and sharp to wet and soft. There was another explosion, and part of Al's skull and hair leaped from the top of his head and skittered off along the floor. Al fell on top of the boy like a spent lover.

It was very quiet in the car.

Claudia lay beneath the seat, hardly daring to breath. She heard footsteps cross the floor, and saw a shod foot come down inches from her face. Someone said, "Claudia?"

A moan of ultimate relief escaped her. "Jesse," she said, and saw the legs kneel, the strong face she knew so well look into hers.

He stuck his pistol back into the waistband of his jeans and tugged his turtleneck down over it, then helped her out from under the seat, and sat with her, an arm around her shoulders. "Are you all right?" he asked.

She looked on the floor of the car at the shattered bodies of Roy and Al, and nodded. "They were going to . . ." She swallowed heavily.

"They're not going to do anything now," he said. "I saw them take you on the train. I grabbed it just as it left, hung on to the back door until it stopped. Then I got in the car ahead of this one. I was watching you through the window. When those kids jumped them I came in."

"The . . . the boys," Claudia said. "Are they . . .?"

"They're both dead." Jesse replied. "They're all dead, and we've got to get off at the next stop. Come on."

He took her hand and led her through several cars until they were in the one next to the front. When the train stopped at 145th Street, they got off. Jesse paused to see if anyone got into the last car, but no one did, and the train pulled out with its burden of death. They stood on the platform and watched it go. She was with him now, and everything seemed safe again. To her amazement, the whole experience had been placed in the back of her mind, as if it were something that had happened months, even years before. The shots, the knife, the blood, all seemed a dream that was over.

"I wanted to tell you," Claudia said, "about Montcalm."

"Montcalm," he said. "Then you know."

She nodded. "On the news. He's dead." She told him about the news stories, about Sinclair and Rodriguez. "They killed the wrong man, didn't they? They wanted to kill you." His silence told her that she was right. "Isn't that enough then?" she asked him desperately.

"Enough? Enough for what?"

Lowland Rider

"To make you come back up, come above again. It's over, Jesse. Can't you see, you've won, he's dead. What you wanted to do down here, you've done. You've done good, but you've done enough. You could stay down here forever and it would never be clean. Haven't you done enough?"

Jesse looked at her for a long time. "One more thing," he said. "Just one. And then I'll come back up. Montcalm may be dead, but I'm not finished here yet."

"Oh God, Jesse, when?"

"Tonight. After tonight. I'll finish it, and I'll come above in the morning."

He would answer no more questions. He rode downtown with her and walked her as far as the stairway that led to 86th Street, then held her as a priest might hold a grieving widow.

"In the morning," he told her again. He turned away when she tried to kiss him, and walked back into the tunnels.

CHAPTER
37

He's anywhere, anywhere he wants to be. He want you to find him, you find him . . .

Rags's words came back to Jesse as he stepped off the stairs and onto the platform. He wanted to find Enoch, but did Enoch want to be found? It didn't matter. He would find him if he had to search every tunnel, every hidden spur, every closed and abandoned station on the hundreds of miles of line. But somehow he felt that he wouldn't have to do that, that Enoch would know, and would rise to the challenge.

It was after midnight now, and the station was deserted. That surprised Jesse. Even on a Tuesday night the Upper West Side was a center of activity long into the morning. Yet there was no one here, no one except Jesse.

But when he looked down at the end of the platform he realized he was wrong. There was someone else standing down there, someone in the shadows. At first Jesse thought that there was a small light from overhead shining on the figure, but then he realized that the light was coming from the figure itself, and Jesse

Lowland Rider

began to walk toward it, knowing who it was even before the man turned so that Jesse could see his face.

Enoch was all in white, a white that blazed with brightness. His face was aglow and smiling, and his hands hung empty at his sides. When Jesse stopped walking, only six feet separated them.

"Hello, Jesse," Enoch said. "I'm glad you've come. I've been waiting for you."

His voice was like doves cooing in barn rafters. Jesse could smell the sweetness of hay, the sharp odor of fresh rain on grass, and exhaled sharply to drive the hypnotic scent from him. He would not be seduced. "I'd have found you," he said, "whether you waited or not."

Enoch nodded. "You would have."

"You know that I'm going to kill you."

"I know you bring my end. My necessary end."

Jesse took the pistol from his waistband. There were still four bullets left. "You are this place's heart," Jesse said. "You are the heart of evil, maybe of all the evil in this city, I don't know. It wasn't Baggie, it wasn't Montcalm, all they did was for you."

"That is true," Enoch said. "Baggie knew it, Montcalm did not. But still, it was for me. And for you."

Now it was Jesse's turn to smile. "For me? Father of Lies, isn't that what they call the devil? You're a poor devil, Enoch, but the only true one this place has. I don't know how you use people, how you twist them to do these things for you, but you do. If it was for money, I could understand it. Not condone it, but understand. But it isn't for money, is it?"

"No. It isn't for money."

"Fine." Jesse nodded. "Then maybe you'll understand that I'm not doing *this* for money. I'm doing this—"

"You're doing this," Enoch gently interrupted, "so that your life has meaning."

Jesse smiled a wry and bitter smile. "Maybe. And maybe so that some other deaths had meaning." Jesse brought up the pistol and pointed it at Enoch.

"And that too is true. Your wife and daughter had to die."

"My . . . my . . . how did you . . ." A red tide crossed Jesse's vision.

"Donna," Enoch said. "Jennifer. It was necessary."

"You *bastard*!" Jesse shrieked, and pulled the trigger.

He fired twice into Enoch's chest at point-blank range, but Enoch did not move, did not flinch. Jesse stepped closer, aimed the gun at Enoch's face, fired again, and Enoch did not move. He pressed the gun against Enoch's temple and pulled the trigger for the last time. The gun recoiled in his hand, and it seemed as though Enoch's flesh parted to receive the lead, then closed up again, clean and whole.

Jesse sobbed convulsively, and the gun dropped from his hand. He began to hammer his fists against Enoch, crying as he did, but Enoch stood like rock, immovable, his flesh unyielding. Jesse pounded his fists against skin more solid than steel, putting every ounce of effort he possessed into this all-encompassing need to destroy this man, this creature, this thing.

And slowly his muscles weakened, his will subsided,

his hatred was drained by exhaustion until he fell against the very being he longed so to annihilate, and he felt Enoch's arms around him, no longer arms of stone, but of flesh, comforting him as he wept.

He looked up into Enoch's face, and saw there all the things he had hoped he would not—caring, sympathy, and a trace of sadness. "What . . . are you?" Jesse asked.

"I am the Axis."

"The . . . the what?"

"The Axis. The pivot, the balance."

"The balance," Jesse said, remembering his own words spoken what seemed like centuries before. "The balance. Between what?"

"Between good and evil," Enoch answered.

"But . . . you *are* evil!"

Enoch smiled, his face full of love, and shook his head. "You do not know what evil is. But you have begun to learn."

Jesse's legs gave out, and he slumped to the cold concrete, his arms wrapped around Enoch's legs. Enoch knelt and sat beside him, holding him again. "Jesse, there *was* purpose," Enoch said. "What happened to you was ordained. But not to bring you down here to kill me. It was to bring you down here to *speak* to me. Not like the others spoke to me and served me, for you are not *like* the others. You came here to be tempered, to be tried in the furnace, to be turned to stone . . .

"To be *apotheosized*."

Jesse had not heard the word in years, and its meaning was nearly lost to him. He looked up, his face streaked with tears. "I don't know what you're talking about. I don't know what you mean!"

"I mean that you will take my place."

Jesse's body trembled as though a train had crashed out of the darkness beside them. But there was no train, there were no people, and there would be none, Jesse knew, until Enoch willed it so. Jesse could not speak. He was afraid to.

"We were all men once," Enoch said, "until we were chosen to be more than men, and we were afraid, just as you are. But when we understood, when we knew, we made our choice, as you will make yours." Enoch paused. "It is the only choice you can make."

"Then," Jesse said in a voice pinched with ignorance, "it's really not a choice at all, is it?"

"When you know," Enoch said, "then it will be the only choice you can make."

"The Axis, you said," Jesse went on weakly. "What does it mean? What is this . . . *balance*?"

"Good and evil, Jesse. We feed the evil so the good can survive. We're God's servants. We do His will."

"Feed evil? I've seen *how*, oh Christ, have I seen. But *why*?"

"Because if it was not fed, if it was not satisfied, held at bay, it would overcome the world."

Jesse pushed away from Enoch's embrace, and Enoch let him go. He crawled several feet away, then said, "I don't believe this. I can't."

"You've seen the power I hold. It comes from God. How else can you explain it?"

"I don't *believe* it!" Jesse shouted. "I see what you do, but I still don't believe it! It doesn't make sense!

Holding evil at bay? That's bullshit! This *is* evil, this place, the things people *do* here, good *Christ*, what greater evil could stalk the world than what I've already *seen*?"

"If I show you—"

"Oh *yes*!" Jesse shouted, pushing himself to his knees. "Oh, by all means, *show* me, Enoch!" He laughed brokenly. "You just show me if you can!"

Enoch stood effortlessly. "Close your eyes then. And see."

Jesse laughed again, the flat, barking laugh of a man close to madness, the laugh of a man who fears no longer. He laughed, and then pressed his eyes closed, a wide, white grin slashed across his face.

And he saw.

He saw the blade of a knife sliding down the front of a body, and skin and breasts laid back like a leather shirt, and arms slipping in under the skin and embracing the living viscera, and wet, red organs slapping against flesh,

saw a young boy with hair the color of honey and skin the color of milk held over a velvet chair, a line of naked, laughing men behind him, each taking their turn, fat, dripping, black candles in their free hands,

saw an old woman hanging by her neck from a rope, her sister, a white-haired and wrinkled crone, jerking on her legs so that the neck stretched, the rope dug under and broke the jaw, the blood pumped from the dead woman's nose, bathing the grinning sister,

saw a soldier in a room full of bound men, castrating each one, then slicing each across the eyes with the same razor, saw priests and nuns drinking each other's vomit, rolling in each other's filth while they prayed the Our Father,

saw a mountain of dead women rotting in the sun, while their children played about them, throwing balls and sticks onto the pile for dogs to fetch, urinating on the faces of their mothers' corpses,

saw limbs and heads hewn off in joy,

saw babies raped and smashed on stones,

saw the wombs of pregnant women sewn up,

saw flesh ripped open and fire forced in the rents,

saw agonies and abnormalities and sicknesses, and founders of plagues and murders thousandfold, and curses and abominations and blasphemies, and excremental baptisms and the incestuous births of monsters and tortures unimagined, and cannibalism and self-mutilation and semen splashed on crosses, and hatred and terror and blood, always blood, drowning everything he saw in red rain.

He saw.

And what he saw drove him beyond fear, beyond nausea, beyond repulsion. What he saw, so much evil compressed into an instant of understanding, took away his words, refused to even allow him to think, to correlate that multitude of sights into one unforgivable whole.

He opened his eyes, and saw Enoch, and Enoch was no longer smiling. On his face was the expression of the crucified Christ. "What..." Jesse whispered, "...what could be..."

"No, Jesse," he said. "Not what *could* be. What you saw was what *exists*, and what has existed. What walks the earth now. I have not yet shown you evil's true face, evil set free. I have not shown you the ultimate potential of evil, the evil that would become reality if not for me, for you, for those like us."

Show me then, Jesse thought. *Madden me. Mold me.*

Enoch heard, nodded, closed his eyes, and Jesse closed his own.

Again, Jesse saw. Nothing was held back, or seen through a dark glass.

This time, he saw everything.

Everything.

When Jesse opened his eyes, Enoch's face was bright with tears. "You see now," Enoch said. "You see what the balance preserves. You see what would otherwise come to pass."

"The death of love."

Enoch nodded. "The death of any love."

Jesse shook his head. "I can't," he said. "I'm afraid. I can't do what you've done. I couldn't. All those deaths . . ."

"You can. You have. You have killed, and today you sent a kind and simple man to murder an insane old woman."

"But how . . ." Jesse choked on the words. "Even if I agreed, how could I do those things? How could I bear to be around those people, those hateful people?"

"Do not hate them, but learn to love them, and they will love you. And serve you. And when your time is finished you will be *full* of love, too full of love to go on, too full of love to stay here anymore."

Jesse ached with the need to understand. "But how

can you feel such love, and still . . . condone this . . . *demand* these . . . atrocities?"

"You do what you must."

"But how can you do it . . . and not feel . . . pain?"

"You can't."

"Oh God . . ." Jesse said softly.

"Imagine my agony," Enoch said, "when I think of theirs. And that same agony will be yours. But you have the strength to bear it. And the strength to make the others serve you. To feed the evil. To keep it below."

"But the *balance* . . ." Jesse said desperately. "You spoke of yourself—and of me, if I take your place—as part of the *balance*. If there is evil, then mustn't there be good? Am I . . . are *we* . . . ordained to do only evil? Will I just be a butcher, a feeder of beasts in some metaphysical zoo? How can I *do* that? How could anyone?"

"You will find your way," Enoch said kindly, then smiled. "There may be more than one."

"Enoch . . . I don't think I can."

"You will. You are already a legend. Now you must become more."

Jesse, on his feet at last, nodded slowly, painfully. "But how? How, Enoch?"

"For that, there is only one way. There was ever only one way."

The whiteness around Enoch began to glow brighter, blinding Jesse, and when he could see once more, Enoch was gone.

But Jesse was no longer alone in the tunnel. Other people stood nearby, waiting for trains, the usual late

Lowland Rider

night assortment, kids, night workers, people who liked the night.

And now a train was coming. It was the IND local, roaring into the station. Jesse heard the rumble of the steel wheels, saw the light growing out of the darkness, the light that presaged the one way of which Enoch had spoken.

A few people saw him move toward the tracks as the train drew nearer, watched him cross the yellow line and stand so that his toes touched the knife-edge of the platform. A woman divined Jesse's intention first, and her cry alerted others, so that over a dozen people saw what happened.

Jesse waited until the train was several yards from where he stood at the platform's edge. He closed his eyes, leaned forward, bit back fear, and despite the roar of the wheels, the glare of the golden eye of the engine that filled the station like the eye of God, Jesse slept.

And Jesse fell.

PART 5

So Jamie Gordon, cursed by God,
Or blest, as some do tell,
Became Death's trusty harbinger,
Who doth man's fate foretell.

And when ye ride the low country,
Gae fast, and nae by night,
Else ye may spy the Gordon bold,
Who causes men to fright.

And if the Gordon cross your path
Your life is at an end.
He hath nae mercy nor nae love,
And nae man is his friend.

For he must ride the lowland dark
Till time itself may cease.
Ne'er Heav'n above nor Hell below
Gie Jamie Gordon peace.

—*Jamie Gordon, the Lowland Rider*

CHAPTER 38

MAN FALLS FROM SUBWAY PLATFORM
Several witnesses saw a man fall in front of an IND downtown local train in the 86th Street station early this morning. The man was identified as Enoch Soames, 33, a Haitian political refugee who had been missing for three years. Soames came to the United States after the deaths of several members of his family in former Haitian President Duvalier's prisons, and disappeared shortly thereafter.

There is some confusion among witnesses, all of whom reported seeing a man dressed in a dark sweater and pants falling in front of the oncoming train, while the victim was found to be wearing white clothing. . . .

—*New York Post*, July 21, 1987

Claudia Dorner found Rags three days after she read the newspaper stories. He was eating a hot dog at the 59th Street station. Although at first she thought he was going to walk away from her, he remained seated on the bench, and moved over slightly to allow her to sit beside him. "Is he dead, Rags?" she asked him.

Rags nodded. "He's dead. He fell in front of that train."

"But it wasn't his body. The papers said—"

"I don't care what no papers said. Fella I know was there, fella named Sam. He saw Jesse, knew Jesse to see him. He said he saw Jesse fall in front of that train. Don't care what they pulled off the tracks, but it was Jesse fell in front of that train."

"But the clothing, and what was in the wallet . . ."

"None of that matters. Jesse's gone."

She stood up. "All right. I just had to be sure."

He looked at the last bite of hot dog, sighed, and held it in his hand. "You gonna write about him now?"

She shook her head. "How can I write a story without an ending?"

Rags watched her for a moment. "He liked you, I think."

"I liked him. I liked him very much." Claudia brushed a stray wisp of hair back from her forehead. "How about you, Rags? Ever coming back up?"

"No." Rags shook his head, and Claudia saw him wince, and noticed that his head was cocked even further to the side than when she had seen him before. "Not goin' up. Not goin' up no more."

She nodded, raised a hand in farewell, and walked back up into the sunlight that seemed unaccountably

Lowland Rider

cold, and the air that smelled stagnant, like damp, endless tunnels.

Two weeks later Rags was riding the Queens line westbound, dozing in the early morning, when he was awakened by the sound of a struggle. At the other end of the car a man with a cracked and worn brown leather jacket was tugging at the suit coat of an elderly, white-haired man. The old man was wheezing asthmatically, and his efforts were growing weaker, until his arms dropped and the younger man was able to wrench a wallet from an inside pocket and run into the next car.

Rags thought about trying to help the old man, but by the time he got to his feet the young man was gone, and his victim had toppled to the floor, gasping for breath. Rags hurried up the length of the car, and saw that the man's face was already blue from cyanosis. His breathing had almost stopped.

There was nothing Rags could do. The man would die within seconds, and Rags knew of no way to save him. The only thing he could do was stay with him until he died, talk to him, tell him that it would be all right, that soon he would be with Jesus forever. Then the door to the last car opened.

Jesse was in the doorway, dressed all in white, his face a mask of sorrow. Rags stared at him, eyes and mouth wide in amazement. Then Jesse began to move toward him slowly, and Rags backed away on his hands and knees toward the door of the forward car, where he stopped and watched as Jesse knelt beside the old man, leaned over him, and put his lips against the blue skin. The wheezing sound stopped, the body shuddered once, and lay still.

Then, for the first time, Jesse looked directly at Rags, and Rags felt a two-fold shock of recognition sear through him as he saw Enoch's eyes staring out of Jesse's face. The illusion lasted for only a moment, and then Rags saw Jesse, and only Jesse, just as if he were alive and human and not what Rags feared he had become.

There was recognition in Jesse's face as well, the sad ghost of a smile at seeing Rags, and he opened his mouth slightly as if to speak, but said nothing. Instead, a look of purpose came over his gaunt features, and he rose from the dead man's side and walked toward Rags, who still crouched on his hands and knees. Jesse knelt beside him and lifted a pale, bloodless hand toward his old friend. The fingers trembled, and Rags could see that Jesse was hesitant to touch him, almost as if he were afraid.

Then something in Jesse leaped into flame as a burst of emotion crossed his face. Rags saw desperate hope, fierce determination, the quenching of doubt, and, above them all, a surge of will that would have physically driven Rags back had not the fingers of Jesse's hand clamped like iron bands onto the cloths around his neck, holding Rags in a grip of fire, a white, cleansing, purifying fire that burned away all Rags's fear . . .

And consumed his tumor.

It did not shrink slowly, like a deflated balloon, nor did it wither and shift, melding with his body. It

Lowland Rider

simply vanished as the knife wound had vanished, leaving his skin furrowed with age, but soft, flat, whole. The cancer had left him.

Now Jesse's hand was soothingly cool, even through the layers of cloth, and for the first time in many months Rags straightened his neck, and looked into Jesse's face, where he saw his own wonder mirrored. Jesse seemed filled with surprise, and even, Rags thought, a certain frail triumph. But there was not enough joy there to balance the sorrow that hung like a mist around his friend, borne of pain so strong that Rags could touch it with his mind.

Jesse took his hand away and stood up. In the instant before he turned and walked back into the last car, Rags saw a tear leave his eye and roll down his cheek, and then Rags was alone with the dead man on the floor.

Rags got up and walked back to the door, looked through it, and saw that the last car was empty. When the train stopped at the next station, he got off and crossed over to the eastbound track. He stood there alone, listening to the sounds of the tunnels, thinking that if it was so hard to be just a man, how much harder it must be to be a god.

"Hope, Jesse," he whispered. "Hope."

Then, slowly, he pulled out the ends of the cloths that swaddled him and unwound them from around his body, first from his neck, then his arms, chest, stomach, and legs, methodically working his way downward until the last piece of fabric came away from his ankles, and he stood wearing only a shabby white shirt and a pair of faded dungarees. He gathered up the rags in his arms and bore them, as gently as if he carried a child, to a refuse container, into which he dropped them a handful at a time.

Then he sat on a bench, bowed his head, and prayed for Jesse Gordon until the next train came, his last train, the train that would carry him up, into the light.